NOVELS

Blackpool Vanishes

Daggerman

The Enormous Dwarf

The Whispering Gallery

Swansong

The Land Where Lost Things Go

Taking Apart the Poco Poco

Fat Hen

Prospect Hill

The Old Spring

Crane Pond

NON-FICTION

Transcendental Utopias:
Individual and Community at Brook Farm, Fruitlands and Walden

Ann the Word:
The Story of Ann Lee, Female Messiah, Mother of the Shakers,
The Woman Clothed with the Sun

Judge Sewall's Apology:
The Salem Witch Trials and the Forming of a Conscience

Fruitlands:
The Alcott Family and Their Search for Utopia

LAURA LAURA

Richard Francis

LAURA LAURA

Europa
editions

Europa Editions
8 Blackstock Mews
London N4 2BT
www.europaeditions.co.uk

A catalogue record for this title is available from the British Library
ISBN 978-1-78770-245-5

Francis, Richard
Laura Laura

Book design by Emanuele Ragnisco
www.mekkanografici.com

Jacket illustration by Ginevra Rapisardi

Prepress by Grafica Punto Print – Rome

Printed and bound in Great Britain by Clays Ltd, Elcograf S.p.A.

CONTENTS

For Jo

LAURA LAURA

AUTUMN

CHAPTER 1

The film had been about a serial killer, to Gerald's surprise. He must have read the wrong review. It was a film of shadows and oblique angles; long periods of quiet, irruptions of violence. More Abby's sort of thing than his. He preferred his terror to be spectral or otherworldly, the sort that suggested more to life than you'd thought. Not about some dreary, obsessive man who did the same horrible thing over and over, like a kind of job.

A clear night in late September. Beyond the small city Gerald could see, or sense, the surrounding bowl of hills, stars poised above them like halted weather. On the breeze, the smell of cooking sausages. For a moment he was tempted to buy one. No, too old to get a hot dog from a stand. He remembered far back, when he was only twenty-seven, somewhere about that, fearing being past the age for flared trousers. Have the courage of your convictions, for God's sake, Abby had said, rolling her eyes.

But you are what you are, so he gave the stand a wide berth. It would be better to have a couple of pints at The Star on his way up the Paragon.

He found himself hugging the edge of the street and to justify it took a sharp right into the lanes, as good a route as any. Immediately, another Bath, gloomy and enclosed, a dark Bath behind the golden façade. He became aware of a faint noise, a sort of throb or pucker of the air. Perhaps his headache returning. Maybe he should go straight home – Abby would be back from pottery by now. Cup of tea. She would envy him the stabbings.

A cardboard cup skittered along in a sudden gust. Just ahead was the narrowest and darkest section of the alleyways. Stepping into it felt like taking a plunge, as if the lane had warped downwards. He had to probe for the pavement's surface with each foot before committing. Then, just out of sync with his footsteps, footsteps, as if his shoes had acquired the faintest of echoes; as if, with each step, he stepped slightly out of himself.

He speeded up as inconspicuously as possible, back stiff, arms barely swinging. He had the impression that he was elongating each leg in turn, reaching downwards through the blackness in search of footing on the slope that wasn't a slope, like trying to hurry on stilts. The footfalls separated themselves from his but continued behind him.

Then a voice. 'Hey! Mate!'

More high-pitched than he would have expected.

'Mate!'

A woman's. But rough round the edges.

Now she was immediately behind him. 'Fucking hell, mate,' she protested, 'you going like the clappers. Robbed a bank? Fuck the fuck.' She was panting.

'Perhaps you shouldn't smoke so much,' Gerald said, still looking forwards at nothing.

A hand grasped his left forearm, spun him sideways, though he continued to walk awkwardly on, crab-like, dragging her.

'What're you saying, mister? What the fuck you on about?'

'I'm on my way home. Leave me alone.' His own whining tone, along with the strange feeling of being tugged, plus maybe the violence of the film he'd been watching, made him feel suddenly desperate. He moved his head impotently from side to side like a bear in a zoo. What the fuck *was* he on about?

Another jerk on his arm, pulling him right round this time. They were at an intersection of the lanes, with a lamp dimly shining. There she was, small, in a too-long red anorak hanging limp. She had two what you might call plaits, except that they stuck upwards like a young goat's stubby horns. Jeans, clown boots.

'Why did you say smoke? *What* did you say?'

'I did say smoke. Stupid of me.'

'Look at me, mister. What's this?' She knocked on the side of her head as if it was a little door. 'What is it?'

'What do you mean?'

'I mean, what the fuck *is* it?' Knock, knock; he could almost hear them.

'It's your head.' An ugly pause while she glared at him. Her face was thin, almost pinched, with a sharp pointy nose. He wasn't hot on faces. Medium-sized eyes. Medium-sized mouth. A face. 'Isn't it?'

'You are fucking with it – that's what it is. My head being fucked with. Why were you on about smoking? Am I smoking? No, I am not.'

'OK, OK, I'll tell you why I said about smoking.' He paused. Suddenly it seemed too complicated. He felt he was losing the thread. Or translating from one language into another. 'My wife.' He whispered it, as if someone else might be listening, as if maybe *Abby* might be listening. Wife was one of those words that could clarify a situation. The pointy nose and the medium eyes peered up at him, the medium mouth sagged open as if to listen too. 'My wife, years and years, one day out of the blue she starts smoking. Never had a drag of a fag before. Not a single one. Now, twenty a day, at least. I don't mean vaping. She inhales all the way down to her toes. She says she's a sufficient age, what does it matter? Dead before it catches up with her. But her voice has gone harsh, a bit harsh, and she puffs. Has a tendency to puff. So I thought maybe you're in the same boat. Sorry.'

He remembered the one time he had smoked himself, when

a boy, about eight. He'd found one of his father's stubs and taken it into the lavatory to give it a try. But he forgot to lock the door, and his sister Ruth came waltzing in. She must have been seventeen at the time, grown-up as far as he was concerned. He stared at her, feeling his ears go red. She said nothing, merely took the stub from him and then crooked her finger. In her bedroom she squashed the stub on a little tin lid beside her bed, took a packet of cigarettes from her handbag, and offered him one. He refused, thinking it might be some sort of trap.

'OK, then,' she said, 'we'll share.' She lit the cigarette, took a big puff, then passed it to him. Afterwards she made him promise never to tell their mother or father what had happened – as if he ever would have. 'Good grief,' she said when they'd finished, 'I forgot I wanted a wee.'

He'd not smoked since. That was the only cigarette he'd ever wanted. Now he felt a hypocrite as he watched the girl. She stood quite still, as if stunned. Her mouth closed as slowly as something enormous closing. He noticed she wasn't holding on to his arm any more but couldn't bring himself to make his escape. It would seem too abrupt, rude almost. Someone walked past them, the swish of a form in silent shoes, like a bat going home to roost.

'Fuck,' the girl said when the passer-by had passed. Silence again.

He had a sudden need to make it up to her, whatever *it* was. 'Would you like—'

'What?'

'I don't know.' Silence again. 'Would you like a sausage?'

'What the fu-uck?'

He sniffed, demonstratively. 'You can smell them, even from here.'

'*Saus*age?' She said the word as if it was incomprehensible. 'What you trying to say?'

'I'm not trying to say anything. It's not a figure of speech. It's just a sausage. I could have one too. I wanted one when I walked past the stand, but I couldn't face buying one just for myself. It made me feel awkward. I felt embarrassed even *not* buying it. We could have a sausage each in a bun. A hot dog. That boy there on Milsom Street was cooking proper sausages in his stall. Not frankfurters.'

'I don't *want* a sausage.'

'Aren't you hungry?'

'I'm always hungry.' The whites of her eyes gleamed slightly, as if able to extract hidden light from the surrounding dimness. There was even a tiny glimmer on her front teeth. 'You're always hungry when you're living on the street. Except when you're pissed.'

'Drinking makes me hungrier, I find, than I was to start with. Beer.'

'I don't do drugs, mister,' she said, almost as if he had accused her of it. 'But I drink some awful crap, you wouldn't believe. You drink what you can get hold of. Even if somebody's pissed in it, which has happened, oh yes.'

'Well, you're not drinking now, are you, so why don't you have a sausage?'

'Because I'm a veggie, that's why. For fuck's sake!' She spoke just as if she'd already told him that.

How *can* you be a veggie, living on the street? 'Perhaps he does vegetarian sausages. The boy. He might, it being Bath.'

She didn't bother to respond. He cast around for what to say next. Really it was her turn since it was she who'd grabbed him in the first place. She ought to get to the point. 'I could give you – I could let you have a fiver. Maybe a tenner. I'm not sure what I've got. Probably a tenner. Would that get you a bed for the night?'

'I don't *want* a fucking bed.'

'What *do* you want then?'

'Come with me,' she said. 'It won't take long. Just come.'
She stepped past him and carried on down the lane. On the
face of it there was no obligation to follow: he could simply
peel off and head home another way. Instead he followed. He
felt as if he was being towed along in her wake.

During his time as a research student in Sheffield, a new
vice-chancellor got himself in a spot of bother. He pulled up at
a red light, and bingo, his passenger door opened and a girl
stepped in and made herself at home. Then the light turned
green, and the vice-chancellor automatically pressed down on
the pedal. But before he had a chance to clarify matters, a
police car nipped past and pulled up to accuse him of kerb-
crawling.

Nobody believed the VC's version, of course. But that series
of events stayed in Gerald's mind, as if they *had* happened like
that, as if he'd witnessed it. The girl appearing by magic, cheap
perfume and a cigarette, short tight skirt. The middle-aged
man in the seat beside her, hands trembling on the wheel. The
squeal of brakes, blue lights flashing, the cop hopping out of
his car and peering through the driver's side window: Hello
sunshine, who's been a naughty boy then? The impossibility of
making clear what had happened, especially since it *hadn't*
happened, like that, anyway.

They came out of the lanes opposite the Guildhall and
turned down towards the Abbey, hunched against the starry
sky. His eyes were throbbing with the effort to keep up. She
seemed to have forgotten her lack of puff and was trotting
now. He had an uneasy sense that it might look as if he were
pursuing her, particularly since he was.

Finally, just before Bog Island, they crossed the road and
ended up by the low wall above the River Avon. She leaned
over it, peering down suddenly intent, like a child playing
Poohsticks. 'How old *are* you?' he panted out as if she'd
deceived him. No reply.

He leaned over too and stared at the arc of the weir, the white water glowing against the darkness. 'Do you know why it's an arc?' he asked.

'What?'

'Why it's not straight across? Why it's bent like that? It calms the water down. It means the water doesn't . . . ' – he couldn't quite think how to put it – 'doesn't need to queue before it drops down. Stops it backing up and causing a flood.'

They remained there, side by side. He stole glances at her while keeping his face pointed at the weir. Hers looked pale under the street lights. He still couldn't work out her age, anything from sixteen to thirty – either way, a child compared to him. 'A council engineer thought of it. Bath was always being flooded. I remember reading about it in the paper.'

Still staring down at the river, she said, 'You're a knobhead, did you know?'

'Often thought I might be.'

She swung round towards him. 'Haven't you been listening to me? *Fuck!*'

'I've tried to. But you haven't said a lot, in fact.'

'Jesus.' She turned away again.

'Look, is it a drink you want? I could get you one. Without any pee in it.'

'The shops are fucking shut. Knob.'

'I suppose they are.' He slid his sleeve up and flicked a glance at his watch. Nearly eleven. As if knowing the time of night had brought it on, he felt suddenly chilled. 'Well then, I'd best be going.'

'Stay here, knob.'

'I've got to go, really I have.'

'Oh yes, he's got to go.'

'I don't know why you wanted me to come here in the first place.'

'See that river down there? See that fucking river?'

'I see it. Of course I see it.'

'Good. Because I'm going to jump in it. That's what I'm going to do. I'm going to stand on this fucking wall and jump right into it. That's what I'm going to do.'

'Don't talk like that.'

'I'm not *talking*. I'm fucking *saying*.'

'Just show me what you wanted to show me in the first place. Here I am.'

'That's what I wanted to show you. Me jumping.'

'So you wanted to jump and me to watch you jump. Can I ask why?'

She was silent, staring out above the water.

'Let me tell you something,' he said. 'Half the people, more than half, who try to commit suicide have no intention of committing suicide. That's what the statistics say. More than half.' He had no idea whether that was in fact what the statistics said, but it must be a fair guess.

'What you saying?'

'You want me to stop you, that's what I'm saying. Talk you down. Which is OK. Here I am, talking you down.'

'You are a total knob. That's for definite.'

'My name's Gerald. If I'm a knob, I'm a knob. I don't mind. Well, I do mind, but it won't stop me talking you down. What are *you* called by the way?'

To his surprise she answered. 'Laura.' She looked reflective for the moment, as if that word brought back who she was, or had been. And in fact he felt arrested by the name, as if it had a certain heft or resonance.

'Well, Laura. First of all, I need to give my wife a call, if you don't mind.' He took out his phone.

She grasped his arm. 'Don't do that. Don't call somebody. I don't want an ambulance. Don't fucking call an ambulance.'

Yes, she was young, quite young. Young at least in the sense of experience. God knows what had happened to her in her life on the street, and in the previous life that had dumped her there, but those weren't experiences in the proper sense of the word: they didn't make you grow up. Made you grow backwards, if anything. True experiences were events that became your possessions. He'd felt that in the past about street people, that whatever things they were guilty of doing, whatever knowingness they possessed when they laughed together, they were in fact more innocent than the people who clip-clopped by them in their suits or high heels. Street people looked with one look at a time, like babies. They were what they were. They got more battered with age, but they didn't mature, being subject to a different category of happenings altogether, ones they couldn't learn from, that no one could learn from.

'And not the fucking police, either,' she added. 'Don't call *any*body. I don't want any fucker messing with me.'

'I just want to call my wife.'

'Fucking hell.' She shook her head as if this was the last straw. 'Doesn't she let you stay out this late? Have you got to run home for your tea? Tosser.'

'I thought I was a knob.'

'What's the difference? Knob. Wanker.' She laughed suddenly like a schoolgirl at a rude joke. 'Go home for your tea, wanker.'

'She'll wonder where I am, that's all. I won't call her, if that's what you want. Or don't want. I'll let her stew.'

'Oh fuck off.'

'If I fuck off you might jump over the wall and land in the river, and there's nobody around to stop you if I don't stop you. By the way, the river isn't all that deep here. You might not even drown. You might just get cold and wet. You might break your legs and have to go to hospital. If you really want to commit suicide, you ought to make sure it does the trick.'

'People drown in the river all the time.'

'That's students. They get pissed and need to have a pee then fall in. And where they do that isn't here anyway.' He was a university teacher all over again, au fait with the dying habits of students. 'It's round the corner past the station, where the water's deeper and the river flows faster than it does here. They have to go that way to get to the residences. The bank is higher too, so however much they scrabble they can't get out, poor sods. Give it a miss, I'm telling you.'

Silence. Eventually she gave a long, shivery sigh. She can't even commit suicide without being told she's doing it all wrong, he thought. She can't even *pretend* to be about to commit suicide without being criticised. Poor girl in a droopy anorak, never given credit for anything.

Once Gerald was on a train with a little boy and his mother sitting opposite. The boy had never been on a train before, and he was excited, pointing at the world unspooling past the window, not at anything in particular but at everything in general, at the discovery that there *was* an everything. But whatever he said was ruthlessly crushed by the mother, who nagged and hectored him for the whole journey, periodically looking towards Gerald for approval, a smug conniving grin on her face. All he could do was look blankly back or not look at all. He wanted to tell her to shut up and be nice, but how do you order someone to be nice? If he told her off she would wait till she was alone with the boy and then take it out on him. It gave Gerald a glimpse of life without latitude.

Perhaps that's the life this girl had lived too. Thwarted routinely so there wasn't room to breathe. In the end the streets beckoned – at least there was air out there. And now his contribution was to thwart her more.

'I'm going now,' she said.

He almost replied, Look, don't mind me. Commit suicide if you want to. I'm sure it will work out fine. 'Where to?' he asked instead. He pulled out his wallet and found a couple of twenties. 'Look, Laura, will this get you somewhere to sleep for the night?'

She took the money, unzipped her anorak pocket, and put it in. 'Arsehole,' she said. She kept her eyes down, but her up-tilted nose pointed at him instead, the way a bird points its beak.

CHAPTER 2

As he plodded homewards up Snow Hill, Gerald thought about what had just happened. Why did the girl go after him? He assumed at the time that she wanted to be stopped from committing suicide, but now he wondered. Could it have been some kind of elaborate con? She'd ended up with forty quid, if evidence was needed. But no, that didn't ring true. The way she had called him an arsehole, not a sucker or dope. It was as if she was disappointed in him, as if he'd missed the point.

A window was open somewhere despite the midnight chill, and a rapper was rapping. Those tumbling impatient words, that pissed-off tone of voice, the strident rhyming, always made Gerald feel panicky, as if he was being accused of something. Maybe the girl hadn't wanted to be stopped from committing suicide after all.

A cat, sitting on a gatepost, gave him a long look, then fled. Maybe what the girl wanted was exactly what she said she wanted. To *show* him. Perhaps for once, and once only, she'd wanted to be *seen*. She already had a low opinion of herself. Never being noticed by anyone must grind you down, whatever your age. To plan to commit suicide with the knowledge that you *still* wouldn't be noticed, that there would just be an anonymous report in the local paper – yes, it would be unbearable. Perhaps all she wanted was just one witness to make it real. He remembered the old conundrum about a tree falling in a wood when no one is there. Maybe she'd wanted him to hear her fall.

Gerald stopped in his tracks. He was only about a hundred yards below his house by now. The lights were off. What do you do when you are thwarted in your suicide attempt? It could give you even more reason to kill yourself than you had already. And in his pedantic professorial way, he'd told her the best place to do it.

Gone midnight. Abby would be asleep in all probability. Gerald turned on his heels and headed back into Bath.

Kids were milling about in Milsom Street and its offshoots. The air still smelled of sausages. Most of the clubbers were drunk to one degree or another, but nobody took any notice of Gerald. He could have been invisible. As he slipped through the crowd, he understood how a ghost must feel, looking at the world from the point of view of being dead.

He headed down to where the river curved west in the direction of Bristol. There was a walkway here, with railings along the side and lifebelts secured at regular intervals. Below the railings a steep bank and then the river, partially illuminated by a sequence of LED street lamps positioned along the narrow promenade. No one here. He peered over the railings at the water moving below. Eddies and currents emphasised its muscular hurry. Halfway across, a huge bough bobbed along, branches bent forward as if doing the crawl. He watched it for a while until he realised it wasn't moving at all, caught somewhere out of sight.

After a few minutes he stepped back and leaned sideways against one of the lamp-posts. What he didn't want was for the girl to come along, clock his presence, and back off to a distance where he wouldn't see her do what she intended to do, if in fact she did intend to do it. After that last experience, this time around she would want to be not-seen rather than seen. There were intimate noises from the river; a breeze washed by. The night was still clear, the stars bright.

Gerald surfaced after who knows how long, head numb,

blinking at the sudden closeness of everything. A boy was walking across the walkway towards the railings. In the faint white light of the lamps he looked oddly retrospective, like a boy on a CCTV playback. He bent down, slipped through the railings, and straightened up on the little ledge beyond. Gerald took a step closer to see what he would do next.

What he did was unzip his flies, feel inside, and bring out his penis. He swayed slightly. Gerald was about to dart forward to grab him, but in the nick of time the boy reached his other hand back and grasped the top railing to steady himself, then began to pee in a thin arc, chittering with relief like you do eating too-hot food. It was as if some small elf or goblin concealed in the boy's trousers had taken out his rod and cast a long line into the river. When he'd finished, the boy gave his penis a shake, pushed his bum backwards to make room, then let go of the railing so he could zip up with both hands, losing his balance again and lunging over the water. Once more Gerald tensed to spring across, but once more the lad straightened up in the nick of time, turned round, swung through the railings, and strode buoyantly off.

Gerald stepped back to the meagre shelter of the lamppost. To his surprise, another boy appeared straightaway out of the night, walked across the walkway to the railings, climbed through, and unzipped himself just as the last one had done. It was as if the boys were computer graphics illustrating a lecture, the very one Gerald had delivered to Laura earlier that night. Once again he tiptoed forward to peer; once again the boy momentarily lost his balance and Gerald readied himself for rescue; once again the elf or goblin cast his line into the river.

Gerald watched the second boy disappear into the night. The young would never learn. Not fair, of course. They learned but then temporarily overruled what they'd learned. He and Abby did the same; it was nothing to do with age. Like when they decided – based on long experience – to have only one martini but, having drunk it, would say, 'Why not?' and have another.

A hand rested itself on his shoulder, so gently he felt no shock or fright.

'Can I ask what you're doing?' came a man's voice, soft enough not to interrupt the calm of the night.

'I was thinking about martinis, if you really want to know. How you always have to have two.'

Gerald turned, and his heart lurched. A policeman was standing there, with a hi-vis gilet over his uniform jacket. His young, mean, intent face peered out from his helmet like a predator from its den.

'What did you say?' Gerald asked. He knew what the constable had said, of course, but needed to restart the conversation. He couldn't stop his voice from wavering, squeaking even. There was something about a policeman close to, a looming quality.

When he was very young, maybe six or seven, a policeman had come to their house after a burglary. Somebody had stolen a bag of farthings. Other things, too, in all probability, though the farthings were what had stayed in his mind. That long-ago policeman was tall, black-uniformed, like an elongated shadow of himself. For months afterwards, years maybe, Gerald dreamed that the policeman had taken his father away. He'd cry out, wake shaking with fear at the injustice of it, at his own inability to protect him. Had part of him *wanted* his father to be arrested? Dad was kind, thoughtful, over-anxious. Maybe something malicious inside Gerald's young self wished him gone, yearned to be free. Maybe it was too hard being loved by someone when you were seven. Maybe the dream policeman was just doing his dirty work for him.

'I said,' said the policeman, 'I would like you to tell me what you thought you were doing.'

'I was . . . ' – Gerald swallowed – 'miles away.' He gave a token laugh at his own foolishness.

'I was watching you. You were looking at those lads having a pee. You went down to the railings so you could get a better look. I got the feeling it was turning you on. Sir.'

'What? God, no. Good grief, no. The last thing, the very last thing. Oh no, not at all.' He was gabbling, like a professor, like a vice-chancellor, like somebody who *liked* to watch boys peeing.

'What *were* you doing then, may I ask?'

'I thought they might fall in. Students, that age. You must know that. They drink too much, need a pee, fall in.'

'So you're standing here all ready to rescue them. What were you going to do, jump in after? Or throw them a life belt?'

'I don't know. Raise the alarm maybe.'

'So is this a hobby? You wait here in case some lad ends up in the water? And meantime watch them get their willies out?'

'No, no. Not a lad. A girl. In case a *girl*.'

'Hang on,' the copper said. He took off his helmet, inspected its inside as if to check there was nothing there to distort what he'd been hearing, then replaced it on his head. He swung his jaw from side to side while he adjusted the strap under his chin, blinking as he did so. 'No girl is going to pee in the river from here. They can't do it, sir, however much they might want to. Or need to. They're built different.'

'I'm perfectly well aware that they're built differently. I wasn't waiting for a girl to pee in the river. I was waiting for a girl to *jump* in the river.'

There was an unpleasant silence. The policeman stared at Gerald. He looked as if he was casting about in his mind for what charge to level. It occurred to Gerald it could be one of many. Loitering. Voyeurism. Public nuisance. Wasting police time. Stalking. How fragile it was, the freedom to be free, to obey your impulses. There was another dark river running alongside him, running alongside everyone, and it was easy to misstep and fall in.

'I saw a girl, earlier this evening. She accosted me, if you must know.'

'Accosted.'

'Yes. A homeless girl. She approached me. I thought she just wanted money, but she dragged me over to the weir. She was threatening to commit suicide. I dissuaded her, but then I felt worried. So I thought I'd better come back to make sure.'

'You thought you ought to come back.'

'I thought I ought to come back. Yes.'

'But this isn't the weir. You didn't come back. The weir is in the middle of town.'

Gerald realised the impossibility of getting across exactly what he ought to say. The trouble with truth is that it's often too complicated to be believable. How would it sound if he admitted he'd told her this would be a better place to jump? Even though he didn't want her to in the first place? Truth can have contradiction embedded right inside it, like quartz in rock, and still be truth. 'I decided to come here instead. She said this was a better place to do it. She told me her name was Laura.'

'Better?'

'Faster current. Plus, deeper. But she hasn't come. She isn't here.' Gerald made a show of looking up and down the walkway. It was for the policeman's benefit but also, beneath the posturing, genuine too. He wanted to check before making his exit, needed to make sure she wasn't somewhere along the riverbank, set on doing something stupid.

The policeman looked up and down in turn, sarcastically. 'Doesn't look like it.' A shake of the head.

'I might as well be getting home then.'

The officer stared at him once more. Presumably a certain kind of lad becomes a cop just in order to be able to give people that look. 'I think you should do that, Mr. . . . ?'

'Walker. Gerald Walker. Professor Walker.' He rarely made use of the title but felt the need of it now. 'Yes. I will.'

They both knew that something more was needed, a clincher. 'And maybe you should stay at home a bit more in future,' the policeman added. 'At night-time, at least. Watch the telly like everybody else.'

'Yes, officer, I'll do that.' Gerald nodded. 'Watch the telly.'

As he walked away he heard the cop's parting shot: 'You'll keep out of trouble that way. Professor.'

It was gone one when he let himself in. The house felt warm and enveloping. As he shut the door behind him, he thought of the girl stretched out in a doorway somewhere, just paving stones or tiles for her mattress. True, she had his forty quid, but he guessed that would be put to other uses.

Unless she was in the river after all.

In his mind's eye he saw her drifting along like Ophelia, transformed, washed clean by the water, at one with it. He wondered if Laura imagined she would do some kind of slow dance with hair spread in long exotic tendrils, flexing with the drift.

Not a hope. For one thing, her hair was tied up into two little stumps on the top of her head – no way it could unravel. And drowning wasn't like that, he knew perfectly well. Once, while cross-country running at school, he'd been thumping his way over a plank bridge spanning a little river and happened to see a calf bobbing in the water, looking back up at him with its dead glaucous eye. The beast was stiff and awkward, waterlogged. It was raining steadily at the time, which it regularly did on those cross-country runs, and that made the sight more comfortless still – even wetter.

You didn't merge with water you drowned in; there was no embrace. Your body would just hang there, angular and hamfisted, bouncing a little with the currents and eddies.

Laura must twist her hair together to make those horns, and the thought of her performing a daily ritual, insisting on her version of the feminine against all odds, gave him a pang of sorrow.

He switched on the kitchen light. Wondered if he should make himself a cup of tea. No, he didn't want to drink it alone down here, in this sharp illumination.

He took off his shoes, turned off the light, tiptoed into the hall, placed them under the clothes stand, made his way up the stairs in darkness. Felt for the knob of the bedroom door and opened it slowly enough to avoid a creak. Undressed facing the pale oblong of the window, groped for the armchair, deposited each item of clothing on it in turn. Moved to the side of the bed and reached under the pillow for his pyjamas. As always in the dark, he imagined someone with night vision watching his blundering movements.

He slid under the duvet and lay there with his heart pounding. It had been a long, complicated evening. Since getting back he'd been bottled up, breathing shallowly, moving silently so as not to wake Abby. The bed was cool, but he liked it like that. As it warmed he would feel his heart calm down and his limbs slowly relax.

But something was wrong. He stretched a hand out towards Abby's side. No Abby.

He was at an age where he feared chunks of his life might go missing. Not long ago he had spent a week trying to remember Frankie Howerd's name. He could see him, hear the voice, remember the mannerisms: the conspiratorial look, the pretence of shock at people's rudeness. And then, suddenly, the name was back again as if it had just been overlooked or approached via the wrong route. 'Give me strength, Gerald,' Abby had said when he told her. 'You've been like that ever since I've known you. You forgot the name of my mother once, back in the days when we were dating. Her surname, which, by the way, was *my* surname too. You said, "Hello, Mrs. . . . " and then just tailed off. Actually I think you said, "Greetings, Mrs.," being you were a bit of a tosser in those days. "He's a funny lad," she said to me afterwards. "Got his head in the clouds." Gave me a worried look. I can see it still. Furrowed her brows. "I suppose he's very clever," she said. People like my mother thought being forgetful was a sign of brains. Your memory's so rubbish you can't even remember forgetting, half the time.'

Had they had a row? Perhaps she was in the spare bedroom. It wasn't in her nature to bear a grudge or to sulk, however strong the language she sometimes threw at him, but just in case he tiptoed up the next flight of stairs and checked.

He went back to their bedroom, only now switching on the light. The room looked even more empty when he could see it. Stupidly, he went over to the wardrobe and peered in as if she might be hiding there, scrunched in the corner behind the hanging dresses with her thumb in her mouth.

How can you lose your own wife, for God's sake?

He had spent hours looking for people, it occurred to him: first the girl, now Abby. The world seemed to be running away from him, leaving him stranded. Like playing hide and seek as a child, counting to a hundred with your eyes shut only to discover the others had gone home to tea.

Gerald rang her number, but there was no reply. Somehow he knew there wouldn't be. She rarely took her mobile out with her. He realised he was shaking from top to bottom. A sob gathered in his throat like something hard he'd swallowed accidentally. It was all too much. Too bloody much. 'Abby!' he called, not too loudly for fear of waking the neighbours on the other side of the party wall. 'Abby!' He went into every room in the house, shouting mutedly. He didn't need to check, in point of fact. When you are alert to it, you can feel emptiness like a presence.

Now what?

His sob dispersed, leaving just a dull ache. Panic gave way to testiness. He could ring the police, but if he did should it be 999 or that other number which he couldn't for the moment remember? A person's disappearance sounded like an emergency, but he wondered if 999 was reserved for actually witnessing a crime. And how interested would they be? He had a notion that a missing adult wasn't regarded as properly missing until forty-eight hours had passed, as if their absence had to mature in some way, like a bottle of claret.

What I'll do, he thought, is I'll go into the kitchen and make a cup of tea after all. Give the world time to return to normal. He had a mental picture of a slight justifying ripple in the fabric of space-time, of the whole scheme of things getting its act together and precipitating Abby home as if she'd never left, like one of those kidnapped people staggering back to earth after being released from a flying saucer.

He went into the kitchen, filled the kettle and switched it on, put a teabag into a mug, and got the milk from the fridge. He sat down at the table to wait. In front of him was one of the squares of paper they kept beside the landline to jot messages and numbers on. Abby had a habit of doodling on them, doing hanged men with their eyes bulging and their tongues flopping out of their mouths. He picked it up. No hanged man, just a message in her loopy writing. 'Gone to hospital.'

'For God's sake,' he said, 'it's my *wife*.'

'Yes sir,' agreed the woman behind the desk. Upswept spectacles; retro maybe. 'I understand. But could you let me know what she's been admitted for?'

'I have no idea. As far as I knew she was perfectly healthy. I was out this evening, and when I got home, not there. Just a message, "Gone to hospital."'

'Did you call her? Perhaps you could call her?'

'She didn't answer. Her battery is probably empty. She's not much into electronics.' That suddenly seemed endearing, Abby not being into electronics.

'She was able to put pen to paper. That's a good sign.'

'You mean her arm hasn't been torn off?'

The receptionist raised her head, stunned at his ferocity. Her spectacles seemed to raise their own eyebrows. Joke, Gerald almost said, but that would have been even more inappropriate, joking.

'Well, I have no record of her being admitted. Try A&E. If she was taken in as an emergency case she would have been delivered there, not here.'

'She's not a parcel, you know.'

'Just trying to help, sir.'

He puffed out his cheeks to exhale, calm himself.

We all end up as parcels, he thought as he scurried along the corridors to A&E, conceding the point now it was too late. Parcelled up in ambulances or beds or coffins. The idea of final things, of Abby's final things, of Abby being, finally, a thing, brought the sob back into his throat.

A drunk with a red dirty face and yellow teeth was singing 'Hey, Mr. Tambourine Man' in the A&E waiting room. There were smells of booze, disinfectant, blood. Wounded and beaten-looking people sat in plastic chairs at odd angles as if blown in on a wind: winos, down-and-outs, kids too, clubbers and pubbers who'd drunk too much or got into fights. An elderly man, pale as death. Not many women – a very fat one, moaning quietly, being comforted by her friend. A small one a few seats further forward, hunched over; could be anyone, a person in a hospital. And then, as if suddenly coming into focus, it was Abby.

'Oh, there you are,' she said, looking up. 'I was trying to read. I bought this magazine in the Friends' shop. But I can hardly make out a single word. This neon looks bright, but it's the wrong sort of bright. Oh Gerald – it was awful, awful.'

'What was, Abby? What have you done? What's happened to you?'

'I'm suffering from shock.'

'What kind of shock? Do you mean electric?'

'Electric? No, no, for goodness sake. Not electric. Just shock. It was Steve.'

'Steve?'

'The potter. Pottery class? He takes it. He's so gifted, Steve. He makes things and brings them in to show so we know what's possible. But all it does is take our hope away. We sit at our work benches potting without hope, the whole lot of us.' She looked slightly to one side, reflecting, then shook her head. 'Anyhow, we'd finished for the evening. I stayed behind for a few minutes to have a word. Then we got thrown out because the caretaker wanted to lock up. We are always the last class, he said. So I said good night and turned to walk home. Steve had to cross over to go down to London Road. I'd just gone a few steps on my way when there was this almighty bang or crunch. Like when you tread on a snail, only magnified. I turned to look. Gerald, it was awful.'

'What happened?'

'He was lying in the road. He'd been knocked down, and the car had run right over his hand. It was squashed into the tarmac.'

Gerald too had once seen or, to be more accurate, not seen, a squashed hand, long ago when he worked in a rubber-composition factory the summer before he went to university. Hot lumps of rubber had to be fed into mills where they were rolled into flat sheets. A man at one of the mills got his arm caught. Gerald ran over towards the screaming. The man was leaning forward, his left ear pressed against the top gleaming roller as if listening to something confidential. His left arm disappeared into the non-existent gap between the enormous cylinders. The man was screeching at full volume but almost mechanically, as if that was just the sound the accident made. Gerald began to step round the mill but was prevented by a grizzled workman who grabbed his collar. 'You don't want to go round there, lad,' the man had told him.

'Ambulance came,' Abby said. 'Police. I had to tell them what I saw, which was nothing. Steve's beard just opened and closed while he was lying there, as if he was miming. Like a fish, if a fish had a beard. I was glad when the ambulance men scraped him off the road and took him to hospital. He's so lovely, Steve is. He made such lovely things.'

'Was it his pottery hand?'

'Both hands are your pottery hand, Gerald. You need the two. Catching hold, one hand. Shaping, other hand. Throwing, both hands. He made a lovely delicate penguin with its egg on its feet. So there I was,' she continued, 'sitting in the kitchen all by myself, bawling my eyes out. You didn't seem to come home. Where were you, by the way?'

'I went to the pictures. I told you I was going to go. I watched a film about a serial killer. You'd have loved it.'

For a second this snagged Abby's attention, and she stared wistfully into space at the thought of a serial killer. Across her line of vision an unconscious young woman was wheeled in a chair by a paramedic towards the inner recesses of the A&E, head lolling, hands hanging limp. Gerald wondered whether he ought to mention his shenanigans with the girl. It would only complicate matters. Also it would seem like some sort of pathetic tit for tat, Abby weeping over gifted Steve, he rushing across town to save suicidal Laura.

'So how did you end up here?' he asked.

'I got fed up being by myself in the kitchen. The funny thing about bawling your eyes out is you get bored after a while. So I wrote you a note and got a taxi. I didn't feel like driving myself. The shock. And my eyes felt blurry. I said I was next of kin, and they told me to sit here and wait. He's being operated on.' She looked at Gerald afresh, as if she hadn't noticed him until now. 'La la, darling,' she said, and smiled her smile.

CHAPTER 3

Abby and Gerald were inspecting the horse, which inspected them back, stamping occasionally. The weather was cold and clear. They were standing in a gently sloping field of tufty grass belonging to the livery stables. The wind was blowing the leaves off a nearby tree, and they zigzagged down the air like pale brown snowflakes.

'My horse,' Abby said. 'Dorothy the horse.' She had insisted on carrying the tackle over her head and shoulders without accepting help from Gerald, waddling across the pasture like a shiny brown beetle. 'I'm used to it,' she'd said, puffing with the exertion.

'I know it's Dorothy the horse. Why did you want me to look at it?'

'Her.'

'Her.'

'If you don't respect animals you become a psychopath in later life. I read an article about it.' She flung the saddle onto the horse's back. 'Hoo,' she gasped. The animal took two delicate sideways steps in response.

'I'm a bit long in the tooth to worry about what I might become in later life. In any case, she can't speak English.'

'That's what you think.'

Abby fastened the saddle's long strap under the horse's belly. Dorothy exhaled as if blowing a raspberry. Gerald bent down, tore off a clump of grass, and presented it on his palm as a peace offering. The horse trotted forward, glanced at it, then stared at him, clearly astonished at being offered what it already owned. Gerald tossed the grass to the wind.

'We used to do that in the Guides to find which direction the weather was coming from,' Abby said.

'What?' Gerald asked. 'I've been married to you all these years and never knew you were in the Guides.'

'I don't have to tell you everything I was or wasn't.'

'You're so unlike any sort of Girl Guide I've ever come across.'

'I was unlike a Girl Guide even when I *was* a Girl Guide. What I was, was the grit in the oyster.' She sighed with satisfaction at the thought, then inserted the horse's bit in its mouth and began securing the reins. 'I only lasted one summer. Going camping did it for me. You can't have a proper wash. But I owe it my love of horses.'

'Did you go riding then?'

'No, just saw some in a field.' She patted her horse on its nose. The horse shook its head again, impatiently. 'I felt like an equal, because I was living in a field too.'

'Abby, why am I here?'

'Good question. Why are any of us here?'

'I mean *here*. Why did you bring me here?'

'I wanted you to be an ordinary person. At least as far as Dorothy is concerned.'

'Just now you were warning me about being a psycho.'

'Someone who doesn't ride horses, I mean: ordinary in that sense. You *don't* ride horses, do you?'

'You know I don't.'

'You may have before we met, for all I know. Or when my back is turned. You didn't know about me being a Guide, after all. You never know things for sure in this life.'

'I have never ridden a horse in all my days. And come to think of it, I don't want to start now.' Dim realisation was dawning. 'Abby,' he added warningly, though it was a warning directed at himself.

Abby looked up at him. She had a thin, mobile face, and with age the tracks left by that mobility, creases round her brown eyes, bags in fact, runnels in her cheeks, lines from her nose to the corners of her mouth, were ever clearer. Her thick hair, bundled in a bun at her nape, was greying now, so that by contrast her skin looked even darker than earlier in her life, verging on coffee-coloured. It occurred to Gerald that Abby's eyes were the same colour as her horse's, almost as lustrous.

She drew a packet of cigarettes from her jeans pocket and put one in her mouth, then immediately took it out again to speak, waving it like a little baton to orchestrate him. 'Just for me,' she said. 'Just this once. You never know, you may take to it like a duck to water.'

'Nope.'

'Oh go on.'

'Abby, I don't want to ride a horse. I have never wanted to ride a horse. Why should I start now? Riding a horse is what *you* do.'

'It's an experiment.'

'An experiment.'

'Yes.'

'To prove what? To see if I break my neck?'

'You won't break your neck, I guarantee it.'

'I haven't got a riding hat. I might break my *head*.'

'I brought *my* riding hat. Look.' She pointed just beyond her booted feet, where it rested on the ground like a large brown fungus.

'I can't wear that. It will be too small. You know how big my head is. I have a large head. I've always had a large head.' It was nerves, making him gabble. Tall himself, he was aware of the sheer height and bulk of the animal standing by him and of its essential otherness, despite being called Dorothy.

'You won't need a riding hat. People never had riding hats in the old days.'

'They never had lots of things in the old days. Hygiene, for example. They died like flies in the old days.'

'Hygiene is a complete red herring, as you well know, Gerald. You're always doing that when we have an argument. You know what I call it? Doing a sideways shimmy. You are prone to doing sideways shimmies. This is a nice soft field. It's rained a lot recently. If you fell on it, it would be like falling on a mattress. A wet, green mattress. And you won't fall on it. I will lead Dorothy by her bridle. She's a gentle old thing, aren't you, Dorothy?'

The horse didn't reply, and there was a moment of silence. Abby took a disposable lighter out of her pocket, lit her cigarette, and inhaled reflectively.

'Abby, please tell me. Why do you want me to ride your horse?'

'Because,' she replied, her voice preoccupied with her exhale of smoke, 'be*cause* I thought Steve might give it a go, when he's healed a bit.' Her eyes flicked away from him, and indeed from the horse, to look at distant hills.

'Steve?' Of course Steve, Gerald thought. Lovely Steve – obviously still lovely even now he'd lost a hand.

'I tried to make a horse in pottery class. We have a stand-in teacher now poor Steve's gone kaput, but she's not much cop. I thought it would unite my two hobbies, riding and pottery. But horses' legs are so thin in proportion to their bodies. I kept thinking about the way Steve did his penguin's feet, with that egg just exactly balancing on them. So fragile. My pottery horse kept sort of bending at the knee. I think I would be better off doing rhinoceroses. Or are they hippos? Things with thick legs. But you can't ride a rhinoceros.'

She seemed to snap out of a reverie. 'La la, darling,' she said, giving him a sharp, bright-eyed look. It was like the one she'd given him when they first met at a party, while he was an undergraduate at Cambridge.

The room was full of people strewn about on the floor and flopping on chairs like stranded fish on a beach, portentously talking or being silent (as if even their silences were significant), and suddenly he became aware of being looked at irrespective of any face, a gaze that was a thing in itself. It took a moment to track it down to a small dark-complexioned person in a pale blue minidress, sitting on a dining chair near the door in an oddly hieratic pose, her legs primly together. Her face was solemn, or at least inscrutable, but there was something droll about the candidness of her gaze, a wide-eyed irony.

Gerald wasn't experienced with girls, and in the Cambridge of that time they were rare exotic fauna as far as most male undergraduates were concerned. Still, he picked his way over and stood timidly in front of her. She raised an eyebrow. Neither of them spoke. He could feel his heart pounding in his chest. Suddenly she rose to her feet, though hardly seemed to gain any height as a result. He was over six foot by contrast, thin and gangling with a large wobbly head, and she seemed exquisite in her smallness, her black glossy hair severely brushed to one side in a sort of wing. 'I'm bored,' she said, as if they were already conversant.

'Me too.'

'You could walk me home.'

'Could. Do just that,' the tension making him speak in gruff English, pidgin almost.

'Come on, in that case.'

Home. She'd said home. He assumed at first that she meant it as a euphemism for rooms or digs but no, it was a semi in the suburbs, the blue light of a TV visible behind the curtains. Even the air on that spring evening had a residential aroma, a suggestion of polish, proper food. During term-time, home existed for Gerald merely as an idea, and the sight of hers gave him a sort of proxy homesickness.

'I live here,' she explained. 'With my mum and dad and my sister. I'm not a student like you. I work in a hardware shop.'

'Hardware?'

'Yep.'

'I *love* it.' He'd almost said I love *you*, the thought of her dispensing saws and spanners was so intoxicating, but had swerved to safety at the last minute. 'Hardware,' he said again.

'Are you a do-it-yourself-er, then?' she asked.

'No, not at all. At school I was so bad at Latin I got chucked into woodwork. Then I was so bad at woodwork, I got chucked back into Latin. That's how I ended up at Cambridge.'

She nodded gravely, as if this was a normal trajectory.

'I love the thought of you selling it; that's what I meant. Perhaps we could go to the pictures sometime,' he added, taking himself by surprise.

She pondered on this for a moment. 'You could meet me after work,' she said finally. Gerald was trembling with relief. 'Maybe next Wednesday? Then we can decide what to see. The shop is called Handyman. My shop. Where I work. It's Mr. Harrison's shop in actual fact. Right by the station.'

He wondered whether to kiss her goodnight. It seemed such a complicated undertaking. He would need to operate himself like a puppeteer his puppet. Before he could do so, she bunched her hand into a fist and punched him gently on the nose. 'La la, fruit drop,' she said to his amazement and skittered up the path to her house.

Gerald raised his foot to slide it into the stirrup, but it wouldn't rise high enough. He had to grasp his ankle with both hands and lift as if his leg wasn't part of him at all, then release one hand to reach for the stirrup and slide it over the toe of his shoe, whimpering with strain as he did so. Once in position, his leg was raised so high that his other foot barely tiptoed on the ground. Despite that, it seemed impossible to raise the second leg in order to fling it over the horse's back, as he had seen Abby do.

He felt Abby's hands on his calf, tugging it upwards. He scrabbled at the horse's mane and hefted himself over, lying along the animal's back and panting loudly.

'Honestly, Gerald, the fuss you make,' Abby said. She went round behind the horse and found the other stirrup for him. 'I was going to ask you to do it with one arm in the air, so it would be as if you'd lost your hand like poor Steve. Just as well I didn't. Hold the reins loosely. I'll take her halter.'

Gerald felt surprisingly high off the ground. The air seemed colder, as if the weather was different up here. At Abby's persuasion, Dorothy moved forward, quite slowly but with the totalising power of an earthquake, every part of her involved in the process. Gerald tried relaxing his body so it moved in sympathy, but that made him feel more insecure than ever, so instead he held himself as stiffly as possible. If you couldn't feel you were part of the horse, you needed to take the opposite tack, contain the beast, resist with every ounce of strength.

'There's no need to keep moaning,' Abby told him.

All he could see, apart from her hand on the halter, was the top and back of her head and the bun on her neck, her black hair streaked with grey and with the pale light from the sun, which seemed to be bouncing in the hazy sky over to the right when he dared peer in that direction. The fields, the trees, the nearby country lane, shifted and stirred. 'If I don't moan, I'll fall off.'

'You should be able to feel the horse's hooves through your bottom; that's the trick.'

'Bottom, did you say?'

'Bot. Tom,' the head replied irritably. It was bobbing too, but out of time with the horse, counterpointing almost.

'What kind of weirdness is that?'

'You can feel the hooves making contact with the ground. You can feel when the going is squishy or when there's a stone. Right through your bottom. Also through your vulva. But you don't have one of those. I don't know how it works with balls, but jockeys seem to do OK. You sort of get sensitised. You'll know it when it starts to happen. That's why I thought it would be good for Steve.'

'How in the name of sanity can this be good for Steve, after all he's going through? Feeling the ground through his balls, for fuck's sake?'

'Because riding a horse is like having four extra limbs. Which must be nice when you've just lost your hand. Think about it. They say horses are good for disabled people. They're very empowering, horses are.'

'Abby, it would be all right if you lost *your* hand, because you know how to ride a horse already.'

'Thank you very much. I'm glad you don't mind if I lose my hand. I wouldn't want you to be upset.'

'What I mean is, when you get on a horse as a non-rider, you feel you're no longer. Clicked into place.' He almost hiccupped with the words as the animal lumbered. 'In the world as a whole.' He looked at the horse's heaving shoulders, if that's what they were. 'And I should think, when someone loses his hand, he'd feel similar. Or she. Like you're partly falling out of everything. Like you're no longer fully locked into position. So if you put the two things together you'd get a double whammy, I would imagine.'

'There's something I've been meaning to tell you,' Abby said. She seemed abruptly to have lost interest in the discussion, as she often did when arguments got too involved. She was not a lover of intricacy, a trait Gerald admired in her, aware he could all too easily get tangled up in it.

'Oh yes?' His heart sank. The sea-sickness, horse-sickness, that had been creeping up on him surged forward, upwards, like the tide. What would she reveal next? The discovery that she had been a Girl Guide had unnerved him – the thin end of a wedge. You could be married to someone forever and still not know who they were, what they'd done. In certain respects she was just as much 'other' as her bloody horse. They had never exchanged pasts when they first met. Abby was so young then, in any case, and Gerald was ashamed not to have had one of his own up to that point. He was reading history without having acquired any. Sometimes there's a need to conceal what you *haven't* done. In any case, Abby's arrival in his life gave him a large enough present tense to inhabit without worrying about what had gone on, or not gone on, before. 'I'm sick of being up here,' he said.

'You'll soon get the hang of it.'

'No, I mean it. It makes me want to throw up. I think I'm going to throw up.'

'For God's sake, Gerald, not over Dorothy.'

'It's Dorothy that's caused it in the first place. You feel sick when you lose your bearings. Sitting here, I've lost my bearings.'

Abby stopped the horse. Gerald swung the leg he had come to think of as his *far* leg back up on the animal's back, released his other foot from its stirrup, and slithered down to the ground. Dorothy did a long rattling neigh to mark his fall. He leaned against her flank while he tried to recover himself. Perversely it was now the *ground* that was shifting underneath him. 'What?' he asked finally.

'I invited Judith. She's coming tomorrow.' Abby looked up fiercely at him. She seemed to shrink in on herself, to make her body immovably dense.

'For God's sake, Abby, you could have warned me.'

'I feel I need moral support, what with Steve losing his hand.'

'I would have thought I could give you that.'

'*She* needs moral support as well. She lost her husband earlier this year.'

'I know she lost her husband earlier this year.' He and Abby had gone to Wrexham for Judith's anniversary celebrations. Champagne flowed, and Ken, Judith's husband, made a speech about the good old days, proving his point by dying a week later.

'Well, we need each other, every now and then. You'd understand, if you had a sibling.'

There was a sudden silence between them, so deep it might as well have been thunder.

'Oh God, Gerald, I'm so sorry,' Abby said, banging her head against Dorothy's flank. 'How could I? I'm such a moron.'

'You never knew her. It's easy to forget someone you never knew.' He was aware of a certain piety in his voice, a wish to make his reasonableness sting.

'I didn't forget her, Gerald. But I've always known her as someone who wasn't there. Who isn't here.'

Gerald's father managed a branch of Littlewoods in Portsmouth and had to catch a ferry from Gosport Hard to go to work across the harbour. Young Gerald loved to think of him on that boat in all weathers, scudding across the sea as if work was a foreign country, wind in his face or puffing at his back. There was nothing heroic in Dad's nature, in fact. He was a small, wary, worrying man. To him, going to work was just a matter of one day after another, which was why, Gerald realised many years later, he had academic ambitions for his children.

When she was in the sixth form studying for her A Levels, Ruth had started going out with a young man by the name of Pete, several years older than she was. Pete hadn't gone to university and had blond hair in a crew cut. As far as Gerald was concerned, that gave him a nautical air like the Gosport sailors, and indeed he worked in a shipyard. Pete knew Ruth's father disapproved of him and couldn't help playing up to it. 'Watcher cock,' he would say when he caught sight of Gerald and then nod and wink at Dad as if they were in a conspiracy together, a conspiracy of commonness, Gerald's father shrinking in response like a salted slug.

One day, at tea, Dad finally took the bull by the horns. Ruth was just getting up to leave the table. 'Look, Ruth,' he said, 'there's something I want to say.'

Something in his tone made Ruth stop abruptly where she was, half up, half down. Dad shifted awkwardly in his chair, nonplussed by the sudden stasis, Mum and Gerald as still as Ruth, intent, all three of them turned to stone. Dad's voice was a peculiar cocktail of nerves and force. 'You have your A Levels in a few months,' he said.

Ruth didn't reply, stayed exactly as she was.

'I don't think it's a good idea . . . ' He paused, then resumed louder. 'I don't want you to see Pete until they're over.' He blushed at his own ultimatum.

There was a long silence. Then, without changing her awkward position, as if suffering from some horrible disability, Ruth replied: 'I'm not seeing Pete. I'm going up to my bedroom to work. See, I've still got my school clothes on.'

'I'm not saying tonight, I'm saying *any* night.'

'Dad, what do you mean? I can't do *any*thing until I've done my exams? Nothing at all?'

Like Gerald, Ruth was tall. He realised she didn't want to stand up straight because that would mean looking down at their father. Despite her rage, it was a kind of good manners.

'When they're done with, up to you,' Dad muttered in reply.

'Dad. Dad. You don't understand. Sometimes, just occasionally, I have to be me.' As if to prove her point, she at last rose to her full height.

In a suddenly self-pitying, whiny voice, looking down at the tablecloth, Dad said, 'But it's only for these months, just for these months. It's all I'll ever ask of you.'

'I'm off up,' Ruth said, 'to swat for my bloody, sodding, buggering A Levels. I hope it makes you very happy.'

'There's no need to swear, darling,' Mum said as Ruth shut the door (quite carefully) behind her. Dad sighed, with relief presumably. He had said what he wanted to say.

One evening, some weeks later, Ruth once again got up from the tea table, tea being what they called dinner in those days. 'I'm going to swot over at Cherry's,' she said. She went off into the hall to pick up her satchel. Gerald happened to follow her out. Perhaps he intended to go up the stairs to his bedroom, or maybe he just liked following her. As she approached the front door, she turned to him and winked. She used to dress up when she was going out with Pete but now was still in her school uniform. That was a disguise, Gerald realised. For a moment he was elated by her defiance but then, as the door shut behind her, felt upset and frightened. Her disobedience seemed to threaten the family. It was as if she was saying she didn't have to be their parents' daughter any more, which meant she didn't have to be his sister either. She was just that 'me' she'd insisted upon. He felt suddenly alone, a foretaste of the huge aloneness to come.

'I'm perfectly well aware she isn't here, Abby,' he said, continuing to speak in a wounded tone contrived to score a point even though he was indeed wounded. He'd noticed this phenomenon previously. You can tell the truth about yourself and still lie, or lie and still tell the truth. 'I know that better than anyone.'

His parents decided he should go to the funeral so he'd know what goodbye meant. He could still see the coffin in his mind's eye, imaging the body inside it like a broken toy being returned to sender. From that moment onwards there'd been a rumble of rage in the background of his life, anger at Ruth for leaving him all alone in his childhood with parents who became so needy, so protective, hatred of himself at the injustice and stupidity of that reaction. There was fear too, at the idea he might have been able to prevent the tragedy. You can feel fear for what happened, or what didn't happen, in the past, he had learned over time, even though it *is* the past. There are always elements that haven't been accounted for.

For years he would lie in bed at night imagining going to his parents and telling them that Ruth was sneaking out in the evenings to join her boyfriend, parked in his Sunbeam-Talbot just around the corner. As if, somehow, that was still possible to do. It was like time travel: go back to that moment and handle it differently. It would have saved her. But of course he could never have told them. They had a cat once upon a time, a little tortoiseshell, which liked to set off to school with him. It would skip at his heels like a joyful dog. But then, quite suddenly, and always in the same place, would stop dead, as if it had come up against a glass wall, looking forlornly through the invisible barrier that marked the limit of its territory as Gerald went on his way.

The as-if world had a barrier just like that. You could see through it, or at least imagine yourself beyond it, but the physical you would stop dead.

If he had told on that wink, he would have been a different person. He would have been the person who had told. A different *he* would have peeled off from the one he actually was and walked away on the other side of the glass wall.

And even if he *had* done that, if he had betrayed Ruth, he would never have known that he was saving her life in any case, because of course she wouldn't have died. He wouldn't even have known he was on the other side of the wall. It would have been worth it to be that person, but he would never have *known* it was worth it, so it wouldn't have been worth it, after all. He would have just been the boy who sneaked on his sister. She would never have forgiven him.

His father sold their car at once, though the accident was nothing to do with it or him. He believed driving was cursed, that life was cursed because it could be contradicted by death. He became even more timid after the accident, preoccupied with the responsibility of fatherhood. He didn't like Gerald going on school trips or joining clubs or swimming out of his depth. He didn't even want him to graduate into long trousers, as if growing up was itself the problem. Gerald stood at the school bus stop on long pink legs like a flamingo.

Abby patted his cheek. 'I'm so sorry I made you ride Dorothy,' she said. He reached out his hand and patted Abby's cheek in return. Dorothy breathed a long sigh through vibrating nostrils.

CHAPTER 4

A toot. Terse but threatening – not to be confused with other toots that warn or greet or bellow in rage.

A large potato lorry was idling in the road while Judith drove her little car forward and back in an incremental succession of awkward angles, trying to fit into a parking space opposite the house. The potato man clocked her efforts with a slab face and dead eyes, looking like his own product. Eventually Judith came fully out into the road. As she was doing so, she caught sight of Gerald waiting in his doorway and gave him a quick divided look, part hello, part wait a minute. The potato lorry edged forwards, assuming she'd given up, then went backwards with a sudden bounce when it became clear she had merely decided to reverse park. This time she succeeded, more or less, and the lorry lunged forwards once more, only to stop with another jerk as she opened her door right in front of it and climbed out of her car.

'Darling,' she exclaimed, running across the road to Gerald, her lips already puckered. Just as she reached the pavement, she stopped in her tracks and turned to give the lorry-driver a wave either of apology or dismissal – it wasn't clear which. He gave a double fuck-off toot in response and roared up the road in a cloud of clutch.

'Well!' Judith said, turning to Gerald and patting his lips consolingly with the flat of her hand to keep her lipstick intact. 'Well, well.' She had on a bright green suit and high heels as red as her lips.

'I don't know how you can drive in them,' Gerald said. He was always at a loss initiating conversation when meeting someone after a while, like a cold machine that needed to be cranked back into life.

She crinkled her nose. 'Badly,' she said and shrugged her shoulders in a way that reminded him of her sister. Judith was small too, though an inch or two taller than Abby, with hair dyed reddish black and brushed down to her shoulders. She was two or three years younger, with a round smooth face.

'Don't think she doesn't have wrinkles,' Abby had said in a sort of briefing for the visit. 'They're just buried.'

'I rode Abby's horse the other day,' Gerald said. 'Also badly.'

'My cowboy,' Judith said.

'Dorothy, name of.'

'We only have sheep up Wrexham way. Sheep, sheep, and more sheep. That comes of living in Wales. I don't think any-one bothers to give them names, given they're all identical to each other. Abby had a friend called Dorothy when she was young. They fell out after a time, like you do. She ended up going to university to study Chinese, I remember, Dorothy did, while Abby was stuck in her shop selling hammers and nails to people. I wonder if it's a sort of homage. Mind you, Abby's loved horses since the year dot. Where is she, anyway?'

'In a field a bit north of Bath.'

'Abby, I mean.'

'Oh. Out. She's out. Talking of which, come in.'

'I need my case.'

'Of course you need your case. Your case!' They crossed the road. Judith opened the boot of her car, and Gerald retrieved the case with a flourish that made her jump back-wards.

'It's got those little wheels,' she told him.

'So it has. Plus it's *pink*.'

'Of course it's pink,' Judith said.

He trundled the pink case formally across the road and waved Judith through the front door.

'I so love your house,' Judith said breathily as they stood in the hall.

'It's just a terraced.'

'A *Georg*ian terraced.'

'You have a four-bedroom detached.'

'But it's in Wrexham, don't forget. You and Abby were so clever to retire down here to Bath. Anyway, nowadays I rattle about in it like a pea . . . ' Her voice tailed off. 'I'm sure people rattle like peas. But it can't be in a pod. They're so snug in their pods. In a box? Rattle about like a pea in a box. All the children gone.' She sighed at the thought. 'The gone children. The husband gone. Gone husband.'

'The children aren't dead, at least. But poor Ken. We were so sorry. Right after your anniversary, too.'

'Oh well, it gave him a note to end on. The big I Am. He always loved being the big I Am, did Ken. I'm sorry you and Abby had to come back to Wrexham again so soon after the party.'

The Big I Was, thought Gerald. It was the sort of gloat that comes with age. 'Talking about peas,' he said, 'that's where Abby's gone. To get some peas. She's cooking lamb in your honour.'

'That would be the Wrexham angle, like I said.'

'She insists lamb has to have peas. You know what Abby's like, insisting. She won't have peas with any other sort of meat, just lamb. So off she went to Morrisons.'

'It's useful to have them in anyway, in case you put your back out. But peas or no peas, the thing about Abby is she's never about. Whenever I come to visit, at least.'

'I don't think she expected you till a bit later. In the meantime I can show you to your room.'

'Ah. Yes. My room.' They stood looking at each other for a moment, the pressure of the word seeming to weigh on them. The 'bed' is silent, Gerald thought. 'How *are* the children, by the way?' he asked to ease the awkwardness.

'The children? Oh, much the same. Jed seems to rise and rise in the supermarket system. He's an area manager now.'

'Good for him. My father was in the retail trade, as you know. Littlewoods. He used to go to work by ferry. Across Portsmouth harbour. It's shorter by water, he always said.'

'Of course, Jed's dad was an area manager too, in the car business. But the thing is, in Jed's case it's a con.'

'What do you mean, a con?'

'I mean Jed's not being true to himself when he rises. He's someone else. The real Jed would never rise. He wouldn't have it in him. He wouldn't even *want* to. Deep down he likes to keep his feet on the ground. Plus he's not clever enough. I love him lots, but he hasn't got the brains. He takes after *me* in that respect.'

'But he *has* risen, so he *must* have the brains.' Judith looked at Gerald in slight puzzlement at this, maybe irritation at being contradicted. 'Just like you have,' he added clumsily. Of course, she hadn't exactly risen. 'The brains,' he clarified.

The look passed away as Judith remembered her previous flow. 'He's so good at pretending to be clever, it's exactly like he *is* clever, so that makes him do clever things pursuant to his work, but he isn't really clever at all. It's just the *pretending* that he's good at. Is that the right word, pursuant? It's a con. He's good at conning.'

'But that's like saying a handsome man is an ugly man pretending to be handsome, even though everyone *says* he's handsome.' Remembering some of the men women fell for, Gerald wondered if this paradox was in fact true.

'Oh, he's handsome all right. Always has been. He makes a

point of it. You know Jed. I'm hoping having little Danny will bring him down to earth.'

'Ah yes, little Danny.' Gerald sighed. It seemed unfair, Judith having a grandchild while he and Abby had never been able to make a baby in the first place. There was another moment of silence. This time Judith looked at him expectantly, her brows, which must have been shaped and darkened somehow, slightly raised. 'And Rita?' Gerald asked at last.

'Oh, Rita. I love her but she's the one who could do with being someone else, to a certain extent, anyway. I'd be a lot happier if she changed her personality. As it is, she hops from bloke to bloke.'

It was a muddy, blustery day in early spring, with sudden spells of sunshine. They had all gone for a walk along a country lane just outside Wrexham. Judith was pregnant with Jed at the time and was walking ahead with Abby, while Gerald was with Ken, who had Rita in a pouch against his chest. The baby twisted herself around so she could stare at Gerald with that unblinking stare of small children, like a snake's. You expect eyes to transmit as well as receive, but hers were just scooping up data. She had two little bunches of hair on the top of her head secured by elastic bands.

Ken was talking about his car dealership. 'You get these punters coming along,' he said, 'and they want to know if the model they're looking at has got this gizmo or that gizmo, and I want to say to them, it's just a box on wheels, like all the other boxes on wheels. Get used to it.'

'I'm surprised,' Gerald said.

'Are you really?' Ken stared at Gerald in turn. He was smiling one of those half-smiles that are just a millimetre from rage. Maybe he was visualising those naïve punters. His chunky face already seemed reddish in those days, or perhaps it was just the wind. The effect was odd, anyway, with Rita's pale disc below her father's red one, like changing traffic lights. 'Why-y?' Ken elongated the word, made it lilt a little to put a challenge into it. He thought he was being patronised.

'Well, you sell cars for a living. I thought you'd be – I don't know. Interested in them.'

'Not everyone can do jobs that are interesting, my friend. The only interesting thing about selling cars is counting up the takings at the end of the month.' Ken gave a strange little growl, like a dog, and hoisted his daughter further up his chest, her mouth, Gerald noticed, comically downturned in dismay, as if she had picked up on the tension that had developed between the two men.

Ken relented a little. 'Now, cars in the old days, when you could take one apart with a spanner, that was a different story.'

'My dad was in retail,' Gerald said, wanting to make it clear there was nothing privileged about his background. 'Store manager. In Portsmouth. Well, more like Southsea. Littlewoods it was. The store. Not there now. He used to go to work by ferry.'

'Good for your dad,' Ken said. 'Yes, well,' he added, to close the topic. It was probably just a bounce from her father, but Rita seemed to nod at Gerald, as if to say touché. In her pouch she must have felt like she was on a ship at sea.

Gerald felt overcome with bitterness that Ken and Judith were about to produce a second child while he and Abby hadn't managed a single one, and now weren't likely to, despite all their efforts, all that fucking, night after night, fuck-fuck-fucking in hopes of a result, their sex-life reduced to a chore – like selling cars, but with no takings to count at the end of the month. It made Gerald want to shout out or take a swing at someone. Not a good idea to take a swing at Ken. Gerald's breath was trembly with anger, or maybe it was sorrow. There was a clump of daffodils growing on the verge, and they too vibrated slightly.

He looked again at baby Rita. There she was in her sling, eyes still intent, her expression now expressionless. She looked – he wasn't sure what the word would be – self-possessed, complete. Perhaps you could only look complete when you were small enough to fit into a bag. He felt a longing for her to be his, one so sharp and deep it almost overpowered him, like a form of lust. Parental lust. Parenthood lust.

The wind felt as if it was fingering his face. Nothing perverted about it, of course not, so why did he feel guilty? Was it that men weren't supposed to feel such yearning, that it was the female domain? He felt he was trespassing.

'I could do without being a grandma, you know,' Judith said. 'It's bad enough being a widow.'

'Labels,' Gerald said. He remembered telling someone recently he was a professor. Who was it? 'Just labels.'

'If you have a bottle of HP sauce,' Judith said, 'it says HP sauce, and it *is* HP sauce.' She sighed as if answering his sigh.

Judith went up the stairs first. She was slimmer than Abby nowadays, more elegant. She took the stairs with a certain skittishness, tottering nicely on her red heels. 'But *you*'ve had to dot and carry,' she said when she got to the landing, turning round to clock Gerald still some steps below, 'lugging my rotten case behind you.' She was a woman alert to male pride, always had been. Abby tended to be scornful about it, but of course she was his wife. 'Is it the room we usually sleep in?'

'Yes, next floor. Onwards and upwards.'

'I suppose those Georgians had flunkeys to lug their stuff, given how they loved staircases so much.'

The bedroom was bright and airy, mellow sunshine streaming in. Judith hadn't been here since Ken's death, too forlorn to drive, presumably. That was the reason for that first-person plural – old habits die hard. Gerald stood side by side with her, staring at the double bed, which looked over-explicit, like an off-colour joke.

'Perhaps you ought to have a rest,' Gerald said. 'After your drive. All that way from Wrexham.'

'Do you know what Ken used to call it?'

'Call what? Wrexham?'

'Call an afternoon nap. He used to say, Do you want an assisted siesta? That's what he'd say. An assisted siesta.' She sighed.

'Ah.' Gerald couldn't tell whether her tone – or her sigh – was elegiac or provocative, maybe both, the traditional overlap of death and sex. He felt his heart pounding, but that might just have been because of the climb with her weighty case.

'Bloody old goat,' Judith added affectionately.

Gerald tested this phrase for further ambiguity. Maybe, maybe not. The ambiguity was itself ambiguous. My God, he thought, history. The different histories. The different sorts of history. The history I invented, in more ways than one. The history between me and this sister. The me, the very *me* I invented. The woman I made out of Judith. The woman Judith made out of Judith. You can people a bedroom, a planet, a whole universe, many universes, just by applying your mind.

'He didn't like his job much, did he?' Gerald realised he was trying to find a symptom of weakness to compensate for the dead man's libido.

'He loved his job. He *loved* selling cars. It was what he was born to do. He got his rocks off on it.'

'He told me once upon a time that he didn't enjoy it at all.'

'You shouldn't believe everything he told you. Ken was a salesman, remember. He was good at giving the customer what he wanted. He just pretended he didn't like selling cars to impress you. Oh dear.'

'Why oh dear?'

'Abby's back. Didn't you hear the door? Bang goes the siesta.'

Chapter 5

The two of them arrived in quick succession at the bottom of the stairs.

'Gerald took my suitcase up to my room,' Judith explained. 'Did you get your peas?'

'It was extremely heavy,' Gerald said by way of supporting detail.

'Knickers,' Judith said. 'Stuff.'

Abby was unfazed. 'I knew it was you,' she said. 'I saw your car.'

'Abby, how could you know it was my car? I've only just bought it. I traded in that big jalopy of Ken's.'

Gerald wondered whether Judith genuinely didn't realise the jalopy had been a Mercedes, or was practising reverse snobbery, or just didn't care. Judith being Judith, any of those was possible. She was a consolidation of mutually exclusive alternatives. She was various.

'I don't know. It just looked like your car. It had an aura. Since you asked, I did get the peas.' Abby would definitely judge cars by their auras.

As if they had now gone through the necessary preliminaries, the sisters stepped towards each other and cheek-kissed. As they embraced, Judith seemed to have become quite a lot taller than Abby, perhaps because of the brightness of her suit. Abby was dowdy by contrast, how she liked to be these days, down to earth in a khaki shirt and jeans, blue socks, brown slip-ons, as if she had in fact been driven slightly into the ground. To

Gerald's surprise, Judith didn't withdraw after her peck, but rested her head on Abby's shoulder and began to weep.

Abby patted her timidly on the back, giving a desperate sideways glance at Gerald. He stepped over and rested a hand on Judith's shoulder.

After a few moments Judith raised her head. 'There, that's done,' she said as if it had been a chore that needed to be completed. 'Can you get my bag, lovey?' she asked Gerald.

'You want it back down again?'

'No, no, not that bag. My *hand*bag, so I can give my eyeballs a dab. I left it under the coat-stand in the hall.'

'I have a suggestion,' Abby said. 'One word. Three words. G and T.'

Gerald fetched Judith's handbag. 'Would you like a sandwich?' he asked.

'A sandwich?' she said, as if it was the most absurd suggestion she could imagine. She opened her handbag, took out a hankie, and started dabbing her eyes with it. 'Do they look bloodshot?' she asked her sister. 'I expect they're like a pair of beetroots.'

Abby gave the eyes a perfunctory once-over and shook her head. 'What are you talking about, Gerald?' she asked. 'I said a G. And. T.'

Judith replaced her handkerchief in her bag and shook her head in turn. Her eyes weren't in the least like beetroots. In fact, they had become oddly radiant, glittery almost, as though refreshed by the tears.

'I thought you might have missed lunch.'

'I missed a G and T a whole lot more.'

'So,' said Judith, lowering herself into an armchair in the sitting room while holding her G and T carefully level.

'So,' Abby agreed. 'Gerald, why on earth are you drinking your beer out of the bottle?'

Why, indeed? To impress his sister-in-law, that's why. Which was also why he was leaning casually against the wall instead of sitting down himself. As if he was young again, as he had been when they first met, without any need for chairs or drinking glasses. Though he hadn't drunk beer from the bottle in those days in any case. That habit hadn't even been invented, as far as he could remember. He felt his cheeks go warm with the stupidity of the affectation.

'Ken used to drink beer from the bottle,' Judith said. Gerald looked at her gratefully. Good old Ken, a man who could make his moves, such as they were, without getting tangled in irony.

'Homage to Ken,' he said. He raised his bottle.

'To Ken,' Abby said, taking a dutiful sip of her G and T. She'd never liked the man. 'A boor,' she'd whispered to Gerald at the funeral. 'Also a bore. What on earth was he doing with my little sis? More to the point, what was she doing with *him*?'

'Earning her plenty of money,' Gerald had said. 'That's what he was doing. So she never needed to get a job the whole of their marriage. That's what *she* was doing. Or not doing.'

'That's all he did make, money.'

'Well, what have *I* ever made? I haven't even made that, not so as you'd notice.'

There was a pause. Only Abby could sit and think about what her husband had ever made, as if there must be an inventory somewhere. 'Castles in the air,' she said, to his delight.

Ken had also made babies, which Gerald also hadn't made. Jed and Rita had been at the funeral, of course, the first time he'd laid eyes on them for some years. They both seemed groomed and grown up, and he felt a pang looking at them (at Rita at least), a sense of belatedness. He tapped his beer bottle against his upper lip as he pondered how you could be haunted, conditioned, by the presence of the non-existent, a dead sister, babies unborn. But that was the whole point of the new kind of history he'd managed to get onto the curriculum at Manchester University some years before he retired, his claim to fame. Everything that can happen, does, as his friend Terence had explained. Quantum history. It proposed places where the non-existent did exist: alternative universes. Where castles in the air could be erected (provided they adhered to the building code of physics). Where every historical possibility precipitated somewhere. There was an astonishing fecundity involved – universe after universe flashing into existence to accommodate the lost, the unfulfilled, and the prematurely dead. What gave the whole project meaning and substance, what caught Gerald's imagination and gave him hope, was the thin incorporeal seepage from one universe to another, intuitions, impulses, ghosts, half heard squeaks and mutterings.

Gerald had come to believe it was wrong to think of this infinite array of universes as positioned side by side in some enormous space. Rather they must be curled within each other in a structure of unimaginable density, so that you lived your life subject to the pressure of unlived lives around and under and on top of you (including your own unlived lives), just as fish are able to swim within the deep tonnage of the ocean.

'Talking of homage,' Abby said, 'I'm making a hippo.'

'A hippo?' Judith replied, impressed. What had filled Gerald with joy from the beginning, from those awkward early visits to the house in Cambridge, was the way in which both sisters could cope with the unexpected, particularly the unexpected information they regularly tossed at each other.

'A horse was too tricky, despite having Dorothy as a model.'

'But a hippo!'

'Fat legs. They're the key. I wondered about a rhino, but theirs are thinner, in point of fact. I Googled them. They look like ballet dancers compared with hippos. They charge around a lot, which keeps them in trim. Hippos just waddle about in water most of the time.'

'She always was the practical one,' Judith told Gerald. 'That's how come the hardware store, I suppose. Personally I couldn't bear going in there. There was always a tinny woody smell in the place. Nothing for sale that you could eat or wear: just hard cold things like cans of paint and chisels. She was ambidextrous, you know, when she was little.'

'Abby was?' Gerald looked at Abby, who was pinging a finger against the rim of her glass, lost in her own thoughts. About Steve, in all probability, and her hippo.

'I think she suppressed it as she got older. It withered on the vine.'

'Is that right, Abby?'

'What?'

'You being ambidextrous.'

'I just grew out of it, I suppose.'

What else don't I know about this woman? thought Gerald. Yesterday I discovered she was a Girl Guide; now I find out she used to be ambidextrous. He felt a stupid twinge of jealousy. What of? What, conceivably, of? Long-ago deftness with her left hand? In any case, jealousy betrayed his whole pluralistic outlook. The thing about quantum mechanics was its generosity, the amount of give it gave. It evoked a multiverse of here comes everybody.

'Why are you making a hippo, did you say?' Judith asked.

'As a tribute to my pottery teacher, Steve.'

'Is he dead?'

'Yes.'

'Abby!' Gerald protested.

'Well, dead as a pottery teacher. He's lost a hand.'

'How funny,' Judith said.

Unshockable Abby looked shocked at this. 'I don't think it's very funny. I don't suppose Steve thinks it's very funny. He got run over, poor man. At least his hand did.'

'What I mean is, we were just talking about your hand

withering on the vine, and now here's this Steve who's lost his altogether. Gone for good. Isn't that a knock on the door?'

'Is it?' Gerald said. Their house had thick walls, so it was not always easy to hear knocks on the front door or the phone ringing when they were seated in the front room. But Judith had always radiated alertness, an acuity of the senses. There was something honed and focused in her expression even when she seemed all over the place mentally – he could picture her snuffling scents in the depths of a forest, in her lipstick and high heels. He and Abby had had to lipread the TV when they visited her and Ken at their place in Wrexham, the volume was so low – though the set was huge, he recalled.

'I'll go and see,' Abby said.

'Chin chin,' Judith said to Gerald when she'd left the room.

They looked at each other conspiratorially. Here it was again, the pressure of the uncompleted past, the past that had failed somehow to make it through to the present. The past that never led anywhere, that was like a shard or a stump in your memory. But in an alternative universe, just a few universes along, or a few deep, it would have grown to maturity, become tall enough to loom over them.

'Chin chin,' Gerald repeated, hoisting his bottle once more and raising his eyebrows at Judith as he did so. Judith wrinkled her nose in reply. They both started when Abby came back in.

'Look what I've got,' Abby said.

Behind her was a policeman. Even though he was holding his helmet, he looked extraordinarily large standing there in the entrance to the sitting room, as if he was some kind of animal that didn't belong indoors. The deep dark blue of his uniform added to the ominous effect, like a cloud suddenly blotting out the sun.

'You've got a policeman,' said Judith breathily. 'I've always wanted one of those.' There was an awkward silence. 'There are hardly any policemen in Wrexham,' she said.

'He was just standing at the front door,' Abby said, as if he had been deposited there like a bottle of milk.

The policeman looked familiar. During the last few years Gerald had come to suspect he had clocked all human types. Every face he saw nowadays reminded him of one seen previously. Growing older, you found yourself surrounded by treacherous similarity.

The policeman gave Gerald a long, steady look. 'Professor Walker,' he said.

Gerald glanced towards Abby, unnerved. She just shrugged slightly, no doubt assuming he was showing general disapproval of the police. She would automatically sympathise, despite her love of fictional detectives. He turned back to the constable. 'Yes. Yes,' he said huskily. He felt his Adam's apple bob. 'That's me.'

'Constable Bennett. You may remember we met a few weeks back.'

'So we did. I was going for a bit of a walk.'

'That's right, you were. You were going for a bit of a walk. Quite late at night.'

'Well, there wasn't a curfew, was there? I went to a film and then I was walking it off afterwards.'

'We bumped into each other while you *were* walking it off, and had a little talk, if you remember,' Constable Bennett said.

'We did, didn't we? Yes.'

'You told me that earlier on you'd been speaking to a young girl.'

Gerald kept his eyes fixed on the policeman's face, but he could hear Abby and Judith reacting, the tiniest intake of breath. 'That's right, I did.'

The constable raised his voice slightly to address the women. 'A homeless person,' he explained. 'By name of Laura, I remember.'

'Did you say Laura?' Abby asked.

'Yes. Laura.'

'How strange.'

The constable turned back to Gerald as if requiring confirmation.

'Laura, yes,' Gerald said.

'Laura,' Abby repeated.

'I thought that name seemed a bit upmarket for a type like that,' the constable said.

'*Is* there a type like that?' Abby asked.

'There but for the grace of God,' Judith put in. 'Did she have an interesting story to tell, Gerald?'

'Her story was she wanted to end her story. She wanted to jump in the river. She grabbed hold of me and more or less dragged me to it. Where the weir is, opposite the Rec. I think she wanted me to be a witness.'

'A witness?' Judith asked. 'I wouldn't like a witness. I think killing yourself's one of those things best left private. You don't want other people watching.'

'She wanted it to feel real,' Abby said. 'Like when I'm galloping across a field on Dorothy and suddenly think, yes! I always imagine a grandstand full of people cheering me on.'

'That's what I thought,' Gerald replied. 'The girl wanted me to still be there when she had gone. What I guessed, anyhow.'

'More likely wanted you to jump in after and fish her out,' Judith said. 'I can't help it,' she told Abby, 'I've always believed in happy endings.'

'Thing is,' said Constable Bennett, 'we *have* fished someone out of the river. Earlier today, a young woman. No ID on her. No clothes on her, in fact.'

'Perhaps her clothes got pulled off by the turbulence of the water,' Abby said.

'I think I would strip off in any case, if I was determined to drown myself,' Judith said. 'Purer, I think, and more romantic.

If you insist on killing yourself you might as well be romantic about it.'

'It could have been foul play,' put in Abby. 'Raped. Then dumped.'

The word rape clanged like a cracked bell. 'So then I thought about what you told me that night,' the policeman continued. He looked at Gerald, something loaded about his gaze. His eyes were very close together. Gerald thought he detected a slight lessening of contempt.

'How did you find me?'

'I looked you up. Only one Professor Walker in the whole of the Bath directory. Easy enough.'

Thanks, Abby, thought Gerald. It was she who had listed their details. When he queried the use of the honorific, she had said, 'For heaven's sake, Gerald, what's wrong with you? Flaunt it.' Given she was the last person in the world to be impressed by a title, it had seemed an odd thing to have done. Perhaps she put it in precisely because it *didn't* matter to her.

'I don't see what I can do to help.'

'You could come down to the morgue and identify her.'

'How can I? I don't know who she was. Only her first name, Laura.'

'Are you sure she was called Laura?' Abby asked.

'That's what she told me.'

'How old was she?'

'Young. A girl.'

'A first name is better than nothing,' Constable Bennett explained. 'If it *is* the girl in question we can put it in Missing Persons and see what comes out.'

'It will winnow the possibilities,' Abby said.

A basement room at the back of the hospital, lit by fizzing neon, with what looked like gigantic filing cabinets installed along two of the walls. No one about, no one alive at least.

'There ought to be *some*one here,' Gerald said to the constable. He got pompous when nervous. 'At all times.'

'They're not going to climb out of their drawers and clear off.'

'Somebody might come in and steal one, though.' Gerald took a sharp sniff, let the air out noisily to fill the unappreciative space.

'Most of the burglars I know prefer mobile phones and bank cards. Easier to carry, I suppose.'

A steel door opened in the far wall, and a man in scrubs with a surgical mask dangling on his chest stared at them. His round specs and bald head reflected the light.

'We were wondering where everyone was,' Gerald said. 'It was so quiet.' There was a pause. 'Like a morgue,' he added. That compulsion to say *any*thing to fill the silence – it came from a lifetime of keeping tutorials on the go. Or maybe it was just the need to ingratiate, in the way a dog might wag its tail.

The man stood perfectly still and remained silent. Gerald breathed loudly again.

'This is the overflow room,' the morgue man said finally. 'We just use it for storage when the death rate is high. In the winter, as a rule, when old people die like flies.' He cocked his head backwards. 'The mortuary as such is through there. What can I do for you two gentlemen?'

'We want to take a look at the river body,' the policeman said. He stepped forward and showed the man his identification. 'This person is called Professor Walker. He might know her.'

'Not *know*, exactly. Met, more like. Just the once, in fact.' Gerald realised he had spoken as if there was shame in admitting acquaintanceship with a dead person. His head fizzed like the neon light. He stretched his eyes as wide open as possible, making his mouth into an O to get them all the way, then shut them violently, hoping to dislodge the ache in the way you shift pressure in your ears when a plane begins to descend. Sure enough, for a moment the interference seemed to fade, but then resumed again.

The morgue man gave a stare, a glare even, perhaps in response to Gerald's popped eyes. He was like librarians Gerald had encountered over the years. Custodians didn't seem to welcome people actually looking at the books in their charge, or the corpses. The morgue man led them to the inner room and across to another wall of drawers. He pulled up his mask to cover his nose and mouth. No mask for us laymen, Gerald noted. Let the death bugs invade.

The man grasped a handle, and the drawer rumbled out on its rollers. There was the body, wrapped in a sheet. The man took hold of its edge and gave Gerald a significant look, like a conjurer about to perform his trick. Gerald's heart thumped, and he stared into the middle distance for a moment, so as not to have to see straightaway. This isn't my first dead body, he reminded himself. As you get older you accumulate a portfolio of the dead. He hadn't seen Ruth's body – only Dad had seen that – but in his first term at Cambridge he'd come across an accident one autumn evening, at a crossroads near his college. A cyclist had collided with a car and was lying on the road, his bicycle nearby, one wheel still spinning, or maybe just spinning in the wind. Even though at this point he'd never seen a body before and wasn't standing very close to it, Gerald knew that the boy – it was a boy, about his own age – was dead. His body was utterly unmoving.

Gerald had felt a peculiar sense of relief, as if seeing a dead person was something that had to be ticked off, like having sex for the first time. No, there was more to it. He felt consoled in some way to know that this was all it was, whatever *it* was. Life, for want of a better word, or death, the two in this case being synonymous. Whatever you did, whatever happened to you, whatever choices you made, you ended up writing finis on the tarmac or your bed, at nineteen or ninety.

Gerald's father died abruptly when he was only sixty-three. It was summertime, and Gerald was back home after his freshman year at university, earning holiday money by working as an usher in the Gosport Odeon. Polanski's *Repulsion* was on that week, the decaying rabbit in the handbag, hands coming out of the wall, blindly wagging like sea anemones in search of prey, the girl slashing her landlord to death with a razor blade. He found out later that back in Cambridge Abby had watched the same film, with great satisfaction. During the half-price afternoon performance the handful of OAPs who had come in just for something to do called out to each other in the darkness, like children lost in a forest.

Gerald cycled home at the end of the evening showing, still wearing his purple uniform with gold epaulettes, like Buttons in *Cinderella*. Dad was sitting in the lounge watching TV. He looked sidelong at Gerald as he came in. 'You don't want to go around wearing those togs at this time of night,' he said and switched back to the screen.

'They're my work clothes,' Gerald told him. 'They don't run to changing facilities down at the fleapit. What's the matter with them anyway?'

'They'll attract attention,' his father said, still glued to the TV. He was eating a custard cream, raising it to his mouth without looking at it, like people do eating popcorn at the pictures. He added, 'There's some funny people about,' before inserting his biscuit by way of a full stop.

Gerald shook his head wearily. Even wearing usher's uniform was a dangerous move, apparently, in Dad's world. Yobbos, highwaymen, sex maniacs – anybody could be out there, waiting to be triggered by the fancy dress. You could get fed up being on the receiving end of so much fatherhood.

Then he glanced across at Dad and realised he was shaking with silent laughter, eyes still fixed on the screen. 'What?' Gerald asked. The mirth was as contagious as a sneeze, and he started shaking with silent laughter himself.

After a few moments his father's laughter subsided. He shook his head vigorously, like a local aftershock. He didn't answer Gerald's question, unless that shake of the head was his answer. He continued to stare at the TV. Gerald leaned over to the coffee table and took a custard cream himself.

His dad began shaking again. 'Wha-at?' Gerald said, on the point of laughing in sympathy once more. Then he realised that there was something not right about the way his father was shaking now. It was too extreme. He looked as if he was getting an electric shock.

'Dad!' Gerald cried. There were shards of biscuit in his mouth. 'Dad! What? *What*?'

The shaking tailed off. Then, as if his father had just been gathering himself for one last almighty shake, his body rose clear of the chair and crashed to the floor, the chair clattering down beside it.

'I thought he was laughing at me,' Gerald said when he described the scene to Abby. 'I thought he was laughing at himself too. But he was dying instead.'

'Maybe he was doing both,' she replied. 'Laughing first, then dying. I don't see why you can't do both.'

She was chalky-faced, her eyes closed.

'We will be carrying out a post-mortem later today,' the man said. 'But there are no external signs of foul play. It looks like she drowned.'

'Right you are.' Gerald's voice creaked like it did when he accidentally inhaled the smoke from one of Abby's cigarettes. The dead face was chubby, and the sheet seemed voluminous and humped where it covered her torso. He could distinctly make out the swell of her breasts. 'She seems fat,' he said.

'They swell.'

'They swell up,' the constable said, as if his job was to translate from Morgue into English.

'The gases,' the morgue man said. 'In this case, water as well. You'd be surprised how much is taken in during the drowning process. Breathed in. Also swallowed.' The drowning process – faux expertise, Gerald suspected. Same as that 'we' he'd used of the post-mortem. There was something obnoxious about the man's knowingness. He was probably not a pathologist at all, despite his surgical-looking gear, just an attendant, proud of seeming clinical. 'But she was quite a large lady to begin with,' the man conceded. He too stared down at where the bosom must be. 'In various places we've noticed some nibbling by trout.'

'How old?'. Quite irrelevant, because Gerald had known immediately that this wasn't Laura. In any case he hadn't been able to determine Laura's age. And she had been almost as small as Abby. But it seemed graceless, disappointing, to rule her out straightaway.

'Late twenties, we think.'

'Late twenties. Right sort of age.' He pretended to inspect the face closely, though the only way he could do so convincingly was by inspecting it closely. A dank smell was entwined about her, perhaps river, perhaps death. She looked extraordinarily dead, and he had to remind himself that in the quantum dimension different fates are at play. All the possibilities, compatible with the laws of physics, unfold somewhere or other. But here and now, what you see is what you get. He tried to picture her in living mode, a refracted image across universes, like a kind of mad cubism.

'No, she isn't,' he said finally.

'Isn't what?' Constable Bennett asked.

Gerald wanted to say, she just *isn't*. 'Isn't Laura.'

Bennett hissed out a disappointed breath. I was his asset, Gerald realised. He was hoping to make progress on this case, show his initiative. 'You're sure?' the constable asked.

'I'm sure. Laura wasn't podgy. I understand about the drowning process, but she would still have been lean. Thin-faced. Bloated maybe, but lean. She's a vegetarian.' He nodded a defiant insistent nod. 'Lean and bloated.' He felt obscurely proud of Laura, as if she was *his* asset.

'Shit,' said the constable. The attendant trundled the drawer back and then carried on doing whatever it was he did do, without taking any more notice of them.

Gerald refused a lift back home. 'I'd like some fresh air,' he said. 'Head's throbbing.'

'Keep away from the river,' Bennett told him.

CHAPTER 6

He walked back through the middle of town – not the quickest way, but he wanted life all around him, to be surrounded by people who weren't dead. He kept an eye out for Laura, of course. Even though he knew the body in the morgue wasn't hers, he had an expectation that if he did come across her she'd be dripping, cleansed, resurrected, that she'd be exactly what she must have imagined she would be after 'the drowning process', as if a fantasy could be flipped into existence by wanting it enough.

Several times he thought he saw a dingy red anorak, but it always belonged to someone else. After a while he found himself looking extra hard at the people in Milsom Street, peering intently at them through the buzzing in his head. It was as if his eyes were gazing of their own accord and spotting flecks of red everywhere in the crowd, red and more red, jumpers and trousers, handbags and hats, like a disease of the retina or an ongoing massacre that nobody else had noticed. But these flashes and patches and specks and spots never resolved into Laura.

He reached quieter streets, and the looking sensation dissipated. His eyeballs seemed to retract into their sockets. As he plodded up Snow Hill, weary from his experiences, he wondered whether Abby and Judith would still be drinking their G and Ts. But no one answered the door, and he had to let himself in. There were two unwashed glasses side by side on the draining board. No note. The glasses had a spur-of-the-moment look. One had a semi-circle of lipstick on the rim. Why hadn't they waited? He was hardly likely to have been gone all afternoon, just looking at a dead body. Perhaps they were so busy being sisters they'd simply forgotten all about him.

When he was about thirteen or fourteen he'd gone on a school excursion to Brighton. It had been a hard-won trip, in the face of his father's fears. He and his particular group of friends arsed around, and then he went into a shop and bought a plate of bacon and eggs made out of seaside rock. When he came back out, his friends had vanished. Gerald had intended for them to eat the plate of bacon and eggs together. He looked at the garish colours, the pink of the bacon, red of the baked beans, vomit yellow of the egg-yolks, and cringed as you do when you make a joke and it falls flat. When there were enough of you around, you were allowed to make quick trips back into childishness. Now, without his mates, the plate was embarrassing. He dumped it in a bin, hoping nobody saw.

It began to rain drearily. He wandered the streets, expecting to run into his friends again. In fact he didn't spot a single one of the boys from his school, friend or foe. The rain, the afternoon, lasted forever. He began to panic at the waste of time, at the futility of the place, at the pointlessness of the waves breaking on the shingle, so grey they were brown.

When finally he squelched his way back to the coach, he discovered that his friends, not knowing what had become of him and with weather closing in, had gone to the pictures. The banality of it filled him with bitterness far out of proportion to the events (or non-events) that had taken place (or hadn't). It only takes a step to go from the inside to the outside of Brighton, to the outside of the world as a whole – to find yourself on the wrong side of its shell, unable to get back in however much you knock and bang.

Those were the lessons he learned during the course of that

empty afternoon, and they stayed with him. Abby was always amused by his dislike of being on his own.

Now here he was, by himself again. He had gone off to look at a dead body, suspected to be that of a homeless person he'd had a conversation with. That was about as lonely an experience as it was possible to have, surely, particularly as the body wasn't even the body in question. It seemed strange that Abby and Judith couldn't be bothered to hang around to discover the outcome. If that didn't snag their attention, what would?

'If that doesn't snag their attention, what can?' he asked out loud, as he sometimes did when there was nobody about. He found himself wandering upstairs. He got to the first landing, where his and Abby's bedroom was, but carried on up. He knocked on Judith's door just in case she was in there having her siesta after all. No answer. Very slowly he pushed it open. There was her pink case, lying on the bed with its little wheels raised up, as if dead. Judith's scent hung in the room, musky and deep. Abby wasn't interested in perfume or cosmetics these days, which was probably why they had such an effect on Gerald.

He was working in the Manchester University library, preparing his newly approved course on quantum history. He'd been introduced to the multiverse over a curry by his friend Terence, a professor in the physics department. The discovery of variability and indeterminacy at the micro level of the physical world had implications for life itself. (Terence forked a prawn and gave it a glare.) Every instant of life marked a choice – going in one direction rather than another. But quantum mechanics allowed for two mutually exclusive options to co-exist. Whenever an option was selected, the rejected one triggered a whole new universe where its consequences would be acted out. Or to put it another way, the rejected one wasn't rejected, after all. That was what made Gerald feel that there was a certain kindness about the quantum world. Nothing, nobody, was left out.

Given that choices were being made every instant, and every person and animal and bug and sub-atomic particle was making them, the number of universes continually erupting into being boggled the imagination. But that, said Terence, was not a problem for science, just a problem for the imagination. 'Scale is only a *product* of point of view,' Terence said. 'Forget point of view and it vanishes as if it never was. Scale is nothing but a bogeyman.'

Gerald remembered a visit to Wrexham, staying with Judith and Ken when their children were still small and playing hide and seek with them. Rita must have been three or four, and when her turn came to be the seeker she methodically lifted up every item she came across, book, coaster, transistor radio, to see if her brother was concealed beneath it, completely impervious to size. From her perspective, scale could be collapsed or expanded at will.

Gerald had always secretly suspected his own mediocrity. *There* was history, growing before his eyes like some terrible fungus, as big as the world, and here *he* was, wondering what to do with it all. His solution had been to be a respecter of facts, a conservative historian with a small c. An overarching thesis simply eluded him, however much he tried to formulate one. He was a plodder. But now he had the multiverse at his disposal.

'What about non-decisions,' Gerald asked, 'where you *don't* do something?'

'Ah, but,' Terence said. 'A non-decision is a decision.'

Gerald pictured a non-decisive universe, a bleak infinity of aimlessness, sloths dangling from branches, tumbleweed rolling, slobs flopped on settees, spiders parked on ceilings. But Terence was right: to decide not to do something was to decide. It was only some time later that Gerald understood the implication for the great non-decision of his own life: not telling his parents that Ruth was sneaking off to meet Pete. Not a non-decision at all, but a decision *not*. On the other side of the glass wall he spent so much of his life pressing his nose against lay a separate universe, one where Ruth survived. Quantum mechanics alleviated his guilt by providing a geography of loss and bereavement. In universes further down the road, she was still alive, or died prematurely in some other way, or had never lived at all.

The department board was suspicious, inevitably. The chair, Brian Chandler, accused him of promoting science fiction, and Gerald had to argue that the proposal was science but not fiction, or at least, as he explained, unable to resist a further qualifier, not fiction in the *made-up* sense. 'Not history in the historical sense, either,' Brian said.

In the end the course went through as a second-year subsidiary option, with simple pass/fail assessment. 'So as not to damage anyone's prospects,' as Brian put it. He had a big yellow face and used sarcasm as a substitute for engaging with his subject. The largest part of Gerald's day job remained the colonial history of America, up to and including George Washington's wooden teeth. The subsid was merely a tiny extra. He'd had to sell it not so much on the basis that it would enable students to explore alternative universes but that it could provide useful exercises in relation to the one we actually inhabit. They could start with leading questions: what kind of world would it be where the Florida recount had given Al Gore the presidency, where Napoleon or Hitler had understood that invading Russia was a bad idea? But then they had to circle back: what does that tell us about the issues at stake, about what actually happened in *this* one? The students took flight only to come down to earth. He felt he was swapping the grandeur of the multiverse for a party game of counterfactuals. Still, the good ones could come to understand that all possibilities had a predisposition to realisation within them, that Archduke Franz Ferdinand, like Schrödinger's cat, could be considered as both alive and dead at the same time.

Sitting in the library trying to reduce these possibilities – these possibilities of possibilities – to a series of pedestrian questions for weekly discussion induced in Gerald a sensation of baffled excitement. After a while it became difficult to remain still and make notes. He decided to walk into the centre of Manchester and browse the bookshops. He was in the mood to look at books without reading them.

It was a bright cool day in early spring, a bounce in the air, daffodils in flower. When he got to Deansgate he was disinclined even to not-read books. He bought a newspaper and stepped into a coffee shop instead.

He was raising the cup to his lips when he saw her sitting near the far wall of the café, staring down at her table. The sighting was so unexpected he couldn't for a moment put a name to the familiar form. He set off across the café while she kept quite still, continuing to stare downwards so their eyes didn't meet as he approached.

'Spring has sprung,' he said, to his own surprise. His voice felt rough, as though he hadn't used it in a long time. His heart was thumping.

'Pip pip,' she replied, still without glancing up. At last she raised her head. She put a cigarette to her bright red lips and looked at him through half-closed eyes. Smoke mingled with her musky aura.

'I didn't know you smoked.'

'I don't.'

'Right.' He nodded. 'How's Wrexham?'

'Somewhere else. For once.'

She'd come on a coach, with a party of women. They were to spend the morning shopping in the big city and go to a matinee together in the afternoon. But suddenly she couldn't be bothered. 'Women, you know,' she said, as if Gerald did. So she'd gone off on her own. 'And here I am,' she concluded.

'Here you are. Me too, it turns out. How are the kids?'

'In school, thank the Lord.'

'And Ken?'

'Ken is Ken. What about Abby?'

'Oh yes, she's Abby all right. She's off at school too, teaching.'

'Well then,' Judith said.

When they got to the house in Didsbury, Judith insisted on having a shower. 'Perfume,' she said. 'Lippy, etcetera. Body. *Foreign* body. You'd better open the bedroom window. There's bags of air out there. Bags and bags of it. *Bags*,' she concluded, shutting the bathroom door.

He was exhilarated, a little appalled, at her practicality. Certainly there *was* plenty of air, unlimited, prodigal air, cascading through the window and washing around the bedroom. The air seemed almost silvery in the light through the partly parted curtains, like the sheen on new foliage.

When she was waiting for her taxi back into the centre of Manchester, Judith said, 'This didn't happen.'

'Agreed,' he replied.

He wondered if the agreement would be possible to honour. How could a historian, even a quantum one, try to eradicate a happening when it had in fact happened? Useless to point out to Judith, or indeed to Abby, that there were plenty of neighbourhood universes where it hadn't. But when Abby came home later that afternoon he was so busy being normal he didn't have time to feel guilty.

A month or two later, an event occurred that eventually helped to clarify matters. He went to Terence's flat to borrow a book. To his surprise Terence came to the door wearing shorts and a t-shirt; he was normally a smart, even dapper, dresser, and in any case the weather was cool and grey. His pale calves had a drift of reddish hairs.

Terence made a pot of tea and drank his seated on the plastic platform at the top of a tiny slide with only three steps, the sort you might put up for a toddler, from where he expounded on quantum mechanics in that abrupt, allusive way of his, knees bent sharply like a grasshopper's to fit his feet onto the top step. While he listened, trying to put together at least some of the pieces of the jigsaw, Gerald was unnerved but fascinated to discover he could see to the top of Terence's thigh, even catch a glimpse of rubbery pink genitalia that grew inside the shorts like some dim woodland plant.

When he'd finished his tea, Terence slid down the slide, got to his feet, brushed himself down, and then they carried on with their conversation. Subsequent encounters in the senior common room were natural and unembarrassed, almost as if the episode had been forgotten. Or rather, a flimsy, spectral memory of it seemed to hover in the air but wasn't vivid enough to push their relationship out of kilter. In the great scheme of things, what had happened didn't matter.

Then, several weeks later, Gerald realised the incident couldn't possibly have taken place. Of course not. What could he have been thinking of? Terence was reserved, almost prim. Never, ever, would he have made such a show of himself. In any case, what on earth would a toddler's slide be doing in his sitting room? It must have been a dream, one that Gerald's brain had accidentally filed under real life. Perhaps in a faraway universe, a little homosexual shoot had thrived in different soil and was now blooming.

But if a dream could pass itself off as real, so, surely, could the opposite happen. What had taken place with Judith had been a real event, but straightaway it had taken on the atmosphere and irrelevancy of a dream. When called to mind (which was quite often), it never felt like part of his lived experience and instead had the quality of erotic fantasy. It was a cul-de-sac, an example of what he would eventually think of as a stump, or shard.

*

Gerald wouldn't try to pursue Abby and Judith, given he had no idea where they'd gone. He sat at his desk and worked on his book, his retirement project.

The problem lay in achieving the correct balance between theory and practice. He was drawn to the task of defining a new, *the* new, historiography, but his knowledge of quantum mechanics was derived mainly from conversations with Terence and confined to some of its consequences and implications, not its weird interior logic. Not even people who understood quantum mechanics understood it, and he *didn't* understand it. And so far, in the two years since his retirement, he had failed to lure Terence down for a visit to Bath. All he could do until he came to advise was rehash the subsid course he'd taught, do-able but dull.

He envied the way Abby could churn out vases and hippos, her enthusiasm for riding her horse. In all ultimate respects, Abby was a nihilist. Didn't believe in God, didn't think life had meaning, etc., but she had an amazing ability to relish the immediate. She didn't so much read her thrillers and detective stories as gobble them whole. Gerald, by contrast, never seemed able to lose himself in what he was doing. There was a Gerald who read and wrote, and there was another Gerald monitoring this activity from the margins, standing on the beach like his father had, to make sure his offspring never swam far out to sea.

It was a relief when there was a knock on the door.

Abby always had to scrabble in her handbag for money or keys so tended to knock if she knew Gerald was in. But when he opened the door only Judith was standing there.

'Oh well,' she said brightly.

Gerald peered over her shoulders as if Abby might be crouching behind her.

'You know Abby,' continued Judith. 'Always somewhere else.'

'So where is she?'

'Potting.'

Strange how a word could hit with such a thud. Gerald felt winded suddenly, short of breath.

'We went to this bloke Steve's,' Judith went on, sitting herself on one of the kitchen chairs. Gerald sat down opposite. 'Abby wanted to show me the things he'd made before his accident. He's got a sort of display in his garage. Hey, tell you what, let's put the lamb in the oven. I'm starving. Do you know what Abby told him? Told Steve? She said, "Somewhere else you still have both your hands. On another planet. That's what my husband says," she said. And *he* said, "What I want, Abby, is to have both my hands present and correct *here and now*. What fucking use are they on another planet?" He uses quite bad language. My Ken never swore. You would have said he was a swearer, looking at him, wouldn't you? But he just grunted when something pissed him off, or growled.' Judith sighed at the memory. 'Anyway, Abby said, "Steve, I could be your other hand. Let's give it a whirl." So I said, "If you two want to pot together, I'll make my own way back to the house and leave you to it." So here I am. It's not really my bag, to tell the truth. I personally thought that penguin with an egg on its feet was ridiculous. I would have thought it was ridiculous even if I'd seen a penguin doing that in real life.'

Gerald rose to his feet, splaying his hands on the table and leaning towards her. 'So you left them to it.'

She patted one of his hands. 'It's platonic, silly boy. Just potting. There's no need to be jealous. He's thirty years younger than she is, for goodness sake. Where's that lamb? Now now.' Gerald had patted her hand in turn, or rather rested his on top of hers. She lifted it as if it was a fish and put it back on the table.

'In the fridge,' he said. He could feel the rush of red to his face.

'Naughty boy.'

'I just thought. Where we left off. That time.'

'For leaving the lamb in the fridge, silly. It needs an air. To loosen up the juices.'

'Don't we all?' The language of seduction was so embarrassing, as if intended to eradicate all romance and dignity. There was a pause. '*You* know,' he said finally.

'Potatoes,' she replied. 'We could stash them all round the leg. I love them roasted like that.'

'What I mean. Resume.' He was using a similar pidgin to the one he'd spoken at that party in Cambridge all those years ago.

'Resume what, Gerald?'

'You know what.'

'Gerald, I haven't the faintest idea what you're talking about.' She rose to her feet and looked steadily at him across the table. 'What we need now is the potato peeler. Dig it out, Gerald, there's a good lad.'

WINTER

I t began snowing as Gerald and Terence made their way to The Star, hard little beads pinging into their faces on the blustery wind.

'Sod it,' Gerald said. 'We should have stayed at home.'

The reason they hadn't was that Abby was potting on the kitchen table, working on pieces that she would take to Steve's kiln for firing later in the week. Her own objects had become more elegant in recent months, sharper in outline, no longer restricted to hippos. 'You boys bugger off,' she'd said, dragging on her cigarette in a way that narrowed her eyes, as if they were dragging on it too. 'Have a pint.'

Ridiculous to be jealous of Abby's new-found prowess, but there was something about the collection on the table that made Gerald's head hurt. They were the fruits of Steve's inspiration, with emphasis on birds and animals. People have pets to compensate for not having babies, and they make pottery to compensate for not having pets, a kind of fossilised family. Abby owned a horse *and* made pottery. Every now and then Gerald had a glimpse of neediness within her robust exterior, or thought he did.

She had never spoken much about their joint disappointment. He had tried to discuss the matter after that long-ago day in Wrexham, when he had experienced a sudden, almost overwhelming, need to be the father of baby Rita, but his description petered out after she had given him a puzzled look, as if she needed to work out what he was really getting at.

Perhaps she was trying to keep the lid on a great body of emo-
tion; on the other hand, perhaps she didn't have a lot to say on
the subject. You could be *that* close to someone, and still they
stretched away from you like an unexplored continent.
Perhaps this, perhaps that. Perhaps he had been projecting his
own feelings onto her.

'Won't you join us?' Terence had asked, with a gentlemanly
sweep of his arm.

'Nope,' Abby said.

'No, no,' Terence replied now. 'I'm in my element. Look,' –
he pointed towards a street lamp flickering with spindrift – 'as
the snow falls against light, it's black. But against blackness,
white. A moral in that somewhere.'

'Which is?'

'Which is.' Terence stopped for a moment. He was wearing
a round-shouldered tweed overcoat, expensive-looking, and
narrow leather boots. Threads of breath twined round his dis-
crete teeth. He stared intently at the thickening snow, as if
decoding it. 'Nothing is itself,' he announced finally. 'That's
the moral. Everything is relative to something else.'

The irony was that Terence himself remained steadfastly
ginger, against whatever background. His head was partly bald
nowadays and currently speckled with flakes, the snow becoming puffier, but the pinkness of his scalp had a gingery penum-
bra, in part the result of a fastidious comb-over. His teeth,
though perfectly clean, were naturally ginger too. Even his
coat, come to think, was a paler version of the same colour,
boots also. Terence had always seemed to Gerald to be a man
unrelated to anything, or indeed, to any significant extent, any-
one.

'Here's the pub,' Gerald said.

'Ah ha,' Terence replied.

The Star was an eighteenth-century building, one of the
oldest pubs in Bath. Its name and credentials were picked out

anachronistically in American-style lettering, its sign a simple star with an elongated downward point. The windows glowed pale yellow against the deepening night.

They entered past death row, a narrow room with a single bench along the wall, into the slightly larger snug, known as the glass room because of the wood and glass screen partitioning it from death row, an open fire blazing away in the hearth. Through an archway was a further room where people were clustered along the bar like piglets at a sow.

'Pub,' Terence said as if clinching an equation. He bought them both a pint, and they sat down at a table near the fire.

'How's the history going, then?' Terence asked when they were settled.

'Oh, you know,' Gerald told him. 'Slowly.'

'A lot *of* it, of course. More all the time. Never stops. Like science, in that respect.' Terence paused and glared at his pint. He had a habit of glaring at inanimate objects, which perhaps explained his mildness with people. 'Like everything,' he concluded.

'Ever more so since we had our conversation that time and I started taking a lateral approach as well.' Gerald remembered a phrase of Abby's. 'A sideways shimmy.'

'I've been meaning to talk to you about that. I might have given you the wrong impression. When I explain things, I have a tendency to seem very definite. I try to inhabit a possibility, which is very quantum of me, I suppose. It might have sounded like an endorsement. But then you got that history subsidiary of yours through your department board, and I was stymied. I didn't like to butt in. It could have put you on the spot. The multiverse. It's a. What a.' He shook his head. 'Makes the mind boggle. Though as one of my colleagues said, it's quite parsimonious conceptually, even if messy on the physical level. But the thing is, it's by no means a given. Not all quantum scientists go for it, by any means. It's mainly the string-theory people who are hooked. Even people who do believe in it don't all share the same picture. In which everything that can happen, happens somewhere. Some people say that's not scientific at all, that it's a theological matter instead, like believing there's a God.' He paused, now staring so fixedly at his pint that one of his eyes, carrying the main load presumably, seemed to bulge with the effort.

'Why *not* God?' Gerald asked. 'You could imagine God as the recorder of total history.' He'd formulated this grandiose idea, God as the ultimate historian, years ago, in an imaginary dialogue with Brian Chandler, but his voice wavered as he said it out loud.

'Well, you could,' said Terence. 'But if by total history you mean all the universes put together, there's a problem. Each of them keeps generating more universes, that's the thing. One after the other. That's what I'm getting at. They breed like rabbits, universes of that kind.' He gazed at his pint again. 'Your God figure would have to be infinite himself, which is not a good attribute for a God. Or for an historian.' He shook his head, then took a quick swig of his pint. 'I'm not saying God ought to be an old man with a beard, but he ought to be *some*-thing. *Everything* looks a lot like nothing at all, that's the snag. You need to be shy of the totality of things to get any leverage. How would an infinite historian hold his pen?' Terence looked triumphantly over towards the fire and nodded as if agreeing with his own killer point. 'His hand would be too big.'

'Oh well, who needs God?' Gerald said. He felt afraid. Terence was his only entrée into the world of quantum mechanics, and here he was slamming the door in his face, or at least politely drawing it shut. Without his imprimatur, what was left?

'It's true, some scientists think there might be some sort of leakage from one universe to another,' Terence said. 'And even evidence of a collision between universes, billions of years ago.

But others say that shows ignorance of what the word universe means. To imagine you can have any sense of what lies beyond one.'

Gerald's heart was now pounding so loudly he feared the other man would hear it. Why on earth hadn't Terence mentioned these arguments before? He was completely out of his depth, always had been. He had pinned his hopes on leakage from afar, ears alert for any distant hints and whispers. There were dead people, lost people, whose voices he needed to hear again, mistakes and failures he needed undone. He had assumed there was some sort of consensus about the multiverse, and that Terence represented it. But if he'd thought it through, he would have realised that quantum mechanics must be the enemy of consensus. There was that phrase, the uncertainty principle. How could you base a book on the uncertainty principle, whatever it was? Those were words that made text wobble and disappear.

Life's work down the plughole.

How much work, and life, Gerald had actually invested was a moot point. In some respects it was a relief *not* to have a life's work on the go. Why should he want to stick out from the mass? 'Oh well,' he said in a barely controlled croak, 'that was all a long time ago. Brrr,' he added, raising his hands towards the fire. 'Water under the bridge. Do you remember my old enemy, Brian Chandler?'

'Bête noire, as I recall. He introduced the graduands at graduation. Big head of hair.'

'His mane. One of those academics with a mane. He had a mirror in his office so he could comb it when nobody was looking. I got an email from an old colleague the other day. Dead and gone.' Gerald sighed, not sure himself whether it was in sorrow or satisfaction. The old bastard had been right all along. 'What did the man say?' he said. 'The past is a foreign country.' Even as he spoke, the thought occurred: What a good title that would have been for my book. 'Perhaps there's an alternative universe in which the multiverse is definitely true.' To emphasise that this was intended as the punchline, he got to his feet and went to buy another round.

'And how are *you* getting on?' he asked cheerily when he came back with the drinks, determined to get the conversation away from himself. His head had a tendency to shake slightly when he spoke, and it was doing that now, giving his cheerfulness the lie.

'You know me. Parked at life's kerb, like always,' Terence said with well-practiced ruefulness. 'World moves on, I stay put. Still in Manchester, of course. Still go into the lab every day. I've retired, but they made me an emeritus, which means I can do what I did before but for no money. How kind. As a matter of fact, it *is* kind. What on earth would I do with my days otherwise?'

'There are worse things than staying put,' Gerald said. Reminiscence came to his aid, and he told Terence about the period between his research degree at Sheffield and his appointment at Manchester University, which he and Abby had spent in Libya. He taught English language at Tripoli University, and she did some private tutoring – it was this experience that led her to enrol as a mature student on a teaching degree when they got back to Britain. They'd lived on a florist's farm in the desert with flowers all growing at once out of the sand – daffodils, roses, freesias, dahlias – as if excused the seasons, water spinners rainbowing spray on them the whole day long. Gerald drove into the university along sandy, pot-holey roads lined with prickly pear, each time passing a huddle of men swathed in blankets and sitting on old wooden crates by the roadside, a little fire on the go to keep their kettle perpetually boiling for endless glasses of *shahi*. When he drove back hours later, they'd still be in place in the afternoon sunshine as if they had invented their very own *there* (or rather *here*), a verge existence where time crept through the ennui of the day as sluggishly as treacle.

'It's funny; I had to go a long way away from home to learn about the pleasure of staying put,' he told Terence.

Terence looked up from his beer and nodded. 'Geography as the antidote to history,' he said. 'You might say.'

'You might if you were you,' Gerald said. 'Which of course you are.' He almost added something to make it clear that this was a compliment but couldn't quite bring himself to. He'd noticed before a tendency to shy away from anything that might smack of intimacy with Terence, long-standing friends though they were. Maybe with others too – how could you tell?

'Space-time claims the exact opposite, of course,' Terence continued. 'Any case, no fun being in a time warp.' He picked up his pint, shrugged, and drained it.

'Oh well, you're in a pub now.'

Terence looked about him. 'Pub,' he once more agreed.

'Though having said that, maybe we'd better make our way back to Abby.'

'She seemed intent on her pieces when we left.'

'She can be very intent, can Abby.'

'When I suggested coming with us, her nope. Pretty firm. How about another pint first?'

Without waiting for a reply, Terence went up to the bar and coincided awkwardly with a young woman in a duffel coat who had just come in, snow flecking her shoulders and hood. 'Oh, so sorry,' he said, and took a stride backwards, slightly bowing and waving her to the bar.

'No, no, you go on. It's only me,' she said.

'In that case you must let me buy you a drink. What will you have?'

'No, you're OK. No worries.'

'I insist.'

Oh for God's sake, Terence, Gerald thought, don't be so

clueless. When he used to come round for a meal in Manchester days he would bring a bottle of whisky instead of wine like everyone else, as if he had to pay extra just for being him. She's in her *twenties*, Terence, Gerald said internally, trying to transmit the words across the room. From her point of view you must just seem creepy.

'I'm fine, honest.'

'Something warming. Keep the. You're coated with snow. Dispel the weather.'

'No. No, I can't.'

His offer, her refusal, had become a politeness impasse, neither side able to give way. 'Don't forget my pint,' Gerald called out by way of a prod. Terence glanced over, then turned back to the young woman, raising his eyebrows at her. Beneath them, his lashes were pale as a pig's.

'Thing is,' she finally explained, 'I'm waiting on a heart transplant.'

There were only the three of them in the glass room, but it felt as if a large crowd had fallen suddenly silent. Once again Terence's head swivelled towards Gerald, aghastness across his face.

'I'm sorry,' the woman continued, as if the prospective heart transplant was her fault, 'but they won't let me drink anything warming.'

Terence shrugged himself back towards normality like a snake forcing down large prey. 'It's so unfair,' he said.

'Lots of people don't drink booze.'

'No, no. The heart transplant. So young. It isn't right. Look at *me*.'

'It is what it is. Sometimes children have to have them, even. Tell you what, you can buy me a lemonade, how's that?'

'No sooner said,' said Terence, doing his best to clutch onto her up-note.

'My name's Alice.'

'Ah ha!' he exclaimed. It didn't occur to him to name himself.

Alice joined them at their table. What else could she do?

'So,' said Gerald, when she and Terence were seated. 'Alice.'

'Yep.'

'Gerald,' Gerald said. Alice looked from one of them to the other, clearly uncertain which she was being introduced to, so Gerald pointed to his own face. 'Gerald,' he repeated.

'Hello, Gerald,' Alice said. 'Is that just the name of your nose, by the way?'

'No, no, the lot. He's Terence. Not Terry. He doesn't like being called Terry.'

'It's not that I dislike being called Terry,' Terence said. 'It's just that Terry would be someone else. I'm too depressive to be called Terry.'

'I don't like being called Gerry, for that matter,' Gerald said.

'I suppose not,' agreed Alice. 'For one thing, you would rhyme.'

'Good point,' Terence said, with a slight shudder.

'When you die,' Alice said, 'I think your name empties out, like a bag of crisps when you've eaten all the crisps. It blows away in the wind.' She waved her hand as if pointing at the fluttering bag.

There was a pause. Terence was muttering to himself, a habit he had, little whinnies and groans and, just audible, 'Bag of crisps.'

'What brings you out on a night like this, Alice?' asked Gerald eventually. 'Since you're not allowed anything warming to drink. Cheers, by the way.' He nodded his pint at Terence.

'Cheers,' Alice said, raising her lemonade but not taking a sip. She put it down and rummaged in her handbag for her phone. 'I've got my mobile. I always have to carry my mobile.

Just in case they find a heart.' She put the mobile on the table. Terence and Gerald both stared down at it as if an alarm might sound at any moment. Odd to think such a small thing could convey catastrophe, and hope. 'I get cabin fever,' she explained, 'sitting at home. It feels like waiting to die.'

'Do you know,' Terence said, 'that's all any of us ever do.' He glanced across at Gerald. 'Speaking for myself, at least.'

'Me too,' Gerald said. 'We're all waiting to die.' He slightly sang the words as if they were a line from a song he'd forgotten.

'So I called my hubby—'

'You have a hubby?' Terence asked, disappointment in his voice.

'I have a hubby. He's on nights. So I called him. I said, "I've got to get out. Just for a few minutes." He said, "Where to, in this weather?" I thought, Where to? Then I thought, here, might as well. Look at the fire they've got.'

They all looked at the fire.

'Do you . . . ?' Terence asked, but tailed off.

'No, no kids. It would be too much strain on the system. Maybe if a heart comes through.'

'*Career*, I meant to say,' Terence said, obviously horrified at being thought so personal. 'Do you have a career at all?' he continued, as if a career was just some sort of accessory.

'No, I don't have a career. People like you two gents have careers, no doubt. Or had.' She gave them each a sad little smile. She had a squarish face with strong features, cropped brown hair, pale skin that may have been slightly blue, though Gerald wondered if he was imagining that. Anyhow, it was cold outside. 'I had a *job*,' she continued. 'I used to work in a garage.'

'Did you, though? Mending cars?'

'Don't be silly.' Terence pinked with pleasure at being called silly. 'A petrol station, behind the till. But I had to give it up. I got too tired. I used to like doing it, meeting people.

You don't meet many people when you're waiting for a heart transplant. Except at the hospital, and they're mostly old.'

'*We*'re mostly old,' Gerald said.

'Yes, but you're in a pub.'

There was a pause. Gerald surveyed the room as if to check out this extenuating circumstance.

'So,' Alice said at last, giving them each a bright look in turn. 'What hobbies do you two have?'

'Hobbies?' Terence asked, obviously baffled. Gerald was irritated at his obtuseness. Alice was deliberately avoiding the subject of careers so that they wouldn't be forced to pull rank. Terence's curse, not being adept at nuance.

'Like what you do in the evening, if there's nothing on TV.'

'Hobbies,' Terence repeated. 'I used to play the piano a long time ago.'

'Ah, the piano.'

'But I stopped.'

'You stopped?'

'Yes, I stopped. For no particular reason. Just stopped. Well, there *was* a reason. I couldn't fit a piano in my flat. I live in a flat. I could have got myself a keyboard, I suppose, but I didn't. You know that way one doesn't?' He sighed. 'Get a keyboard? Ironic, when you think about it. There's music, just a structure in the air. And here's a piano, too big to get through the door.'

'So what do you do now?'

'Let's see. Physics,' he said finally. 'Theoretical.' Another pause. For God's sake, Gerald thought, couldn't you have invented something, like students do on application forms – reading, walking, theatre, stuff everyone pretends to do? 'Quantum?' Terence concluded, as if expecting a nod of recognition.

'Well, *you* know how to enjoy yourself,' said Alice. She turned to Gerald. 'What about you?'

No way he was going to use the word quantum, particularly now. Nor, for that matter, history. If only Abby had been here she could have said pots and they'd be away. 'Cooking,' he said by way of association, catching himself by surprise.

'Cooking?' Alice asked, her eyes brightening.

'I like cooking.'

'That I didn't know,' Terence said. Nor, in fact, did Gerald. It was something he occasionally did when Abby wasn't in the mood and they couldn't be bothered to go out or have something delivered.

'What sort of things?' Alice asked. 'Cooking-wise?'

'Knowing my friend here,' Terence said, 'and colleague, my guess would be enterprising, at the very least. Former colleague.'

'Not cottage pie then.' She sighed. 'These days I have to have everything I eat measured out in advance, just to stop my heart getting more clapped out than it already is.'

'Like tennis players,' Terence said. 'They travel around with their own nutritionists, I believe.'

'Just like tennis players.'

'I like to rustle up a homemade pizza from time to time. But my big thing is Chinese,' Gerald said.

'Ambitious,' said Alice.

'Oriental, at least,' Terence put in.

'I had to find a gap so as not to compete with my wife. She's pretty good.'

'A chink in her armour,' Terence said.

'I wouldn't go that far. I'm not sure she has one of those.'

There was a compact, even compacted, quality about Abby which seemed to preclude chinks. When young she had been physically slight. He remembered a breezy day when they were walking along the Backs in Cambridge not long after they had started going out together, his sense that she could be swept away by a gust at any moment, that she was teetering on the very edge of the wind. But even then, despite that lift and lightness, she gave the impression of being more herself than others were, Gerald included. Whatever it was she was, it wouldn't be diluted by the impact of other people.

One way this showed was the impossibility of impressing her. It never entered her head there might be a gulf between working in a hardware store and being a Cambridge undergraduate, and because she didn't see it, it wasn't there, to Gerald's frustration at times. He longed to be a snob, like so many of his fellow students, but she would have none of it. Of course at the time her imperviousness made it all the more mysterious, and magical, that she had chosen him.

'I don't do it often, to tell the truth,' he continued. 'My favourite recipe is Stir Fry of Three Deliciousnesses.'

'Ah!' Terence exclaimed, as if he'd been waiting for those very words. 'Is it scheduled for tonight?'

'Never gave it a thought, to be honest. Abby was going to cook something, but she may have got distracted. She sometimes gets distracted. Perhaps we should get a takeaway.'

'What *are* the three deliciousnesses?' Alice asked. She looked across the table with an eagerness that made her seem very young, as if she was trying to solve a riddle in a fairy story. As you grow older you lose the possibility of strangeness. You become used to the world. Her enthusiasm made Gerald want to respond in kind, as you must do when you read a child a bedtime story and you get into the spirit of the thing – not that he'd done that very often. He'd read a story to Jed and Rita once, but the two of them had immediately fallen asleep. 'The first is either cod or chicken,' he said, assigning each a finger, 'take your pick.'

'Cod,' said Terence, as if there really was a choice to be made.

'Chicken,' Alice said. 'More bite. God, I've felt so hungry ever since my heart failed. It drives hubby bananas.'

'He should be more sympathetic,' Terence said.

'He just wants me well, I suppose.' She cocked her head as if listening to this explanation, checking it for accuracy.

'Next, scallops.' Gerald ticked it off on a third finger, as if there were too many deliciousnesses to hold in his head. 'And finally prawns.'

'That's four deliciousnesses,' Alice said. She counted his fingers, pointing at each in turn. 'One, two, three, four.'

'No it's not,' Terence said. 'The first two were either/or.'

'Prawns,' Alice said reverently. 'I used to love prawns. They have bite, same as chicken. More so. I wonder if I'm allowed to eat them. Just a few, that would do it. I can eat fish all I want, so maybe. I'll probably dream about prawns tonight.'

'Wouldn't that be rather nightmarish?' Terence asked. 'I think they agitate their little legs to swim.'

'Not if they're safely stuck in a curry, they don't.'

'I believe they have quite a lot of fat in them,' Gerald said.

'I suppose they must have,' Alice said regretfully. 'They'll need it to keep them cosy. Under the Arctic floes.'

'It might be good fat, though,' Terence said. 'There's good fat and bad fat, I understand.'

Abruptly, Alice got to her feet, as if she'd remembered an appointment. She opened her mouth to say something, then didn't say it, instead standing perfectly still, her mouth remaining open. A couple chose that moment to come into the glass room, stamping their feet and brushing the snow from their shoulders, speaking and laughing in breezy outdoor voices. Behind Alice's stillness their activity seemed manic.

Alice reached down and took her glass from the table as if she had just realised she was thirsty. She raised it towards her mouth but before it arrived there dropped it to the floor, the lemonade unfolding above it like a parachute. Gerald heard its smash in intricate detail, a dense crunch with a circle of tinkles around it, like a sudden crystal flower. Slowly, Alice began to topple backwards. The incoming people beyond her were static, as if photographed.

Terence plunged across the table. The extremeness of the movement seemed to contradict his whole nature as if, Gerald thought afterwards, he had turned into a Terry after all. Beer flew, and Gerald gasped as it hit his groin. Terence was now straddled over the table, reaching into the room, but Alice was beyond his grasp, falling like a tree. When she hit the floor she bounced a little. It was at that moment that Gerald understood once and for all that his sister Ruth couldn't be alive in some other universe. The dead were dead.

He got to his feet and stepped over towards the body. He had to waddle because of the wetness of his trousers. She lay between the pub tables, completely still. They had been talking about prawns, and now, as he looked at the closed box of her head, Gerald imagined prawns trapped inside it, stuck in her dead brain forever, unable to move their little legs, the last things she'd ever thought about.

The people who had just entered the glass room strode forward.

'For heaven's sake!' exclaimed the woman. She had one arm in, one out of, the sleeves of her coat.

'She's in a bad way, Jes*us*!' the man said, pointing at Alice's body with his boot. 'You better do something! *Jesus*!'

Two thoughts came into Gerald's mind. The first was that Alice had been dead before she even fell, so there was nothing to be done, ever. The second was that these people seemed to think she was his particular responsibility. They had no sense of being under any obligation themselves. These thoughts coalesced into a single one: *fuck off*. He tried to open his mouth to say it, or maybe to say something even worse, but his jaw was locked shut.

Terence, though, knelt down beside Alice's head. He looked up at the man. 'Yes,' he said, as if agreeing with him.

He pointed at the snowy anorak the man was clutching. 'Snap snap,' he said, snapping his fingers in sync with the words.

The man seemed to withdraw instinctively, as if at an unwanted pass, but then grudgingly handed it over. Terence raised Alice's head and spread the anorak over the tiles beneath, a curiously tender action, like tucking a child into bed. Then he placed his hands on her chest, on her breasts even, and began pumping up and down, leaning over from time to time to fasten his mouth to her still open one.

Gerald felt a stupefying wave of contempt and hatred for the couple, so much so he wanted to strike them, kill them even. He wanted to say, she was waiting for a heart transplant, you imbeciles, and drive home each word, each syllable, with a blow of his fist. You fucking imbeciles. But his mouth was still shut tight, and he couldn't move his arms.

The landlord came through from the bar. 'I've rung 999,' he said. 'Ambulance on its way. And police.' He looked down at Alice. 'Her eyes are still open,' he said in shock. 'Oh dear. Oh dear.' He put his forearm up to his own eyes as if to shield them from the sight. 'Oh dear, oh dear,' he said again.

Gerald understood exactly what shocked him, the awfulness of eyes that can be seen but not see, the lack of reciprocity, the nakedness of them.

The Star was only a few hundred yards from the ambulance station, and a vehicle arrived within minutes. Blue lights flashed beyond the pub windows, and two paramedics rushed into the room. The couple turned to buttonhole them, but the ambulance men brushed them aside. 'Sir, sir,' one of them said to Terence, easing him gently away from Alice. 'There's a good chap.'

Terence got to his feet. 'It was her heart,' he said. 'Heart failure.' He glanced forlornly at Gerald. His comb-over was erect in a series of punkish spears. Gerald remembered with a pang how thick and dense Terence's hair used to be, a burning bush. He realised he must use gel to keep the remaining strands snug on his scalp, but now it was having the opposite effect. His head looked like a child's drawing of a sun.

'Defibrillator,' one of the paramedics was saying to the other, who pulled two pads out of a small box. The first paramedic pulled up Alice's jumper, tore open her shirt, stuck one pad on her chest and the other on her side.

Gerald could move again, now help was here. He patted Terence's arm and pressed him gently downwards onto a seat, then sat down himself. The drying beer on his genitals felt unpleasantly sticky.

'That's my coat, by the way,' the officious man said, pointing towards the anorak cushioning Alice's head. It wasn't clear whether he was taking credit or demanding it back.

'Keep clear,' one of the paramedics said abruptly. The man stepped away, looking indignant. The defibrillator fired, and Alice's body bounced in response.

'Gerald,' Terence said, 'tell me something. Why did she stand up? We were talking about prawns and she just stood up.' He aimed a pleading look just below Gerald's eyes, as if too ashamed or frightened to make direct contact. Gerald realised what he was thinking. That if she had not stood up, if she could have been persuaded not to stand up, if, in another universe, a universe that went in a separate direction just a few minutes ago, the thought had never crossed her mind to stand up, then she might still be alive. Sadly, there wasn't another universe to hand. It was like that moment when you clonk your car, and you think, OK OK, just let me rerun these last few seconds and everything will be as it was.

The defibrillator fired again, and once more Alice convulsed in a sad parody of resurrection. 'I think she stood up to try to get away. Same as leaving her house in the first place. She was sort of on the run.'

'But she stood perfectly still.'

'There was nowhere left to go.'

Another siren sounded, and a few moments later a police-woman came into the glass room. Once again the couple tried to explain what it was they wanted to explain, their own significance in the world, ultimately. The policewoman raised a flat hand as if the self-justifications were just so much traffic. 'What's going down?' she asked the paramedics.

'No life signs,' one of them replied, looking up from beside Alice and shaking his head.

A policeman now followed his colleague into the room, having parked up, presumably. She turned to him. 'No life signs,' she said.

'What happened?' he replied.

'What happened?' she asked the paramedics.

'Cardiac arrest,' the first one replied.

'Cardiac arrest,' the policewoman told her colleague. It was as if they were standing not in a small room but in a field somewhere, communicating across distance. An unconscious response, Gerald guessed, to the fact that the dead woman, wherever she was, was so far away.

'Excuse me?' he called out. The policewoman glanced at him, then began to raise her hand once more. 'She was dead before she hit the ground,' Gerald explained quickly. 'She couldn't—'

'And who might you be?' she asked.

'Oh no!' exclaimed her colleague suddenly. She turned to stare at him. 'It's him again,' he went on.

'Him who?'

'Professor Walker, that's who. Would you bloody believe it?'

There was shock and a look of distaste on the man's face. Once again, a dull report from the defibrillator. Gerald felt as if his own heart had been shocked. Please, he thought, please don't start. Don't start. The constable was so indignant, Gerald could imagine him blurting out something.

'They were sitting with her!' the officious man called out.

'Were they just? In that case I can tell you something,' Bennett said to his colleague. 'I'll bet you a fiver that the deceased lady is called Laura.'

'Her name is Alice, in fact,' Terence said, taken aback by the constable's aggressive manner. He turned towards Gerald. 'Laura,' he repeated. 'Don't you think that's strange? Laura?'

'And who might *you* be?' the constable asked him.

'They were sitting with her. The woman who died,' the officious man repeated, as if pointing out the accused, 'both of them.'

'My name is Terence Marshall,' Terence said. 'Professor Marshall.'

'Another one,' the constable said, 'of course. And *were* you sitting with her?'

'Yes, we were,' Terence replied.

'So you knew her?'

'No. No, we didn't *know* her. We knew her name was Alice.'

The policewoman asked, 'If you didn't know her—?'

'Except her name was Alice,' Bennett said. 'By the way, I owe you five quid.'

'I don't gamble,' the policewoman told him. 'If you didn't know her,' she asked again, peering down at the pair of them, 'how come you were *sitting* with her?'

There was a brief pause. 'I bought her a drink,' Terence confessed.

'What made you do that?'

'I'd brushed against her by the bar. Rather brusquely.'

There was a pause. The policewoman kept her face expressionless. 'Brusquely?' she said.

'I felt awkward about it. I felt I had been a bit rough. The call of the beer, I suppose. So I offered to buy her a drink. A lemonade, as it turned out, was all she wanted. She explained she couldn't drink alcohol because she was waiting for a heart transplant.'

The medics looked up at these words, and the defibrillator fired again. The policewoman watched as Alice settled back into deadness, then nodded thoughtfully.

'Which is what I was trying to say,' Gerald said. 'She just fell to the ground. Her heart gave out. She said it herself, she was waiting to die.'

'You seem to hang around dying women,' Bennett said.

'I beg your pardon. What do you mean by that?'

'Last time I saw this gentleman,' the constable told his colleague, 'was in the morgue, checking out a dead body.'

'That right?' She turned to Gerald, raising an eyebrow.

CHAPTER 8

Prawns, real and imagined, marked the end of the multiverse, but also its beginning.

Some years previously, Gerald and Terence had gone for a meal at an Indian restaurant in Manchester's Curry Mile. Abby and Judith were in London together, to shop and see a show, as they did from time to time, with Ken looking after the kids back in Wrexham.

'What would you recommend?' Terence had asked the waiter. Terence was wearing a well-cut grey suit, oddly formal for an Indian restaurant, indeed for Manchester in general. There was a kind of pathos in the trouble he took to dress the part, or so thought crumpled Gerald, whatever part it was. Terence's hair, atop his outfit, flared like flames from a sconce. 'I like to consult the horse's mouth,' he explained to Gerald.

'There is no horse,' the waiter said. 'Chicken, lamb, and beef.'

'No, no. I meant you, not the menu.'

'Me?' The waiter glared down at Terence.

'As the *expon*ent of the menu,' Terence explained, oblivious. 'In that capacity.'

'He just wants to ask you what you recommend,' Gerald said.

'Yes,' Terence agreed. 'To gloss. Read between the lines.'

'To tell him what's best,' Gerald put in quickly, glossing 'gloss' before the waiter could take any more offence.

'How do I know what's best? Some people like one thing,

others like another thing. You might be a man who likes chicken or a man who likes prawn.'

'I do like prawns, come to think,' Terence said. 'I find chicken rather bland.'

'Prawn curry then,' the waiter said. His tone was heartfelt. Even Terence could tell it wasn't open to argument.

'And I'll have saag gosht,' Gerald said.

'Saag gosht,' Terence repeated when the waiter had gone. He shook his head sadly. His long gingery eyelashes gleamed in the light from the ornate wall lamp, giving an impression of tearfulness. 'I'd forgotten about saag gosht. I got wrong-footed by the thought of chicken. It's my favourite, lamb is. I wouldn't say I was greedy. At least I hope not, food not being an important part of my life, except insofar as it's essential of course, but I always become nervous about ordering the wrong thing. It's a question of enacting one's priorities. Of getting decisions *right*. More a disciplinary matter than a lust of the flesh.'

'How about this? We share. Half and half.'

'You mean the cost?'

'Not the cost, the curries. Half prawn, half saag gosht. What do you think?'

'Ah. Good idea. It would have the bonus of letting us divide the bill exactly by two. Prawn curry as fish course, saag gosht the main.'

When the curries arrived, Terence promptly helped himself to his share of the prawn, spreading it out on his bed of pilau rice. To Gerald's surprise, he then tapped each prawn in turn with his fork, counting rapidly under his breath. 'Fourteen,' he announced when he got to the end. 'You need to check out the ones remaining,' he told Gerald, 'see if they tally.'

'Do you know,' Gerald told him, not sure whether to be annoyed or amused, keeping his voice exactly on that boundary, 'I don't give a toss whether I have eighteen of the little buggers, or twelve. Or twenty-five, or *ten*. They're just a bunch of prawns as far as I'm concerned.'

'Well, maybe they do have a collective identity. Like a coral reef. Sea creatures also. I'm not really au fait with the habits of prawns, whether they herd together. But think about the way a shoal of fish changes direction in utter unison. If Karl Marx had had any sense he would have used watery analogies. I'm . . . I don't think I'm mean any more than greedy. Hope not, certainly. My trouble is just being wedded to accuracy. I can't stop trying to make my sums come out bang on.'

'That's the result of living alone, I suspect,' Gerald told him. 'You have no one on hand to blur your edges. I'd probably be playing the historian all the time, bleating on about the past, if I wasn't married to Abby.'

'The irony is that the calculations I do professionally can't ever be.' Terence shook his head at what the calculations weren't. 'I have to live with the uncertainty principle. Nailed down with any finality. The calculations, I mean.' He impaled two successive prawns on his fork as he said this, nailed *them*, in fact, staring at them fixedly as if they were embodiments of the uncertainty principle, or perhaps refutations of it. 'Any more than you can nail down a spring day. That's the sort of world we actually live in,' he explained, 'even though we don't see it.'

'One that's not nailed down.'

'One that's not nailed down. Exactly. Or inexactly, rather. When we're working with very small particles, they seem nailed down while we're actually dealing with them. They seem to be *there*, so to speak. But our sense of them being there is simply a function of looking. As soon as we aren't looking, they're all over the bally shop.'

'You shouldn't just drop dead in the middle of a conversation,' Abby said at breakfast.

'I don't think she had any choice,' Gerald said.

'There's always a choice. That's what life's about.'

'But it *isn't* life, is it?'

'Lack of choice is what *death's* about,' Terence said. He stared at his slice of toast as if waiting for it to reply. 'Death,' he finally repeated, sotto voce.

'There's such a thing as willpower,' Abby said. 'When all else fails. What were you talking about, anyhow?'

'Prawns,' said Gerald. 'Terence was mentioning the way they swim by waggling their legs.' Gerald nearly described his fear that the last thing you think about as death overtakes you is locked in your brain for good, that the poor woman might have a monstrous prawn looming towards her forever more, like some creature in a sci-fi film. This was the sort of thing you could discuss with Abby, as a result of her non-hierarchical outlook. She would draw on a cigarette and ponder its merits. She would probably refer him to the gigantic locusts in *Quatermass and the Pit*. But the presence of Terence made Gerald feel too inhibited to broach the subject.

He had become aware in recent years, as his own end grew more imminent, of a developing tendency to try to picture the process of dying, and this habit had intensified since that evening when Laura accosted him. Perhaps because he felt she had a romantic view of suicide, he'd over-corrected and become morbid. Given that when you die, time comes to a stop, he feared being forever imprisoned in the moment of death, stuck in that last split second as if it was a dungeon, while for those who remained the moment passed in a – in a split second, and then time in general, time measured in hours, days, years, resumed and they all marched along with it, leaving you behind.

That was why it had been a consolation to have other universes to fall back on, where life might be continuing or death was definitively over with, or rather both of those at once. He would always associate the loss of the multiverse with that young woman's death in The Star, when beer flew across the table and snow fluttered down outside.

'She made an interesting point about names,' Terence added. 'She said when you die your name empties out, like a bag of crisps. When there aren't any more crisps left in it, obviously.'

'You see? That's what I'm getting at,' Abby said. 'Her willpower was going in the wrong direction.'

Gerald thought of his sister Ruth's headstone, back in their home town of Gosport. Yes, just a name, an empty name, separated from the anonymous body below, Ruth Walker, 1938–55, beloved daughter of. A blank space had been left below it, and in due time the names of their father, then, years later, their mother, had been carved there. Gerald hated the thought of the two of them lying on top of Ruth, suffocating her somehow, infantilising her for always. This was a girl I shared a cigarette with, he wanted to tell their unhearing ears. Or rather, a girl who shared a cigarette with me. Sometimes people put photos of the dead on gravestones, but that made them no more real. They were photos of people who didn't exist. He envied those who believed the soul rose up after death, not visibly of course, but somehow able to *modify* visibility like a flaw in glass, encoding the essence of the deceased. 'It wasn't willpower,' he said, suddenly angry. 'Ruth didn't want to die. It never entered her head.'

'I wasn't talking about Ruth,' Abby said quietly. She reached across the table and patted his arm. 'Anyway,' she continued. 'Today I'm going to Steve's to fire my objects. Then I shall take Dorothy for a trot. The snow doesn't seem to have stuck, and she'll be getting cabin fever in that stable. What are you two boys up to?'

'What *I'm* going to do later,' Gerald said, 'is make a stir fry of three deliciousnesses for this evening.' They had come back so late last night that they'd made do with cheese on toast. Abby had been absorbed in her potting and was covered in white powder when they finally arrived, a room-temperature snow-woman. Gerald decided while lying awake in the small hours that something should come of the conversation that had taken place in the pub. Cooking the dish that Alice endorsed so enthusiastically would be a sort of homage or wake.

After breakfast, he and Terence walked into Bath town centre along the canal.

'Your wife,' Terence said when they'd been going for a while. He looked at the water while saying the words, letting them hang portentously in the cold air that lay over it. Gerald felt himself recoil – Terence's phrase sounded like the overture to one of those male conversations. Terence was very masculine in his way, despite a life of, so far as Gerald knew, more or less celibacy. Notwithstanding his mild manners, you could almost think of him as a predator, particularly given his tigerish colouring, at least if tigers wore tweed. All Terence had ever done, to Gerald's knowledge, was fall in love with barmaids at fifty paces, then bemoan their inevitable inaccessibility, but of course predatoriness precedes the act of capture. If it never makes a capture, then perhaps, year on year, it ramps up.

'That bloke,' Gerald countered, pretending to have embarked on a separate train of thought before clocking Terence's.

'What bloke?'

'That one.' Gerald pointed at a battered-looking canal boat moored against the bank. There were logs and sacks of coal on its roof, and a tin chimney puffing smoke. Fingers of snow lingered on the towpath, so the effect was snug, in a grubby sort of way. A porthole exactly framed a grim black-bearded face peering out at leg level.

'Heavens.' Terence leaned towards Gerald to whisper as they walked on past. 'He looks just like a pirate.' Gerald felt the warm curlicues of Terence's words in the folds of his ear.

'He was a street person,' he explained. 'He made a living selling pictures of pints of Guinness. Basically just the outline of a beer glass with blackness inside it and a white head on top, scribbled in crayon. Some with handles, some straight. They were surprisingly popular.'

'*I* don't find that surprising,' Terence said. 'That's the thing about art, I suppose. It makes things portable. Through time. Painter paints a picture of someone. Person dies. Picture is still there, centuries later. Plus through space, of course. I once got off a train in Norwich when it was pouring with rain. I didn't have an umbrella with me, but in my pocket I had a *photo* of my umbrella. Well, the photo was of me, in point of fact. It was to put on a book flap. Though why any reader should want to know what a physicist looks like is beyond me. But leaning against the table where I was sitting, desk in point of fact, was my umbrella.' He paused and thought for a moment. 'No use for keeping out the rain, of course. It was furled, in any case.'

'A double whammy, then. You can't drink a picture of a pint of Guinness, either.'

'Good point,' Terence agreed.

Terence was like Abby in one respect, Gerald realised: he too was non-hierarchical. Because he saw the world without preconceptions, he made no distinction between obvious and original. In fact they both had the ability to make the obvious *be* original. Perhaps that was why Gerald loved the two of them. 'Anyway,' he continued, 'the postman used to deliver letters and postcards to the park bench where he slept. People bought him pies and coffee. Then an American admirer came along out of the blue and asked him what would make him happy. He replied that having a canal boat to live in would do the trick. So the American bought him one, and here he is.'

'Well,' Terence said. He shook his head at the strangeness of the anecdote.

'There's a twist. Which is he looks bloody miserable all the time, as far as I can make out. I think he was happier before.'

'That's what happens in fairy stories, as I remember. People get their wish and then regret it.'

'It's a no-win situation,' Gerald said. 'Because if you *don't* get your wish you regret it too.'

He wished now he hadn't chosen this particular route of evasion. Talking about life on the street, in conjunction with the chilly wetness of the canal, had brought Laura back into his mind, teetering on the Bog Island parapet. In fact she hadn't been that precarious. They had just stood by the wall and talked. But when he thought back, even her fucks had a lyrical resonance. The details of their encounter had turned into a myth inside his head. The peeing students from later that evening framed the scene like a pair of satyrs or cupids.

In any case the evasion was to no avail. 'Abby,' said Terence obstinately. 'She's a phenomenon, Abby. Phenomenon.'

'I suppose she is.' It was difficult to know whether to be modest or boastful on behalf of one's wife. 'She's . . . ' Gerald couldn't quite sum up what she was, the long lifetime of it, of her.

'Yes,' Terence said, as if the ellipsis was itself a description. 'She is.'

They walked on, skirting muddy puddles on the towpath, the occasional clump of rotting snow. 'Life force,' Terence said, 'whatever that is.' As per habit he muttered the phrase again, 'Life force,' and sighed.

I know what you mean by life force, Gerald thought. Sexiness: that's what it means, at least when loaded with Terence's yearning. Abby had it, always had. Age was neither here nor there. Of course she no longer had the ethereal quality she'd possessed in youth. She had become larger in outline and yet at the same time more compressed, denser, as time went on. But what she was was centred on her gender, always had been.

'You forget, you know,' Terence went on. 'Since the pair of you moved down to Bath, *I* forgot. You know how life goes on day after day. You become a bit numb. Then seeing her again, you remember. It's more or less a shock, is how I'd put it. Good shock. One comes under her sway, even an innocent bystander like myself. You're a lucky man, Gerald. Don't you forget it.'

'I am,' said Gerald. 'I won't.'

'That's right.' Terence gave him a quick sidelong look with those ginger eyes of his. 'If only she'd had an unmarried sister, that would have done the trick.'

'She does, as a matter of fact. At least, a widowed one. Judith.'

Terence stopped in his tracks. If he'd heard of Judith in the past, it had presumably been as a married woman. Gerald wondered if Terence would secretly prefer that. 'She lives up in Wrexham,' he said.

'Does she, though?' Terence replied. 'Wrexham. Not a million miles from Manchester.'

'Judith thinks Wrexham is a million miles from anywhere.'

'Is she like her sister? To all intents and purposes?'

'A bit. And a bit not. Like siblings in general.'

'Ah.'

Gerald knew from the tone invested in the tiny word that Terence had followed the direction of his line of thought, the direction that led inevitably to Ruth. You could tell Terence had never had siblings of his own. You couldn't imagine him being like anybody else, or for that matter, the opposite. He had no one to resemble and no one to contrast with.

'But she has the life force all right,' Gerald continued. 'In spades.'

They split up when they reached the town centre. Terence intended to have a Bath bun then potter about for a bit while Gerald bought some ingredients from an oriental grocery and went home. He had got hold of some dumpling skins in order to make dim sum for starters in his steamer. They should be cooked just before eating, but he didn't want to risk that with Terence and Abby looking on. He decided to experiment with them now. If it worked, he'd warm them up in the microwave later on.

He made a sauce of black beans with chopped spring onion, chilli, and garlic, and put a dollop in the centre of each skin. While he was doing so, he thought about how animated Terence had been with poor Alice, and now this interest in Judith. Gerald couldn't help resenting it – feeling jealous, in fact, which was about as ignoble a reaction as it was possible to have. Being possessive about Judith was a betrayal of Abby, and begrudging Terence his wispy longing when the man had so little in his life apart from physics was crass. I'm treading both of them into the ground, Gerald thought, wife, friend. And here I am, at my age, leering after my sister-in-law who has in any case 'forgotten' our mad moment.

There had been a crack in the continuum that afternoon, and they both happened to slip through, that's all. Judith was right to forget it. Perhaps she really *had* forgotten it. Once the crack sealed shut again, who was to say what had happened on the other side? Your life might be full of events, relationships, and experiences – myriads, cascades of them, pullulating years, centuries, millennia, of them. A lifetime was an absolute unit – you have always existed, and the world in all its fullness is co-extensive with yourself. We are bounded infinities. But it could be that your narrative, your history, only accepted certain authorised events, that a ghostly editor was at work shaping your existence for general consumption so that when you looked back on the past all you saw was a truncated, abbreviated, version. Perhaps he'd been to Outer Mongolia, to Tierra del Fuego, without even knowing it. Perhaps that was why he almost always understood what other people were talking about. He'd been everywhere himself, been everybody.

God, he thought, I'm internalising the multiverse, swallowing it like a spy swallowing secrets. He could sense panic encroaching and sat down at the breakfast table, took deep breaths, tried to collect himself.

After a few minutes, he rose to his feet and picked up a bowl of raw prawns he had left to defrost on the work surface. With a shaky hand, he placed them one by one on the waiting skins, each resting like a tiny pale courtesan on its own blob of sauce. He put a pan of water on the gas to boil and placed his bamboo steamer on top like a wonky pagoda. When the water began to bubble, he turned it down to a simmer, squeezed the dumplings shut and placed them in the steamer.

While he was waiting, he wandered over to the kitchen window and stared out at the courtyard. The sky was suffused with pearly light. Once upon a time, he and Abby had moved to the Shropshire countryside, and he commuted long-distance into Manchester to teach while Abby got a job in a Market Drayton primary school. The good life was their plan, at least for a year or two. Without ever saying it out loud, they both had a notion that with the enormous example of the countryside all around, Abby might get pregnant. But nature, or the Shropshire version at least, turned out to be disappointing. It did so little, at least while you were looking. There is nothing more sluggish than vegetables. The current light reminded him of this, because so often during that period the sun seemed opaque, as if you had to peer out at the day – even when you were actually outside and *in* it – through the frosted glass of a bathroom window. The whole environment was dimly grey and brown and green. They returned to Manchester childless and defeated.

A baby would have brought us together, he thought now. Stupid. It could just as well have pushed them apart. In any case, he and Abby were as together as any couple he knew. Except that at this very moment she would be firing her objects in Steve's kiln while Steve patted encouragement with his remaining hand.

It was satisfying being stupid, letting your thoughts run away with you, akin to the pleasure you get scratching a sore place till it bleeds. A moment of extremeness could rasp your surfaces clean. He knew where this irrationality was coming from: self-inflicted punishment for his anger at Terence in respect of Judith.

The dumplings must have been on for long enough by now. He stepped back to the cooker and raised the lid of his steamer, peered in. Buggeration. They had all opened up again, wagging gaping beaks at him like fledglings in a nest. He could make out plump prawns in their dark cells, like the tongues of birds, like maggots in an apple.

Still, they might taste all right. It was worth giving one a try. If the dumplings proved edible, he might be able to squeeze them shut once more. He put a hand in to take one out of the steamer, cried out. The heat was agonising.

He pulled his hand back so sharply the whole tower toppled over with the dignity of a large collapsing building, its rapid slowness exactly to scale, and landed on the floor, vomiting dumplings in every direction.

Gerald tucked his hand under its opposite armpit and wandered about the kitchen bent over, squelching dumplings underfoot as he went. Abruptly, he pulled himself together. 'Pub,' he said aloud, conscious he was quoting the greeting or verdict or explanation, whatever it was, that Terence had made as they entered The Star the previous evening.

He went to the Fairfield Arms for a change, the other direction from The Star and slightly nearer, and passed a gloomy hour talking to the barman. On the way home he was taken aback to make out Abby ahead of him, tottering along with the aid of a stick. He hurried to get level.

'Whatever's the matter?'

When he was a student, he had a friend who bought himself a walking stick and limped about enjoying the sympathetic looks he got, or imagined he got, from passers-by. Abby's walking stick seemed equally insincere, a stage prop.

'Thanks very much, swine.' She didn't glance at him but continued to hobble forwards. 'Swine,' she said again. This time her eyes flicked over to make sure the word had gone home.

'Where did you get your stick?' he asked, as casually as he could.

'The chemist's. Where do you think?'

'It looks quite . . . ' It had a duck-beak handle in iridescent colours and a black shaft with a matching iridescent band round it two-thirds of the way down. 'Smart?' he suggested.

'Completely horrible in every respect, but it was all they had.'

They continued on their way for a few moments, Abby emitting a small groan with each step.

'What I don't understand,' Gerald said, 'is why you need one in the first place. What on earth happened?'

Abby stopped to face him. 'I'll tell you why I need one. I need one because after a hard morning's firing at Steve's, I decided to come back home to make myself a sandwich before going off to ride Dorothy. I went into the kitchen, and next thing I knew I was arse over tit. I cracked the back of my head on the floor and nearly knocked myself out. When I sat up and looked around to find out what the hell was going on, I seemed to be in the middle of a shoal of octopuses. For which, much thanks, as I said. Then when I got to my feet, I discovered my ankle was sprained.'

'Oh Abby, I'm so sorry. I was making dim sum for tonight,

but they went all over the shop. I was so fed up I went off to drown my sorrows. I couldn't face collecting up the little bastards straightaway. I just thought, sod it. I had no idea you were coming home for lunch. By the way, it was silly of you to walk up to the chemist with a sprained ankle.'

'I didn't walk, I limped. I wanted to find out how buggered I actually was.' Abby fumbled in her bag and brought out a package. 'The answer was, quite buggered. Look, I've bought myself a tubular bandage. I've always wanted to wear one of those.' The thought seemed to cheer her up a little. 'It's especially for ankles, they said, so I suppose it's been designed to go round a corner. If you want to eat Chinese, go to China, is my advice. Failing that, a Chinese restaurant.'

'You cook *Indian* quite often.'

'There is a difference. Which is, I don't scatter my curries all over the floor for people to slide about on.'

When they got home, Terence was already there to open the door, wearing an apron that was too small and feminine for him.

'La la, darling,' Abby said. 'What gives, monsieur?'

'The kitchen floor was in a bit of a state, so I've been clearing up.'

'What a treasure! Isn't he a treasure, Gerald?'

'He's a treasure,' Gerald agreed.

They went into the kitchen. It had been dowdy with clay or plaster of Paris or whatever it was Abby used in her potting, as well as with dumplings, but was now sparkling clean, laboratory standard. When Abby explained her plight, Terence pulled out a chair from the breakfast table for her to sit on. To Gerald's surprise, he then knelt down beside her as if about to propose. He took the shoe off her injured foot and gently felt his way round her ankle. It was as if giving the kiss of life to Alice last night had convinced him he had a licence to be intimate with damaged women. Who do you think you are, Gerald wanted to say, Prince Charming? Me?

'It *is* a bit swollen,' Terence said. He pivoted Abby's foot a little. 'But I don't feel it grinding.' He glanced up at Gerald. 'I was first-aid officer for the physics department,' he explained. 'I went on a course.'

'Hey ho,' Abby said. 'That's a relief. I wouldn't want it to grind. I'll go upstairs in a minute and put my bandage on. I'll need to take my tights off first.'

Terence carefully slid the shoe back on. Gerald wondered if it was the first female shoe he'd ever handled.

'Yoicks,' Abby said while he was doing so. Then: 'Pass me my stick, Gerald.'

She got to her feet using the stick to take her weight. Terence stood up as well. He brushed his hands together and then wiped them against the apron as if he felt the need to remove any trace of the moment of intimacy. 'Well, gentlemen,' continued Abby, 'I will retire for a few minutes, and adjust.'

'Do you need any help going up the stairs?' Gerald asked.

'I don't think our stairs will take two abreast. Don't you worry, I'll hop.'

'It's very hard using a walking stick to go *down*stairs,' she said when she returned. 'That's one thing I've learned from sliding on those dumplings. You have to lean forward so much you nearly topple over. Up is a picnic, though. Anyway, look at my bandage.' She tugged up the leg of her jeans so Gerald and Terence could look at it. 'The funny thing is it makes me feel sporty even though I can hardly walk at present. Like I've earned it. Anyway, I'm off now to ride Dorothy.'

'For heaven's sake, Abby, you've just sprained your ankle and you haven't even eaten.'

'You're not stopping me, Gerald. Dorothy will be waiting.'

'Abby, Dorothy is a horse. She doesn't *wait*. She doesn't expect things. Things just happen, in her world.'

'Things just happen in my world too, from time to time. But it will be quite useful trying to ride with an injured ankle –

practice for if ever I manage to persuade Steve to give it a try. I'll find out what it's like not being four-square.'

'Riding might be bad enough, but driving there will be even worse. How on earth will you do that? Tell you what, *I'll* drive you.'

'You stay here with Terence. He doesn't want to see my horse.'

'I don't mind seeing your horse,' Terence said.

'I'll be fine, don't worry. I will have to yell out in agony every time I brake, so the thing to do is avoid braking.'

'Abby—'

'Except in an emergency, of course. Toodle bye, both.'

Gerald had the odd feeling the three of them had been performing on a stage in front of an audience of who-knows-who, of themselves, perhaps. Maybe it *was* a sort of flirtation, one that operated in every direction, a low-voltage electrification of language and act triggered by the presence of the third party. Certainly when Abby departed, there was an awkwardness between himself and Terence, as if they had been up to something secret or shameful.

'By the way,' he said when they were seated at the kitchen table drinking tea, 'how did you manage to get in? I was at the pub drowning my sorrows, and Abby was at the chemist's buying her elastic bandage. And when we came back, there you were in your pinny, having sluiced the kitchen floor. Abby's pinny, rather, not that I've ever seen her wear it. I think Judith must have sent it to her one Christmas.'

'Usual way. Used a key.'

'I didn't know you *had* a key.'

'Abby lent me one when I first arrived. So I could come and go.'

Gerald was conscious of analysing everything being said. Did giving Terence a key, telling him to come and go, have any significance? No, none that he could think of. Stupid, stupid. Just because the man had taken hold of his wife's foot, expressed interest in her sister. Only last night he, Gerald, had been talking with a woman who suddenly died, mid-conversation. That, surely, was about as familiar as you could get, but it had hardly disturbed Abby's equilibrium. It was quite difficult to imagine what would.

'Tell you what,' said Terence, 'I was taken aback when that policeman mentioned Laura. It caught me bang in the solar plexus.'

'Laura?'

'You remember. He bet that Alice was called Laura. I thought to myself, why on earth does he have *that* name in mind?'

Why on earth do *you*? wondered Gerald. He hadn't told Terence about Laura yet. 'I *told* him, of course, that's how he knew it.'

'You told him? Why on earth did you do that?'

'He was asking about it. About her.'

'But it was years and years ago. This is not part of that business of dredging up misdeeds from the dark ages, is it, that is all the rage nowadays? Me Too, I think they call it. I so hope it isn't.'

'Hardly years and years. A few months.'

There was silence. 'I think we're at cross-purposes, old man,' Terence said.

'Are we?'

'You seem to be thinking of a recent Laura. I'm talking about the Laura of years back.'

'What Laura would that be?'

'Oh for heaven's sake, Gerald. She almost cost you your marriage. *That* Laura. Your student.'

Gerald felt his cheeks go red. Had Terence confused him with someone else?

Terence was expecting a reply. 'I'm surprised you remember all that,' Gerald said, which in its own way was the truth.

'Of course I remember it. I'm not going to forget it, am I? You came to my flat and. You just stood there. And. I had no idea what to do for the best. It's not my forte, helping out in times of distress. Or giving advice on matters of the heart. Even less. I think I told you so at the time, or words to that effect.'

CHAPTER 9

I t was fine,' Abby said. 'I had to mount her from the wrong
side, so I wouldn't put my weight on my buggered ankle,
but once I was aboard, no problem. What do you think?'
Abby looked down at her bowl of deliciousnesses and tapped
the rim with her fork as if to get their attention. She always
refused to use chopsticks.

There was silence.

'What do you think?' Abby asked again, raising her head.
She looked intently at Terence.

'What?' he said with a slight jump as he realised she was
waiting for him to reply. 'I'm sorry, Abby, I thought your question was rhetorical. What I think is how remarkable to mount
a horse when your ankle is . . . ' He pondered a moment,
searching for the mot juste. He was holding chopsticks, which
he opened and shut like a pair of pincers as if to tease the right
word out of the ether. 'Buggered,' he finally said, presumably
unable to find a synonym that wasn't either pompous or cor-
rective. He articulated the word with care as if it was in a foreign language he hadn't quite learnt.

'Correct,' Abby said. She sighed with satisfaction at the
achievement. 'But no longer. When I got off Dorothy, I discovered my ankle was as right as rain again.'

Which suggests, thought Gerald, that it wasn't particularly
buggered in the first place. Abby tended to make a fuss about
minor cuts and bruises, though in other respects she was the
least hypochondriacal person he knew. At various times in his

life, he'd imagined he was suffering from brain tumours, heart palpitations, neurological symptoms of one kind or another, but Abby would dispel them immediately he confided in her, as if her healthy scepticism was itself contagious.

He had been wondering, in fact, whether to tell her about his recent headaches, but hadn't done so so far, perhaps afraid that this time the magic wouldn't work. Since Terence had informed him of the existence of another Laura in his life, he'd also begun to fear that perhaps he was getting Alzheimer's and that the headaches were a symptom. How could a person just disappear from your memory?

Last night, he had woken in the small hours and lay thinking about this long-lost Laura. He could nearly remember remembering her, as if his mind had just chosen to switch tracks somehow. She seemed to loom over the bed, like a darker shadow in the black room. He could almost make out, woven into Abby's steady breathing, a whisper from the past. He kept thinking of Judith's words at the end of that afternoon they'd spent together in Didsbury: 'This didn't happen.' Perhaps her assertion wasn't just a statement of intent, a plan or metaphor. He remembered the idea he'd formulated the other day. Maybe you experienced *every*thing there was to experience, then retrospectively selected a particular route through and jettisoned the rest, the byways and picnic areas, the landscape stretching away on either side of the road. Ultimately, though, the whole world must exist somewhere in your head, because there was nowhere else for it to be, which was why, when you died, the world came to an end.

He had lain beside Abby for hours, thinking Laura, Laura, haunted by possibility, saddened by loss, even by the loss of loss, though he wasn't sure if the loss was of Laura or of his own memory of her.

'Good lord,' Terence said. 'That's certainly a result. By the way, Gerald,' he went on, obviously assuming that that line of conversation had come to an end, 'you don't think the police will come knocking at the door, do you?'

'Why on earth should they?'

'I bought Alice the last drink she ever drank. Forced it on her, more or less. To that extent, I suppose I was implicated. What if the fizziness of the lemonade over-stimulated her heart? Or the sugar content?'

'For heaven's sake, Terence.' There had been a perverse hopefulness in Terence's voice. The man wanted to feel involved with somebody even if it was only in her death. 'I don't think you can be slammed in the slammer for buying a woman a lemonade. In any case, she didn't drink any of it.'

'Oh yes,' Terence said, disappointed. 'That's right.'

'It just shows,' said Abby. 'You get up on the back of Dorothy, and she takes you somewhere else entirely. It's like she has wings. Like that horse in mythology had. That's why I want poor Steve to ride her.'

'Abby, wherever Dorothy canters to with Steve, he still won't get his hand back,' Gerald said, aware of his own patronising tone. 'There is buggered, and there is amputated.'

'Dorothy is a good name for a horse,' Terence said. 'Down to earth.'

'Abby named her after a friend at school who ended up reading Chinese at university,' Gerald told him. He turned to Abby. 'Maybe you gallop to China,' he added, taking mean satisfaction in squashing her flight of fancy as revenge for the obsession with Steve. He raised his own chopsticks, pleased at calling to mind this distant piece of cause and effect, even though the calling to mind was a cheat, given he'd only heard about Abby's friendship with Dorothy a few months ago. He needed to convince himself, or at least pretend, that he still had access to the dim and distant past.

'Dorothy?' Abby asked. 'Do you mean Dorothy Maddox? You mean Dorothy Maddox. Good grief, Gerald, I haven't thought about her for a lifetime. How come you know about Dorothy Maddox studying Chinese? Judith told you. Judith would. Judith was Dorothy's friend, not me. I wouldn't name my horse after Dorothy Maddox for all the tea in China, if you want to know what I think about China, or about Dorothy Maddox, rather. I don't ever think about China as such. Judith wasn't Dorothy's friend in point of fact: she was her admirer. Dorothy didn't *have* friends. She only wanted admirers, and Judith was a year or two younger, the perfect age to have a crush. Mind you, Judith carried on falling for people even when she grew up.'

'So she still falls for people?' Terence asked hopefully.

'From time to time she does, yes. She married a very uninteresting bloke called Ken, for example, who's dead now. I used to think he might be a psychopath.'

'What made you think that?' Terence took this sudden twist more in his stride than Gerald would have expected.

'Because he was so boring. I imagined he must have a hidden dimension in his life, like those sort of people do. A cellar somewhere with women imprisoned in it. But it turned out he was just uninteresting.'

Terence inspected a prawn held delicately between his sticks, then suddenly ate it like a trout eating a fly. Gerald could almost hear his brain ticking over: if she fell for a very uninteresting bloke, maybe she'll fall for me, a little fog of ambiguity hovering over the issue of whether this was because he would be more interesting, or more uninteresting, than the late Ken.

Gerald and Terence walked along the sunny side of the Paragon towards the centre of town. A cool breeze blew. Gerald said he had nowhere special in mind, just a wander, but in fact he intended to head unobtrusively to a specific destination, a set of steps leading up to a chapel in Manvers Street, near the railway station.

'Perhaps you can advise me,' Terence said as they made their way past The Star.

'Oh yes?'

'I could drop Judith an email, telling her I've been staying with you, good friends, go way back, and so on, so forth, happen to be visiting Wrexham next week, wondered if you might fancy a coffee. What do you think? Abby's sister.'

'I do know who Judith is.'

'Yes, of course.' Terence sucked in his cheeks and sighed. They walked on in silence for a while. 'You would have to give me her email address, of course.'

'*Would* you be visiting Wrexham the following week?'

'No, no, of course not. Yes, I would. I mean, I would be visiting the place in *order* to have a cup of coffee, assuming she agreed.'

'A bit devious, Terence.'

'Surely you have to be a bit devious, in this sort of business? Make your moves.'

Terence must have spent much of his life working out ingenious overtures only for them to disappear into the sand, like some bird doing an intricate courtship dance that involved the placement of pebbles or the wagging of twigs, while the female obstinately looked the other way at males with brighter colours or longer tails. But tempering any sympathy was Gerald's anger at Terence's designs on Judith. His only motive could be that she was Abby's sister. He was planning adultery at one remove.

'Did we really talk about my marriage being at stake?' Gerald asked as they peered in the window of Toppings bookshop on the corner of Broad Street. Featured was a pyramid made up of copies of a novel titled *Stories We Tell Ourselves*, which seemed to his jiggling nerves like a deliberately staged little allegory.

'Your marriage?'

'When I was with that student, that time?'

'Laura?'

'Laura, yes, Laura.'

Gerald had prided himself on not getting involved with students, unlike certain of his colleagues. But as the morning had gone on, he was developing an uncomfortable awareness of the first Laura's passage through his mind, like some asteroid that dented the night sky before the human race ever looked upwards. Perhaps the new Laura had summoned him on behalf of the one before, acted as a sort of surrogate – just as Judith substituted in Terence's mind for Abby – her voice, chock-a-block with fucks, calling to him with the distorted diction of a puppet, her hand clutching at him in Bath's dark lanes on behalf of a hand that clutched him years ago. Maybe love's imperatives were fuelled by deflected energy, like the moon.

'We certainly did, Gerald. When I let you into my flat you could barely speak. Your eyes were wild. I thought for a moment you were having a stroke. You gibbered like a monkey.'

'Did I? Gibber?'

'Did you gibber.'

'I'd forgotten.'

'Forgotten?'

'How extreme it was.'

'Extreme.' Terence sighed.

Something was coming back to Gerald as they spoke, glimpses of a face, just an oval really, like an identikit face that hadn't been filled in yet. Framed with auburn hair. A sense of long-forgotten perturbation. Research student. Yes, that was it, that was her. A research student. Of course he'd had quite a few of them over the years. Jonathan Edwards – she was a student doing a thesis on Jonathan Edwards, the great religious philosopher of colonial America. A woman student, something poignant and brave in the tableau, pitting herself against that relentless mind in full flow as he argued for the freedom of the will under the scrutiny of an all-knowing God while Indian arrows whizzed around his head. Gerald, abashed at the complexity of the discussion, pointing out to her that he himself was simply a historian of colonial America, not a theologian or philosopher, gradually losing his grip on the dissertation that was being written under his supposed guidance. How could he even have imagined he'd forgotten her? There she was, in touching distance, a flickering girl able to think thoughts he couldn't think himself.

People were scattered over the steps of the Manvers Street chapel like mushrooms and toadstools in a field. Their clothing, faces, all tended to the colour, almost non-colour, of dirt. No Laura, no one even young, though the old weren't necessarily old.

Gerald came to a standstill in front of them, pretending to be preoccupied with his conversation with Terence. A man on one of the lower steps was holding a can of lager, a comfortless drink in this searching wind. Further up, two men were joshing a bag lady who looked from one to the other in obvious bewilderment but with a knowing grin glued to her face so as not to let her confusion show. A man was counting his change, dropping coins from one hand to the other.

Terence looked baffled as Gerald turned into a sort of tour guide. Isambard Kingdom Brunel built the station at the end of the road. Burgers were on sale in a grill you came to just before you got to the bus depot, gourmet ones, dill pickle, Monterey Jack. By contrast, a veggie restaurant was just up the road, known for spicy chickpea stew. Cop shop right next door to the chapel. On the other side, a famous bookbinder. 'I had some colonial American books rebound there.'

Jesus, Gerald thought, one of them was my first edition of Jonathan Edwards on the freedom of the will, bought in

Hay-on-Wye in the hot summer of 1976. A whole pile of colonial American books, lacking boards but otherwise intact, for almost nothing. The kid at the counter said, 'These are pretty old, five pounds each,' the figure plucked out of the air as if their being old meant they weren't worth much, a sentiment it turned out Abby agreed with. He remembered showing the Jonathan Edwards to someone before eventually having it rebound, sliding it out of its archive envelope, her head leaning over it, fascinated, light brown curls, shampoo smell.

His own head throbbed as if cranking up this memory was painful to the brain. He stopped talking for a moment to collect himself. In any case, he had lost the thread, if there was one. There was a sour edge to the air as it flowed towards him from the street people, the step people, unless he was imagining it. Your senses could slander, and it was easy to demonise down-and-outs. But my God, the teeth in all these dingy faces, stumps, tombstones, black holes. Still, it was interesting how a bunch of loners and losers was able to gel into an ad hoc community. Despite everything, they laughed more than other people did. 'Despite everything, they laugh more than other people do,' he whispered, nodding towards the steps.

Terence cocked an ear to check, in that fastidious way he had. 'True,' he said. 'But it seems mirthless. More a sort of shouting.'

Yes, sneers and rage were folded into the laughter. Sorrow too. Having nothing and nowhere and nobody, apart from fellow sitters on the chapel steps, must surely fill you with perpetual, low-level panic.

'Excuse me,' Gerald suddenly said in a louder voice, addressing the man sitting on the second to bottom step drinking lager. The man was wearing an unravelling brown beanie on his head and an old donkey jacket. Gerald chose him simply because he was nearest. He didn't want to project his voice to the steps in general.

The man slowly raised his head. His chin and nose approached each other like Mr. Punch's. No horror teeth, no teeth. His mouth didn't look like a feature at all, just a tiny crack giving access to his head. 'What?'

'I was just wondering—'

'You talking to me?'

'Yes, if that's all right.'

The man looked one way then the other, smiling his toothless smile at imaginary colleagues sitting each side of him, then took a swig of lager as if the interaction was over.

'I was wondering if you know someone.'

The man lowered his can then looked blandly up at Gerald. After some moments, he did a double-take, as if it had only then sunk in that they were still conversing. 'I don't know no one,' he said.

'Know is the wrong word. *Met* someone. Seen them about. On the street.'

'Acquainted with,' Terence said, 'someone.'

'You what?'

'Acquainted,' Terence repeated, glancing sideways at Gerald, confidence draining from his voice. His reserves weren't large. This morning Abby had asked, over breakfast, 'You know what you remind me of, Terence?'

Terence looked up from his muesli like a schoolboy waiting to get his homework back. 'What?'

'A bumblebee. Those ones in little ginger coats.'

'Not ginger!' Terence's eyes widened in an effort to show he was being jolly and robust. 'Auburn, my mother always said to say. If anyone asks, she used to tell me, tell them auburn. '

'Fuck a duck,' said the man on the steps. 'If I told you everybody I was acquainted with. Name of the game here. Acquainted.'

'Not everybody,' Gerald explained. 'Just one. Woman called Laura. A girl, really.'

'A girl.' The man scratched the side of his beanie as if 'girl' was a challenging concept. He said it West Country, to rhyme with curl.

'Called Laura.'

'Laura.'

There was silence. 'I keep expecting you to say Alice,' Terence said, to Gerald's annoyance. He'd told Terence about the second Laura, but Alice inevitably took up all his attention.

'Alice?' asked the man on the steps.

'No, no,' Gerald told him hastily. 'Laura. Alice is someone else. Was.'

The man on the steps became enraged, out of the blue. It was like watching a sharp change in the weather. He rose to his feet and went up to Terence, standing directly in front of him and staring up at his face. Terence, as usual unable to make eye-contact, turned his head to look over the man's shoulder, which infuriated him even more.

'Here,' the man said, 'look at me, buster.'

Terence's eyes slowly moved in the man's direction, took a quick look, and scuttled away again. He repeated the word buster under his breath.

'Are you having a laugh?' the man asked.

'Me? No,' Terence muttered in response. 'Not a laugh. As such.' He gave a feeble grin, as if trying to demonstrate the difference between a laugh and a not-laugh, still gazing towards a non-existent horizon.

'He was talking to *me*, in any case,' Gerald said, 'not you.' He wondered for a second if he should add that Terence had a habit of seizing on the odd word and muttering it to himself but thought better of it.

'What's your problem, then?' the man asked Terence, pushing his face even nearer his. 'Don't want to talk to me? Rather talk with your mate here?'

Terence gave a frightened glance in Gerald's direction, as if to confirm they were in fact mates, then switched back to the man. They were almost nose to nose, Terence's sharp and alert, the man's poignantly red and basic. 'No problem,' Terence said, adding, 'Oh. Beery.' He gave an exaggerated sniff and hunched his shoulders, perhaps to suggest this was intended to be an amusing observation. Gerald cringed at the flailing attempt to – to what? To be frankly personal, as if he and the man knew each other well enough for such frankness, to take a small liberty when it was blindingly obvious no liberty was on offer.

The man paused a little as the word 'beery' sank in, then suddenly plunged forward, placed both hands on Terence's chest, and shoved.

Terence stumbled backwards a few steps, caught his balance, then rubbed the front of his overcoat as if trying to brush the man's handprints from the tweed. To Gerald's astonishment, he then stepped forward and performed a mirror image of the man's attack, placing his own hands on the front of the donkey jacket and giving a push. Somehow Gerald had expected a theoretical physicist would be theoretical all the way down.

The man staggered backwards in turn, bent over as if winded, then rushed forwards like a bull at a gate, barrelling into Terence's chest. Terence recoiled but, just as the man straightened up, swung his arm in a large arc and caught him on the left ear. The man raised a hand to hold it, pushing the beanie askew on his head. He stood still a moment, looking woebegone. Terence in turn waved his own hand to dispel the impact then rubbed it with the other one.

As if at a signal, both men stepped backwards away from each other, like a couple at the end of a dance. The man pulled his beanie back in place, replaced his hand over his ear, and resumed his seat. 'Make your minds up,' he said as if the fight had never taken place. He turned his head to face up the steps. 'You know a girl name of Alice?' he called up to a fat man a couple of steps above. The fat man shook his head. He was wearing a peaked cap that was too small for him and made the face hanging beneath it globe like an aubergine.

'No, no,' Gerald said. '*Laura.*'

'Oh bloody hell,' the man said. 'Laura,' he shouted.

'For Christ's sake,' said the fat man. 'Fuck off.'

'I think we've drawn a blank,' Terence said.

'I think we have.'

Terence nodded his head slightly at the man on the step, as if to conclude business, but the man was now busy taking a swig from his can, still with a hand clapped to his ear as if listening to a distant sound. Terence and Gerald walked away past the police station. 'Tell you what,' Gerald said, 'since it's here, let's go in.' He turned back.

Terence stopped in his tracks. 'Do you think so? Face my demons, sort of thing?'

'What demons would they be?'

'Well, I just exchanged blows with a vulnerable man. Not good.'

'You could argue he just exchanged blows with you. Plus you're a vulnerable man yourself.'

'And someone died before my eyes. Just the other night. Years go by in Didsbury without anything happening at all.' He sighed. There was an odd satisfaction mingling with his regret. 'Bath,' he added.

'Tell me about it.'

A glum-looking middle-aged policemen was seated at the reception desk.

'Is Constable Bennett about?' Gerald said.

'What do you want with Constable Bennett, if you don't mind me asking?'

'He knows about . . . what I've come about. We discussed it before.'

'You can't pick and choose.' The policeman gave Gerald a long look. His eyes had a pale, sucked appearance, greeny blue, almost transparent. His cheeks sagged.

'No, no, but—'

'I mean, you aren't entitled to your own personal copper,' the sergeant explained. The idea amused him, and he gave out a deep rumbling sound, shaking his cheeks as if someone else had made the suggestion. 'At your beck and call. It doesn't work like that, the system.'

'No, of course not. It's just that he knows about it. About her.'

'He's not here at the moment, Constable Bennett isn't. He's out. I can't tell you where; that's police business. He's out, far as I can go. So I'm afraid you'll have to make do with me, if you have no objections.'

'Of course not.'

'I'm pleased to hear it. Because if you do, tough. I'm *it*, for the time being. Plus I'm a sergeant, slumming. We don't have enough junior staff available, not since austerity bit.'

'That's good. I mean, it's fine.'

'I'm glad it's fine.'

'It's about a girl named Alice.'

'Laura,' said Terence.

'Make your minds up.'

'Sorry. Laura. Alice is somebody else. Was. She's missing.'

'Alice or Laura?'

'Both, in an ultimate sense,' Terence said. 'All three, even.'

'Beg pardon?'

'That's another story,' Terence muttered. He twisted his shoulders as if he wanted to screw himself into the ground. 'Altogether.' The sergeant stared at Terence. His eyes, thought Gerald, had looked at too many people, for too many years.

'Alice died in a pub the other night,' Gerald said.

'Did she really?' the sergeant replied. 'Worse places to go, if you have to go.'

Terence sighed with relief that the name Alice didn't ring a bell.

'Laura,' Gerald said, placatingly. 'Laura.'

'Laura,' said the sergeant. 'As long as you've made your mind up.'

'I was wondering if there'd been a sighting.'

The sergeant flipped open a notebook. 'Laura what, when she's at home?'

'I don't know. Just Laura. The point is, she isn't at home. She's on the streets. You know, like those people who sit on the steps of the chapel next door. Only they don't seem to know her. I asked them.'

'Oh yes. I was watching out the window. I saw there was an exchange of views taking place.'

'I punched the poor man on the ear,' Terence said. 'To my shame.' He hesitated. 'Left ear,' he added as if to confess in full.

The sergeant looked at Terence appraisingly, then out of the window towards the steps. 'He probably won't bring charges,' he said.

'I'm worried about her,' Gerald told the sergeant. 'She told me she was going to jump in the river.'

'Oh dear. And what's your connection?'

'What do you mean?'

'I mean, is she a relative, for example? A friend?'

'Do you have to be a relative? When people throw themselves in rivers? Or nearly do?' Why am I being sarcastic? Gerald wondered. It's counterproductive. Nerves, just nerves. 'No, no. Not at all,' he said in an apologetic voice. 'She's a stranger.'

'How come you know her, then?'

'I don't *know* her. She just plucked me out. I suppose she had to tell *some*one she was going to jump in the river, and the someone was me. But it makes me feel responsible. I was wondering if there were any sightings.'

'We did have a woman who jumped in the river, a few months back. Or was pushed.'

'Oh yes, Constable Bennett took me to the morgue to see if I could identify her. If it was the same one. Laura. But it wasn't. Did you manage to find out who *she* was?'

'Never did. She stayed a nobody, poor sod.'

'We all become nobody. When we die, I mean.' Gerald was remembering what Alice had said about the bag of crisps emptying out. But to be an unclaimed body seemed to him more extreme still, as if there could be degrees of non-existence.

'Thanks for that thought,' the sergeant said. 'That's bucked me up no end. I don't think we've fished out any other women in recent months.'

'She could be snagged at the bottom somewhere,' Terence said. 'Laura, I mean.'

The sergeant gave him another weary look. He turned to his computer and began to type, then inspected the screen, mouthing what he could see there. 'There's no Laura been reported locally,' he said to Gerald. 'Is there anything else?'

'Surely Constable Bennett would have put her name down.'

'You didn't even know this young lady, by the sound of it. Constable Bennett probably thought there wasn't enough to go on.'

'I saw her – that's enough, surely? I was a witness. She wanted a witness.' Gerald had a sense of belatedness, as if he'd let the girl down. 'I want to declare her missing. Officially missing.'

'Definition,' said the sergeant. 'If you're on the streets you're missing. By definition. You've gone AWOL from your life.'

'With all due respect,' said Terence. Gerald's heart sank. At a certain point Terence's eyes would snap into focus, and he would gird his brain almost visibly, ready to pounce. 'That implies,' he continued, his voice taking on a slightly deeper, hortatory timbre, 'that you have an *intended* life, so to speak. A default one. A teleological arc, as you might put it. Do you see? Platonic, even.'

The sergeant looked up with bland pale eyes. Gerald had the sense that he could explode into rage at any moment, just like the man on the steps. 'In reality,' Terence said, 'all the decisions you make are binary, same as a computer. Go or stay, yes or no. Your life is just a matter of where they take you, one decision after the other. You zigzag through your life.'

The sergeant pointed his head inquiringly towards Terence, looking sidelong at Gerald. 'Yes,' Gerald agreed. 'He's always been like that.' He didn't look at Terence himself, too ashamed at this small betrayal, necessary though it was to keep the sergeant onside. At least Terence hadn't said that the discarded choices were believed by some to trigger new universes.

'What I'm saying,' said the sergeant, with creaking patience, 'is you can't go missing if you're missing already.'

There was silence for a moment. The sergeant looked down at his desk; Gerald looked at the sergeant; Terence looked away somewhere.

'All I'm asking,' Gerald said finally, 'is to declare a certain person, Laura by name, missing. A person I once encountered. That's all. It's been weighing on my mind. *She*'s been weighing on my mind.'

'OK, all right,' the sergeant said. 'Listen. Hear me tapping into my computer.' He tapped at his keyboard. 'I've put Laura down as her surname, seeing as we don't have a surname. The problem is,' he said, looking up at Gerald, 'what to put for her given name. If I don't put one in, it'll just beep me when I press return.'

There was a pause as the three of them thought about this.

'Laura,' Terence said. 'Laura *is* her first name, after all.'

'That would make it Laura Laura,' the sergeant said. 'But it's better than leaving it blank, I suppose.'

'Laura Laura.' Terence turned to Gerald. 'Two Lauras.' He raised an eyebrow rather jerkily, as if he had never raised one before. Gerald said nothing.

'Laura Laura.' The sergeant sighed. 'What age would you say she was, this Laura? These Lauras?'

'Difficult to say,' Gerald replied. 'Older than she looked, I suspect.'

'Gerald, Gerald,' Terence said in a loud aside, like a defence lawyer advising his client in an American courtroom drama, 'that's not possible, when you think about it. What you are describing *is* how she looked, surely? She can't have looked *old*er than she looked. How she looked was in fact how she looked.'

'Late twenties,' Gerald said.

'Late twenties,' repeated the sergeant, giving Terence another quick look. 'And what did she look like, apart from older than she looked?'

'Ah. She was wearing a red anorak. Reddish. And jeans. Fair hair. She had two little . . . stumps, poking up. Of hair. Like little plaits.'

'Stumps? Stumps.' The sergeant continued typing. 'Stumps. Got it. And what *else* did she look like? Apart from the stumps, of course. Which might have been here today and gone tomorrow, to tell the truth.'

'They looked a bit more permanent than that. Semi-permanent, anyway. Part of her look. They looked as if they would stay where they were for a while. She was small. About up to here.' Gerald put the flat of his hand just under his chin, as if pretending to cut his throat. 'Up to here, about.'

'My friend being on the tall side,' Terence said, 'my guess would be a bit over five feet.'

'Thank you for that input,' the sergeant told him. 'A bit over five foot. Very precise, considering you weren't actually there. You *were*n't actually there, were you?'

'No, I wasn't actually there,' Terence said. 'It was just simple deduction. Professor Walker here is something over six feet tall. He placed his hand—'

'Her face,' Gerald broke in. 'She didn't have – she had a not very memorable face, as I remember. Like one of those identikit faces, before they're filled in.' Sod it. He realised that was what he'd thought about the *first* Laura. 'You know, just a face.' Something came back to him. 'Her nose poked up, like a bird's beak, I remember thinking at the time. Sort of cocky. Little bird.'

'Cocky nose,' said the sergeant, still typing. He paused to scratch his own, as if reminded of it. It was even larger than the one belonging to the man on the steps, and bluish, rather genital, and it seemed to give way flaccidly under his scratching fingers, as if lacking bone. Do noses *have* bone? Gerald suddenly wondered. Skulls have no noses at all, so presumably not. But they must have *some*thing to hold them up (except for the sergeant's). As so often, Gerald thought, How could I get to my age and not *know*?

'That should help,' the sergeant said. 'And what date was she last seen?'

'It was September.' Gerald couldn't remember the exact date, so made one up. 'The fifteenth.' What difference would it make?

The sergeant tapped some more. 'Done it,' he said. He angled his monitor so Gerald could follow what he read out. 'Laura Laura. Late twenties. Last seen September 15 2018 wearing red anorak and jeans. A little over five foot, fair hair done with two stumps. Pointed nose. I put pointed instead of cocky. I thought cocky might be misunderstood.'

'Good thought.' The ingredients seemed rather meagre to make a person out of. 'Thank you. I'm very grateful.'

'Talking of the right word,' Terence said, 'what about stumps? People might be baffled.'

'Can you suggest a better one? I have no idea what those things are called.'

'No,' Terence admitted. 'I have no idea either.'

'I did say plaits,' Gerald pointed out.

'Plaits go down, in my experience, not up,' the sergeant said. 'Let's leave it at stumps.' He looked back at the screen. 'The description hasn't brought up any previous entries,' he said. 'No cross-references.'

'Ah,' Gerald said. 'Pity. Thanks anyway.'

'By the way,' the sergeant added as they turned to leave. He leaned across the desk and lowered his voice. 'Constable Bennett is a cunt.' He tapped the side of his nose. 'Take it from me.'

SPRING

CHAPTER 10

Early spring, low-wattage sunshine, a chilly little breeze. Abby insisted on having coffee outside so that she could look at her tulips.

'I mean,' Gerald said, 'how much time do you need to inspect a tulip? Let's go in.'

'I'm not inspecting tulips. I'm looking at them. It's not the same thing.'

'All right. Looking at them. Now you *have* looked at them. Done and dusted. They look like flowers that've been looked at. So now can we go back in the warm?'

'They have to have time to sink in,' Abby pointed out. 'Anyway, I wanted to tell you something.'

'You could have told me indoors.'

'I'd rather say it out here. Someone is coming to dinner. By name of Steve.'

'For heaven's sake.'

There was an unpleasant pause. Abby glanced at Gerald then looked away. She'd known how he would react, which made him not want to react in that way. She hummed some song or other under her breath while he was gathering his thoughts.

'I would have thought you see enough of him as it is,' he said finally. 'Potting.'

'That's not the same thing. He's a friend.'

'Your friend.'

'Maybe he'll be your friend too when he comes to dinner.'

Gerald sighed. He might as well concede gracefully. 'Did you ever get him to ride Dorothy?' he asked, as if politely interested.

'Not yet. He took a rain check.'

Rain check wasn't something Abby would say. It would be Steve's phrasing. People can take up residence in each other's minds, speak through their mouths.

Stop being melodramatic, Gerald told himself. She's just *quoting* him; that's what he happened to say when she tried to get him on the back of her horse – wisely, when all was said and done, assuming he didn't want to break his neck.

'Best to cook him something he can eat one-handed,' he said. 'It would be embarrassing to have to cut up his grub for him.'

'Unexpected problem number a million,' Steve said. 'When you've lost a hand you can't hold a bottle of wine and an umbrella at the same time.'

He was standing on their doorstep, rain beating down. He had a thin face with quick black eyes and black hair parted firmly to one side like Hitler's, strong nose (i.e. big), and one of those large modern beards that look Victorian. He was wearing jeans and a leather jacket, one sleeve of which hung loosely at the bottom. He raised up a bottle of wine with his left hand as if it was an offering.

'Let me take it,' Gerald said, taking it. 'Thank you very much. Oh, *grand vin*, just the job.' He put the bottle on the hall table. 'Come in, come in.' Say it twice in hopes of sounding welcoming. Steve was handsome, in a routine sort of way. Maybe that was the only way to *be* handsome. I wouldn't know, thought Gerald, spindly, wobbling head. Steve was solidly built, firm-chested, well organised as a structure except for the bit of him that was missing: compact, really, just like Abby was.

He stepped in, and they stood in the hall facing each other, rather close together. 'Welcome,' said Gerald. 'I'm Gerald.'

'Steve. Hello Gerald. '

Gerald raised his hand but of course couldn't shake, so used it instead to pat the man's shoulder lightly. It was odd how you were inclined to make intimate gestures towards people you didn't take to. 'Welcome,' he repeated.

'Wet, wet, wet,' Steve said, 'to coin a phrase.'

'Let me take your jacket. Oh lord, your trousers.'

'Better not take *them*,' Steve said. 'Not this early in the evening. Nice smell.'

'Abby's cooking boeuf bourguignon.' Abby had decided this would be easy to eat one-handed, as long as she didn't use big chunks of beef like they did in France. 'I take your point,' she'd told Gerald. She was going to serve it with mashed potatoes. 'It'll go perfectly with the claret you brought,' Gerald told Steve.

'Between you and me,' Steve said, winking, 'Château Plonko. But don't tell the boss. There's a safety pin in my left-hand jacket pocket.'

'Is there? Oh, OK.' Gerald rummaged in the pocket and found it. 'Here it is.' He looked at Steve, perplexed. Steve flapped his dangling shirtsleeve at him. 'Oh, I see. Do you want me to—'

'No, no, give it here.' Gerald passed the pin to him and Steve flicked it open. 'You'd be surprised at some of the things I've learned to do one-handed,' he said, pinning the sleeve up. He gave a slightly leery wink.

'Here you are,' said Abby, coming through from the kitchen. She was dressed casually, sailor-type slop, jeans: making-art clothes, her hair in a severe bun. She was wearing an extraordinarily large pair of bright red oven gloves which gave the impression of gigantic hands, tumescent ones even. Not tactful, Abs, Gerald wanted to say. She went up to Steve and patted each of his hairy cheeks with these paws. 'La la, choochie-face,' she said.

'La la, maestro,' Steve replied. 'She does my work for me these days,' he told Gerald. 'And I take the credit. Good deal.'

'Let's go into the kitchen,' said Abby, 'so we can talk while I'm cooking.'

Gerald had noticed before that as soon as someone mentioned being able to talk, an awkward silence inevitably fell. Abby didn't seem to notice. She was at the stove stirring a big casserole pot with a wooden spoon, still with the oven gloves on.

'A drink!' Gerald said, suddenly remembering. 'What'll you have?'

'A beer, if you've got it.'

'A beer. Good idea. What about you?' he asked Abby.

'Whayte *wayne*,' Abby said, still stirring. She always said the words in what she took to be a Bolton accent in honour of a friend who came from there, her voice rising fiercely on the second word.

'Two beers, one whayte *wayne*,' Gerald said. He poured Abby's and offered it to her. She nodded for him to put it to the side of the cooker. He got out two glasses for the beers.

'I'll have mine from the bottle, if that's OK,' Steve said.

'Easier, is it? With the hand. I mean, without the hand. Sod it. Sorry.'

'No difference, mate, with or without. I've always drunk it straight from the bottle, ever since I was a nipper. Saves washing up.'

'Ah well, if you insist,' Gerald said, passing him a bottle. He poured his own beer into a glass. Abby turned away from her cooking, slid off one of her gloves, and picked up her drink with a suddenly tiny hand. 'Cheers,' she said.

'Cheers,' Steve replied.

'So Steve,' Gerald said. 'Have you always been a potter?'

'No, not as such.'

'Oh.' There was an awkward pause. 'What *were* you then?' Gerald finally asked.

'Am,' said Steve. '*Am*, by Jove.' He said Jove sarcastically, as if he thought it was an exclamation Gerald might use himself. 'I only lost my hand, you know, not my whole life. I'm just on hold for the time being, professionally speaking. A man cannot live by pots alone.'

'Your profession being . . . ?'

'Teacher. Arts and crafts. At the college. Just the college. What they used to call the tech. Not at university like you brainboxes.'

'I'm not a brainbox,' said Abby indignantly, once more stirring with her back to them. 'I only taught tiddlers.' She gave a dry little laugh. 'Let's face it, I'm never going to set the world alight.' She turned back towards the room. 'So, Steve, how's stump?'

'Abby!' Gerald exclaimed.

'No, no, relevant question. Stump is good, Abby. Stump is doing OK. A little eruption or two, but on its way.'

'I knew someone,' Gerald said hastily, 'when I worked at a rubber-composition factory, who lost his hand. It was a holiday job. On my part, that is. He was a lovely man.' Maybe this reference to the rubber factory was to counterbalance being a brainbox. But his remark was greeted with another silence, as if neither Steve nor Abby knew what to make of it, or cared. 'He used to take me fishing,' Gerald added, to his own immediate horror. What on earth made him blurt that out? It was the sort of thing a particularly dim criminal might say on the hoof, trying to spice up an alibi. Gerald hadn't known the man at all, certainly had never gone fishing with him. The poor bloke had only ever been a figure bent mutely over a rubber mill, at least until he was bent screaming over it.

'Before or after?'

'I'm sorry?'

'He lost his hand.'

'Oh. Oh, before. Yes, before.'

'Pity. I'd like to learn how to fish one-handed. You could have given me a tutorial.'

Thank God, thank God, thought Gerald.

'Why I asked about stump,' Abby said, 'is because when it's totally healed, Steve will be able to get himself a prosthesis. And when he can use his prosthesis, he will stop being on hold and can teach his arts and crafts again. La la, people, dinner time!'

'I gather,' said Steve, spooning his stew, 'you've been having adventures.'

'Me?'

'Him?' asked Abby. 'Gerald doesn't have adventures, do you, Gerald? When we used to go to Greece, he went snorkelling while I shagged the waiters.'

'Ho ho,' Steve said. He wagged his spoon at Gerald. 'Division of labour.'

Gerald looked at Abby in amazement, sticking a grin on his face to buy time. What could she mean? He had a sense of history being rewritten, or rediscovered. Now he thought about it, he did remember a waiter when they were on holiday on Crete one time, a big looming fellow like a bear, with black curly hair, maybe a black beard even, Abby trading quips with him, she laughing, the waiter meanwhile deliberately, ponderously, straight-faced. She'd always had a thing about waiters. 'The only chance I get for a man to do whatever I ask,' she'd said once.

She hadn't meant it, of course; it was just the sort of thing you say. And now, what she had just said was also just the sort of thing you say – that *Abby* would say, at least. It was heat of the moment, like him claiming to have gone fishing with the rubber-composition man. Gerald told himself she was trying to impress Steve, prove she was a goer, or had been. Compensate for the difference in their ages, probably a difficult gap for a woman to cope with. Even in a simple friendship the woman was likely to feel at a disadvantage. Or maybe she was just making a joke.

Shirley Valentine, he remembered. Of course, of course. He felt a glow of relief. It was a film reference. They had gone to see *Shirley Valentine* years ago. Why, he had no idea. It wasn't their sort of film at all. Maybe they'd mistaken it for *The Shining*. 'Snorkelling can be quite adventurous, in its own way,' he said good-humouredly. 'I saw a conger eel once.'

'I must be attracted to Greeks,' Abby said. 'My first boyfriend was a Greek. Well, half a Greek.'

'That must have been a baptism of fire,' Steve said.

'He *was* a bit of a handful,' Abby said, 'in more ways than one.'

'I didn't know you had a first boyfriend,' Gerald said. He was so shocked he almost lost his voice but tried to convert his whisper into a tone of mild interest, like someone being polite on the way to the gallows. One shock after another. His head began to throb.

'Blimey,' Steve said, 'did you think *you* were the first? Young love.' He wagged his spoon as if picking a song out of the air. 'I suppose that's what it was like in Cambridge, in the olden days.'

Gerald glanced at him in quick hatred. That was, of course, exactly what Cambridge *was* like in the olden days.

'What do you think I was doing at that party, Gerald? It was an undergraduate one, wasn't it? And I was working in a hardware shop in those days, remember.'

'I remember *that*,' said Gerald sullenly.

'I went to the party with my *boy*friend. He was very good-looking but a bit of an arse, when all was said and done. You must have seen him there, Gerald. Blokey bloke? Slightly obnoxious? He was reading engineering at Churchill College. He came into our shop once upon a time to buy some tool or other. He was always making things, being an engineer. He made me a record player that worked, so he wasn't all bad. But we had a terrible row on the way to the party, and when we got there he spent all his time chatting up some girl or other, to prove a point. So I thought, sod you. He was high maintenance at the best of times. The record player was all right, though. Judith and I used to listen to the Beatles on it. We would jive in my bedroom. He was called Demis. Like Dennis, only spelt wrong.'

Demis. There was that fat singer Demis Roussos who used to warble wearing a sort of tent, a marquee almost. Could Abby be improvising again? On the other hand, how *did* she get herself installed at that party? Gerald had never asked himself that question before. Women in the Cambridge of those days, before the male colleges went co-ed, were in such demand they would hardly have needed an invitation. And Abby was Abby. At least, that was what he'd always believed.

'Sounds like she got you on the rebound, ole boy,' Steve said.

'Not to worry,' said Abby brightly. 'I've been rebounding for half a century, give or take. Give or take a waiter or two, I mean.'

'Anyway,' Gerald said, as if suddenly tiring of the topic, 'what *was* this about my adventures? Considering I don't *have* adventures,' he added.

'Except for that conger eel, don't forget,' Steve said. 'It was just something I heard on the grapevine.'

'Which was?'

'Yes, what did you hear on the grapevine, Stevie?

'What I heard,' Steve said. He scooped a spoonful of mashed potato into his mouth. 'Excuse, I couldn't resist,' he said after a moment. 'So buttery. What did I hear? What I heard was . . . oh shoot, it's not really for mixed company. Goings on, what I heard.' He put his spoon down and picked up his glass of red wine, took a considering sip, nodded in fake-judicious approval, mouth down, drops of wine like blood splatters on his bristling beard.

'I think not,' said Abby. 'My Gerald doesn't go in for goings on. Do you, Gerald?' She gave him an amused, rather challenging look, then turned back to Steve. 'In any case, I'm not mixed company. You have to take me neat. Everybody has to take me neat.'

'Not necessarily the goings on you might think went on. Isn't that so, Gerald?'

Gerald said nothing, just looked at him across the table with as much hatred as he could fit into his gaze. His eyes seemed to pulse with the rhythm of his headache. Steve wasn't looking back. He had put down his glass and was drawing circles on the tablecloth with his forefinger. 'Watching young boys?' he asked.

'Oh for God's sake!' Abby must have told him. He couldn't recall telling her about the boys, but he must have done. 'I was actually looking out for someone else entirely. They weren't boys in any case; they were students.'

'Ah. That makes it OK, then.'

'I don't like your implication. But the person I was looking out for was a girl. A suicidal young woman. She'd accosted me in the street an hour or two before. I thought she might go to that part of the river and throw herself in.'

'A waif,' Steve said, 'like they have in silent movies.'

'Oh yes,' said Abby, gleeful at getting a film reference, 'with her basket of flowers. Then the words come up on the screen. Would you care to buy a posy, sir? Tear trickling down her cheek. The crinkly sort of hair they had in those days.'

'Stumps,' Gerald said. Steve jumped a little at the word.

'She wasn't some moon-faced girl with a tear trickling down her cheeks.' Though of course that was pretty much how Gerald had envisaged her, or rather had envisaged her envisaging herself, as she headed towards a damp, pre-Raphaelite conclusion. 'She was a fiery girl with stumps on her head. Like little horns. I don't know the word for them. And she said fuck all the time, all the fucking time.' He looked at Steve triumphantly. I'll give you *adventures*, he thought. The drum in his head was beating loudly now. 'Fuck fuck fucking *fuck*.'

'Well, that went well,' Abby said. She was standing at the sink washing up.

'I don't understand why you don't use the dishwasher,' Gerald said. He was sitting at the table nursing a cup of tea. His headache had faded somewhat.

'Because it's full, and I can't be arsed to empty it. Anyway, I like to get my hands in hot water. It reminds me I've still *got* hands. Unlike some poor sods I could mention.'

'But you're wearing Marigolds.' The rubber gloves looked as huge on her as the oven mittens had done, reaching almost up to her elbows.

'Best of both worlds. Wet and dry at the same time. You can sort of feel the wetness through the dryness.' She raised her gloves and inspected them as if struck by this thought, then put them back in the sink. Had she bought all these gauntlets specially? To show – what? To show how *hand*ed she was? A kind of ambidextrousness of basic anatomy, two hands not one? 'Why did you shout obscenities at Steve, may I ask?' she called over her shoulder. 'Bastard.'

'I didn't shout obscenities at Steve. I repeated obscenities other people had shouted. Another person had shouted. There is a difference.' I could ask *you*, he thought, I could as well ask *you* why you told Steve about the boys? Why you told him about that false accusation that was made? That was an obscenity in its way, an obscenity of another sort.

'You lost your rag, that's what you did. Steve must have thought you'd gone mental.'

'I'm not very interested in Steve's opinion, to be frank.'

'I'm taking him riding tomorrow, to show there's no hard feelings. Fixed it while I was showing him out.'

'I had the impression he didn't want to go riding in the first place.'

'Well, he *is* going riding. Call it tough love. He agreed this time because he wanted to make sure we're still tickety-boo. I knew he would. That's the way it works. Sometimes I think you haven't the faintest idea how it works. You're jealous, aren't you?'

'Of Steve? No, I am not jealous of Steve, for heaven's sake.' A man who pots penguins, he thought, but didn't say.

'Of Demis, I mean. My old boyfriend, my prehistoric boyfriend who built me a prehistoric record player. Plus a bunch of waiters in a foreign country.'

'Abby, I'm not jealous.' Not a lie, he told himself. It wasn't jealousy. As such. What it was was a sense that he didn't know Abby after all, that a part of her had indeed inhabited a foreign country, several foreign countries. Her life wasn't accounted for fully. Unless it was all a fiction, to impress Steve. But what did that imply *about* her relationship with Steve?

No life could ever be fully accounted for, of course not. But there were more gaps in his knowledge of Abby than he had ever realised or allowed for. And gaps were the enemy. Gaps were the fucking enemy. Lacunae, you might say, speaking as a historian. Fucking lacunae.

They'd been having a week's holiday in a rented cottage in Oxfordshire. As luck would have it, a heatwave set in. Perhaps that was why they had become irritable. When you're in a new place, Gerald noticed, you see each other with new eyes. He and Abby were at home for hours every evening and weekend, just the two of them, and yet it took being somewhere else to be able to assess what that really amounted to, the weight of their relationship in pounds and stones, in tons.

The sun blazed down day after day. It was as if they'd travelled to a foreign country. The lawn in the cottage's little garden had already gone brown and patchy. There was the smell of distant barbecues. Gerald and Abby lay naked on top of the bed like two large items being offered for sale in a shop, seals maybe. This suggested a certain availability, particularly in the morning, sunshine through the curtains as thick as custard. Gerald was taken aback when Abby told him she didn't want to have sex.

'We're supposed to be on holiday,' he said.

'Yep. Holiday from sex.'

'Abby, sex is hardly work.'

'Isn't it? You're the one who bleats on about how we fuck and fuck and never produce children. That sounds a lot like work to me.'

There was a long silence as they lay there giving off heat. Sometimes you fly into a rage; other times a rage just creeps up on you, insidious as the tide. 'How *stu*pid,' Gerald found himself saying. 'Sex without offspring is recreational sex. Look it up in the bloody dictionary.' Hating himself as he spat the words out, particularly as she'd hit the spot. He always took refuge in being an academic in times of crisis, wrong-footing himself with pomposity.

'I was just an assistant in a hardware shop while you were being a student at *Cam*bridge,' Abby said. 'I never got to know the meaning of long words.' She was lying on her side, facing away from him, her bum blatant. 'Like sex, for example,' she added.

Gerald laughed, but it wasn't a release from his anger, just part of it. The laughter came out despite himself, distorted into a whinny. 'Fuck you,' he said, as viciously as he could.

'No thank you,' she replied. 'Let's just have a rest for a day or two. For a week. Is what I'm saying.'

Of course, they often abstained for a day or two, for a week, for longer, much longer, in their normal lives. It was the way of things for everyone, surely, those becalmed periods. There were other issues that would take priority at such times, like worrying about work, or reading interesting books. But on holiday it should be different, shouldn't it?

'You've only got one willy, when all's said and done,' Abby said.

What could she be getting at? 'So?' he asked eventually.

'So,' Abby replied, ending the discussion.

They normally had fruit and cereal, but that day, perhaps by way of apology, Gerald decided to cook eggs and bacon. He hurried out to the little shop at the end of the lane where he bought his paper and got some from there. While the eggs and bacon were frying, he opened the door into the garden and let the warm breeze in. There were flecks of sunshine on the kitchen lino. Somewhere outside a bird was singing, a blackbird perhaps.

Abby arrived, dressed in t-shirt, shorts, and trainers.

'What's this?' she asked, looking at her plate.

'A peace offering,' Gerald said.

'No it's not. It's a fried egg.'

'That too.'

'For heaven's sake, Gerald. You know how I feel about fried eggs.'

'I thought you liked fried eggs. You eat them when we're staying somewhere.' He paused. 'And here we are, staying somewhere.'

'I eat them when I have to eat them. They make me shudder. There's something so yellow about them. You must have clocked me when Judith doles them out for us, surely? Doing a controlled shudder? I can hardly bear to watch the way Ken gobbles them up.'

'Oh for God's sake,' Gerald said, his rage coming back full force. How could you be married for years and not know that fried eggs made your wife shudder? 'If you don't want to fucking eat it, don't fucking eat it. Don't eat the bacon, either. I expect that's too fucking pink.'

'It is, as a matter of fact. That's the exact shade the bacon is. Fucking pink.'

There was a pause. Gerald was panting, or pretending to pant; he wasn't sure which. He went to the back door, leaned against the frame, and stared out as if he was taking an interest in the world. From behind came whimpers and groans as Abby ate her egg and bacon, doing controlled shudders with each mouthful. After a while he began to laugh, keeping it bottled in at first so he was doing controlled shudders too. Sure enough he could make out little squalls of laughter coming from Abby in response, tucked in amongst the groans. After a while, he said, 'I mean, Abby, how many willies did you expect?'

Later that morning they went for a walk along the Ridgeway and past the Uffington White Horse. The heat was bruising now, the day almost airless, and it was strange to see the animal's etiolated body in full flight, as if being blown along the crest of the hill in a tempest. Gerald wanted to say something about the paradox of an image of movement staying static for three thousand years but knew that, however phrased, it would come out sounding pretentious. Abby had possessed a bullshit filter from the word go, and this had been a testy morning. The image was difficult to resolve, even from close above it, as if the animal was intent on galloping out of vision. It was bigger than one's eyesight.

'Horse,' Abby said reverently and sighed, as a toddler

might. She gazed at it as if it was the first horse in the world, which it almost was.

'Some people say it's a dragon,' Gerald said.

'Oh for goodness sake. Dragons don't gallop in that way.'

'Dragons don't gallop at all.'

She gave him a swift acid look and turned back towards the horse. 'It makes me want to ride,' she said. 'So much. Before I die.'

'Why don't you, then?' Gerald asked. 'You talk as if you're going to pop your clogs any moment.'

'Because,' she said, 'you can't ride in Manchester. It can't be done.'

'Of course it can be done. On the outskirts, anyway. In north Cheshire or out towards the Pennines. There are bound to be riding schools. It's jodhpur country out there.'

'I don't want to go to a riding school. I have enough of schools as it is. And I certainly don't want to wear jodhpurs. I'm too short to wear jodhpurs. I'd look like a hobbit. What I want is a horse of my own. You can say till you are blue in the face that you can keep a horse in a garage in Didsbury, but you can't. Anyway, we don't have a garage in Didsbury.'

This was a common feature of rows with Abby, finding yourself called upon to defend something you'd never actually said. It wasn't that she lied, just that she jumped a few stages in the discussion, stages you'd never have arrived at under your own steam in the first place. 'True enough,' he said.

There was a wood nestling against the lower slopes of the Ridgeway, and Gerald led the way down towards it. Abby, with her dark complexion, didn't seem to find the sunshine oppressive, but Gerald could feel his cheeks had reddened, and the tops of his ears were sore. They had only gone a short distance into the shade of the trees when they found themselves entering a glade. In the middle of it was a mound with an entrance of standing stones. They came to a stop and stared at it in silence.

'I know what this is,' Gerald said eventually. He found himself whispering, as if in church. 'I remember reading about it. It's Wayland's Smithy.'

'Is it?' Abby replied, also in a whisper. 'Is what?'

'Wayland's Smithy. That's what it's known as. I think that's an Anglo-Saxon name. But in fact it's a neolithic long barrow. You know, a tomb.'

'A tomb.' Abby sighed in satisfaction. 'Perhaps they galloped here on the horse. Those neoliths. Galloped along along the hill-tops, then came down into the woods. Like elephants going into the jungle to die.'

'It's several thousand years older than the horse, the barrow is.' Still, as so often, Abby seemed to have hit upon a truth of sorts, the horse caught in mid-leap, mid-life, the barrow so final and still, the full-stop at the end of a sentence, its entrance guiding you into a dead end. And of course it *was* called a smithy. 'People believed if you left a horse here, along with a coin, Wayland would have shoed it by the time you came back.'

Gerald began to walk round the barrow. Even though the sun reached here, the surrounding woodland seemed to keep the air cool. There was a gentle hum of insects, like audible silence. He had only gone a few steps when he stopped. In front of him, sprawled side by side on the short grass, lay a couple. They looked disorganised, as if they'd just fallen out of a tree, like fruit. Courting couples tend to snatch glances from the corner of their eyes to check if you're impressed, but these were deeply asleep, eyes firmly shut. They seemed trapped in the sunshine like insects in amber.

Abby touched the bare leg of the male sleeper with her toe. He didn't respond. 'Out for the count,' she whispered.

They tiptoed round the couple then stopped abruptly. Ahead of them lay some more people, this time a family group, mother and father and two children, also scattered arbitrarily upon the grass, all of them deep in slumber.

Abby inclined her head to one side by way of asking Gerald to bring his nearest ear in range. 'It's like one of those cults,' she whispered, 'where everybody is made to drink poison.'

These people were breathing, however, taking long but shallow breaths, like a soft tide lapping at the shore. 'They're asleep,' he whispered back.

Some distance beyond the family, a lone boy, about twelve. He was lying on his side, one leg thrusting forward, the other back, caught in mid-stride like the white horse itself. A few feet to the far side of him lay an elderly couple on their backs. She had a little hat of white, tightly curled hair and a dark blue dress down to her ankles; he wore an old-fashioned grey suit with waistcoat and tie, despite the hot day.

'They look as if they've been here since 1948,' Abby said.

'Perhaps his watch has stopped,' Gerald suggested. The old man was wearing a fob watch, its chain straddling his waistcoat. Gerald and Abby seemed to have wandered into a place where time had been suspended, a lacuna in history itself. 'What are they dreaming about? That's the question.'

'Tell you what, whatever it is, they're all dreaming the same dream.'

'How do you know?'

'Because they all have the same look on their faces.'

'Their faces look blank to me.'

'That's what I mean, same look. You know when you go swimming and leave your clothes in a little pile on the beach? That's what they've all done. They've left their personalities behind them and drifted off.'

Gerald remembered a time when he was young and went to swim in a dream-like sea off West Wittering, the water warm as blood just as the air was in this enchanted glade, swimming out, far out – until his father grabbed his arm and made him return to the land. To his mum, to the picnic, to life, to whatever you might want to call it. Gerald looked down at Abby, who was still gazing at the prone OAPs. What she'd said seemed freighted with his own experience, with images drawn from his past, as if she could somehow remember his memories. Sometimes he couldn't remember them himself, let alone find an entrance into hers.

As if sensing his stare, Abby glanced up at Gerald. She raised a hand towards his face and crooked her forefinger. Then she turned back and tiptoed over the old lady, one leg at a time, and continued, still high-stepping, across to the fringe of the glade, just where it entered the wood. There was a slight depression in the soil here, a sag like you see in churchyards when a grave has given way, a dell, he supposed it should be called in a place like this, Elvish being the appropriate tongue.

Abby's hand was raised above her shoulder, finger still crooked, summoning him forward. As he approached, she lowered herself into the dell and lay down. He assumed she'd decided they should fall asleep along with all the other denizens of Wayland's Smithy, but then she raised her buttocks and slid down her shorts and pants. She peered up at him as she kicked her trainers off, then the clothing. 'Come *on*, then,' she said, still whispering but loudly, almost. 'One thing I always adore, sex in the open air.'

Abby turned slowly round as though the word lacunae had struck her an unexpected blow. He must have said it out loud. Her eyes looked at him as if they were looking from a den, a cell, an enclosed, separate space. Judgmental, assessing eyes, not Abby's usual eyes at all. She rested her Marigolded hands on her hips and ran her new eyes over Gerald as if totting him up, making an inventory.

'Let's see,' she said after some moments. 'How about that research student you had, way back when? Had being the word. I don't think seeing that conger eel *was* your only adventure, was it, Gerald, even though you always make out you wouldn't say boo to a goose? Talk of brainboxes, *she* was a brainbox, and I don't mean the eel. From what you used to say, at least. The biggest brainbox of the lot. Cleverest student ever, you kept saying. You used to drool over her. I thought you were about to do a bunk. Hand in hand. I thought you were off to Gretna Green. What was her name? Laura, that's right. I remember her coming round to our house, when you had your research students back for drinks. Is there anything I can do, Mrs. Walker? If there's one thing that creeps me out, it's people who want to know if there's anything they can do. In a little chirpy voice. Anyfin I can do, Mrs. Thing? I thought, good grief, *men*. What is it about men? Do they really lust after women with chirpy little little-girl voices? Yes, there *is* something you can do, Laura, now you mention it. You can pass the olives, and when you've done that you can stop trying to go to bed with my husband, that's what you can do.'

While Abby was speaking, a strange thing happened in Gerald's mind. Laura, the original Laura, the real Laura, stepped into it fully formed, and here she was, installed in her own lacuna.

They were sitting in his office, at his desk. They were talking about Jonathan Edwards on the freedom of the will, trying to follow his calmly logical confrontations with all the paradoxes involved. Or rather, Gerald was trying to follow, while Laura led. They actually had his first edition in front of them, dated 1756. Her head was bent over it, her curly auburn hair tending forwards, one small pink ear in his line of vision. As he recalled that detail, he remembered how, a few months ago, he'd noticed his own ears had grown, one of the curses of old age. They now had long dangling lobes that looked as if they ought to be kept out of sight, like one's epiglottis, and the ears as a whole had developed a rubbery texture, like fake ones that had somehow been fastened to the sides of his head. Since that discovery he checked them nervously in the mirror every morning.

Laura's small mouth was reading out some of the words, her intelligent lips, poised lips, lips that could address obscurities, chisel out meaning, articulating the abstruse, abstract reasoning, the fine line between being a prisoner of God's total knowledge of what is to come – 'Future events are always in God's view as evident, clear, sure, and necessary, as if they already were' – and laying claim to possibilities of your own, to freedom of action: 'Man is entirely, perfectly, and unspeakably different from a mere machine, in that he has reason and understanding, and has a faculty of will, and so is capable of volition and choice.' Her precisely formed chin, just enough of it to be assertive. Even her chin, intelligent. Sporadic freckles, like brown stars. Now he could recall individual freckles, scattered over her upper cheeks. One freckle exactly *there*, like the head of a nail or screw holding her whole face in place.

For Edwards there was only one life. God knew what you would choose, though it was still your choice. Other possibilities were so many abortions, lying in the ditch. His was a one-life universe, not a multiverse.

'Plus another thing,' Abby said, 'what about you going to bed with my little sister?'

He thought he was keeping a secret from her, but she'd known all along. She had been keeping a secret from *him*.

This morning she was off riding with Steve, which gave him space to think about it in all its unpleasantness. While she was in the same house, he hadn't dared. He was hunched in on himself, taking up the smallest space possible. As this was an internal manoeuvre (what wasn't, in his life? – maybe in everybody's life), it was his brain that had to do the hunching, dwindling to the size of a pea, leaving just enough neurons available to go to the lavatory or make a cup of coffee. Abby, meanwhile, went about her business without referring to it again. She didn't seem to want an answer to the questions she had asked. Perhaps the questions were answer enough in themselves.

Had Judith told her straightaway? What tone of voice could she have possibly have used? Contrite? Complacent? Would Abby have seemed formidable, or vulnerable? Maybe both. Too Abby, that's what Abby was, always had been. Abby up to the rim. As she'd said, not mixed. Neat.

He'd noticed over the years that Abby had a way of knowing things she couldn't know, as if she had an extra sense or sensitivity, like birds using magnetism to navigate their migrations. She would have been able to detect what he'd been up to just by looking at him, being with him, decoding the words he used, smelling him even, despite the window of their bedroom being open to the Didsbury afternoon.

All these years she's been keeping a secret from me, he thought bitterly. *My* secret.

Then there was Laura. She'd known about Laura too. Which was more than he had himself: that was the injustice of it. Here he was, resenting the fact that parts of Abby's life were a mystery from his point of view while all along his seemed to have been an open book to her. Over the years, he'd lost his sense of the reality of what had happened with Judith and mislaid completely what had happened with Laura. They had been events outside his marriage, and they were, in some way he couldn't quite get at, irrelevant. They never happened, to use Judith's words. And yet that wasn't the case as far as Abby was concerned. The marriage she was in was altogether larger, baggier, than his.

The phone rang.

'Guess where I'm speaking from?' came a voice.

'Wrexham,' Gerald said.

'Good heavens, how did you know that?'

'I just did.'

'It's Terence here.'

'I know that too.'

'I'm in Wrexham.'

'So I gathered.'

'I might as well ring off, as you seem to know everything already.'

'Bye, then.'

'The point is, I took to heart what you said about my plan.'

'Which plan was that, Terence?'

'The plan whereby I would tell Judith that I happened to be coming to Wrexham and wondered if she would like a cup of coffee.'

'Oh yes, that plan.'

'*Mauvaise foi*, I think you called it.

'I don't think I did.'

'Perhaps that was me, then. But you gave me the hint.'

'So what *did* you do?'

'I rang Judith up and told her what my plan had been. Then I explained to her that I had realised it would be *mauvaise foi*. Yes, that *was* me, now I recall. I decided that would be the best way to put it. Incidentally, *mauvaise foi* is a concept in quantum mechanics. As Einstein said, God does not play dice with the universe. I didn't explain. I thought that it would overcomplicate matters. That it was you who had put me right. I think she was a bit baffled in any case, to tell you the truth.'

'Surely not.'

'You may well say that. She is pretty on the ball, in fact. I have to run to keep up. Except for theoretical physics, maybe. That's always a tricky area, apart from those in the know. It's a bit of a club, between you and me. We all read the same equations. But in terms of my strategy, she floundered a bit. Of course it had been abandoned; that was the whole point. That's what made it tricky to follow. But still, we had coffee together anyway. I think she had heard tell of me from Abby, so it wasn't completely, what do they call it? Blind. It wasn't totally blind.'

'Let me tell you something about that pair of sisters, Terence. They're never totally blind. Just the opposite. Take it from me.'

'Good point. Anyway.'

Terence seemed to run out of steam. Gerald could picture him lost in thought, forgetting that he was still holding the handset. 'Is she there?' he asked.

'Who?'

'Judith, of course. The person whose house you're in.'

'Oh, Judith. No. She's out. She's gone shopping. I offered to go with her, but she said no. She said she wanted to buy something surprising for the evening meal. That's why I'm ringing you.'

'It won't be *that* surprising. There are limits to what you can get in Wrexham.'

'No, no. I just wanted to talk to you while she's out. Ask your advice. The thing is, we've hit it off.'

'Good for you.' Despite everything – because of everything – Gerald felt annoyance rising in his chest.

'This time she's asked me to stay over. Do you think this means? I wouldn't want to. But on the other hand. Of course it might never have entered her head. There are some women who are not bothered by that kind of thing, as I understand. She may feel like that. I wouldn't want to.'

'I don't think you need worry on that score. She's not one of those women.'

'How can you tell?

'I can tell.'

'Really? Oh, I see. Extrapolating from her sister. Got you.'

'I don't need to extrapolate from her sister, Terence.' For a second Gerald was on the brink of telling Terence what had happened between Judith and himself. That would be vulgar beyond belief, like a teenager boasting about sexual con-quests, real or imagined. But he *want*ed to be vulgar. He wanted to feel the sting of aggression. It would crush Terence. For the moment he even wanted that, wanted some-one to be more crushed than he was. And then it passed. He remembered who he was – who he mainly was, at least. He had travelled back from an adjacent universe in the little spaceship of the self.

'I just think one can tell, with a woman,' he continued. 'Just as a woman can with a man, obviously.' Now remembering who he was to such an extent he insisted on treating the sexes equally. 'I'm sure *you* can tell, yourself.' (Also *Terence* equally.) 'It's a matter of trusting your instinct. That's why you phoned me in the first place, wasn't it, because of your instinct?'

'Instinct is one thing. The question is, experience.'

Suddenly a trembling came into Terence's voice. 'I keep remembering the last time that I chatted to a woman. Up, chatted up a woman. Before Judith, I mean. Was to that poor Alice woman in the pub, and she dropped dead immediately, more or less.' He made an odd noise down the line, part hiccup, part sigh, part sob. 'Not a good precedent, is it? Even now I keep expecting that policeman to knock at my door.'

'That is entirely irrelevant, Terence, as you know perfectly well. You didn't chat up Alice, for starters – you were just being polite. In any case, you're well beyond the chatting up stage with Judith, by the sound of it. What you're doing, you're trying to give yourself a let-off.'

'A let-off?'

'You're trying to find an excuse not to take the plunge.' A certain accidental physicality in that phrase gave Gerald pause. He had a fleeting image of Terence taking the plunge, taking the plunge with Judith, *into* Judith, a glimpse of nakedness, of diving, and felt a wave of nausea rise in his throat. He swallowed it down. 'It's a different sort of experience you're talking about here,' he added huskily.

'The point is, Gerald, my experience of *that* kind has been pretty disastrous too. Sometimes I cringe. Also few and far between. Spotty, you could say. I may make a pig's ear of it, to be honest. The danger is of lacking finesse.'

'Terence, be yourself. Just be nice, and all will be well. Judith will appreciate you for who you are.'

So says the expert on human relationships, Gerald thought glumly when he put the phone down.

It rang again a few minutes later.

'Terence,' Gerald said, with that slightly strained but good-humoured patience that you use. There was silence at the other end, bafflement implicit in it. 'Hello,' Gerald asked. 'Is that you, Terence?'

'No. It is not Terence.'

There was another silence, except for the sound of Abby puffing.

'What is it, Abby?'

'What it is, Steve just fell off the horse.'

Gerald experienced a moment of pure joy.

'Well, he didn't fall off, to tell the truth,' Abby continued. 'He was never on. I hoisted him up, you know, like I did you, but he sailed straight over Dorothy's back and down the other side. You were right, Gerald, it was because he only has one hand. He sort of held his stump aloft.'

'Stump?' Gerald asked. 'He held *stump* aloft?'

'I said to him, it's not the Olympic flame, for goodness sake. I think he wanted to keep it clear, to avoid further damage. He can't get a prosthesis until it stops erupting. But it prevented him getting a point of balance. I should never have hoiked him. I could feel it wasn't right while I was doing it. You'd have thought he was flying. Stump still up, while he was in the air. I didn't know I had the strength, to be honest. I don't think smoking can do you any harm at all. And landed on the other side.'

'What happened, then?'

'I just told you. He went—'

'No, I mean, *to* him. To Steve?'

'He's hurt his leg. He landed on his leg. But not in a good way.'

'Is he badly hurt? Have you called an ambulance?'

'I don't know. He's groaning a bit, but quite quietly. Quietly groaning. I don't want to call an ambulance. I think he's all right. Basically. He can't have a buggered leg as well as a buggered hand, can he? It would be too much.'

'I don't think it works like that. In this world you can have a buggered everything.'

'Anyhow, can you come out and give me a hand with him? We're in the usual field. And bring my walking stick, that one I bought when I slipped on your dumplings.'

As soon as he put the phone down, it occurred to Gerald that Abby would have taken the car. She must have forgotten that fact in the heat of the moment. He was glad of an excuse not to go. Abby had brought about this mess; let her fix it. Find some stick in the hedge that could function as a staff. In any case Steve was *her* friend, not his, certainly not his. Abby was a fucking Girl Guide, when all was said and done.

Just as he was putting out a hand to the phone again, it rang.

He picked it up, paused for a moment collecting his thoughts.

'Is that you?' came a quiet voice down the phone.

'Abby, why are you whispering? Is it worse than you thought?'

'What? Is what worse?'

'Is Steve worse?' An ambulance would solve the whole problem. Get an ambulance, be done with it. Cart him off to A&E again, where he belongs.

'Steve? Do you mean the potter? Potter Steve?'

'What?'

'Penguin Steve, I call him. Gerald, this is Judith here.'

'Oh for goodness sake. I thought you were Abby.'

'People say we talk a lot alike.'

'I think it's because you're whispering. Why *are* you whispering?'

'The reason I'm whispering is Terence is here. Your friend, Terence?'

'I know Terence.'

'He's in the sitting room, doing his laptop. He spends a lot of time doing that. When you look over his shoulder it's not even English. I mean, it's not even *language*. It just seems to be numbers of some sort. Also signs. I can't make head nor tail of it. I think there may be some Greek letters in it somewhere.'

'Judith, Abby isn't here at the moment. As you will have gathered. I've got to—'

'No, I don't want Abby. I want you.'

Gerald's heart pounded. For a moment, he thought, he thought . . . There was a certain promise in the phrase *I want you*. He thought perhaps the proximity of Terence had made Judith appreciate *him*, feel the need to reach out, confide, to remember what they had had, insofar as they had had it. Oh God, he thought, after all that was said last night. I'm incorrigible. He had always pictured himself as restrained, essentially monogamous, but perhaps he was some sort of obsessive after all, a sex addict, even. How ridiculous, not to know whether you were one or not.

'Well, here I am,' he said.

'I don't want Terence to hear. We've got a bit of a thing going, to tell the truth.'

'I see.'

'I like him. He's much cleverer than Ken ever was. Not that that is how you should judge. But he's so interesting to talk to. I don't understand a word he says, or not many of them, anyway. I told him I was going to give him a surprise tonight.'

'OK.'

'I bought some escargots. We have a new delicatessen that's just opened here. Just in a tin. I thought he might like them. He seems to speak French from time to time. Followed by lamb, needless to say.'

'I'm sure he'll love them, Judith. Look, I'd better be – Abby's expecting me, to tell the truth. I have to—'

'No, it wasn't the snails I wanted to ask you about. He'll have to like them or lump them. I'll serve them up as best I can. I think they already have garlic added. They have instructions on the tin, although they're in French, of course. But I still have my old dictionary from school. No, the point is, what I wanted to ask you about is, he's staying over. For the first time. I'm so worried about doing the wrong thing. You know. I don't want him to think I'm forward or anything.'

She paused. Perhaps she was remembering that Didsbury afternoon as well. She hadn't been forward then, any more than he had been. Forward was the wrong word. It wasn't the same as inevitable. Fated, even.

'With old Ken,' Judith resumed, 'you just had to wind him up and watch him go. But Terence is a different kettle of fish, of course. A more sensitive type.'

And where am I in this pantheon? Gerald wondered. Nowhere, that's where. 'I'm sure you have no need to worry,' he told her. 'Just be nice to the poor old sod.'

'I always try to be nice.'

'I know you do. You are.' He said this as sincerely as possible, if it *was* possible to be sincere on purpose, wanting to remind her of the source of that knowledge.

As soon as he'd finished the call he dialled Abby again. 'Abby, how *can* I come? You've got the car.'

'Are you still there? For goodness sake, Gerald, haven't you left yet?'

'Abby, I haven't got the car!'

'Well, get a taxi. I just need you to help Steve get back to where I've parked. He doesn't seem as bad as he was, but I don't think he'll be able to walk without help.'

'And what am I going to tell the driver? Take me to a field? With a horse in it?'

'Gerald, everything in this world is *some*where. Even ants, probably. Look in our address book under S for Stable. Or maybe L for Livery, I forget which. It will tell you where Dorothy lives. It will even tell you her post code, in case you should ever want to write her a letter.'

From a distance the threesome looked like something in a pastoral painting, the sun shining down, the horse peacefully cropping, the man sitting on the grass nearby, and the small form of Abby standing at a little distance, smoking. The effect was enhanced by the fact that no communication was going on, except for a blackbird singing furiously from the hedge.

As Gerald drew nearer, Dorothy lifted up her head and saw him. To his surprise, she immediately began to amble over, snorting through her nostrils as if in greeting. It was almost as if she wanted to get her side of the story in first. Even though she was now presenting herself as a sort of ally, she still intimidated Gerald. There was such a lot of her to step round, particularly as she rotated with him in apparent affection.

Steve looked up as Gerald approached, the horse undulating companionably beside him. 'Fuck,' Steve said. 'You taught me that word. Comes in very useful. Fuck. A. Duck.'

'I'm sure you knew it already. How's the leg, then?'

Steve just glowered up in response. The injustice of it, thought Gerald, given I was the one who warned Abby that taking him riding was a bad idea. It had never felt so pleasant to be wrongly accused.

Abby stepped over. 'Look,' she said to Steve, 'Gerald's brought you a walking stick. It's got a duck's beak handle. Admittedly it's pretty horrible, overall. Let's get you up and see if you can hobble over to the car with it.' She looked across at Dorothy, who was now peering down at Steve with fat lugubrious eyes. 'It's a pity we can't make use of the horse, with having one on tap,' she added.

'Abby!' Gerald said.

She took a pull on her cigarette. 'I don't need any instructions from you about how to behave,' she said. 'I was only lifting the atmosphere.'

'Well, how about having an instruction from *me*?' Steve asked. 'Here it is. I have hurt my right leg, Abby. Also I have lost my right hand. I fell off a fucking horse and I got run over by a fucking car.'

'You didn't exactly fall off the horse,' Abby pointed out. 'You were never on her in the first place.'

'What I'm trying to tell you is that there is no way I can grab hold of the duck's beak handle of the walking stick Gerald so thoughtfully brought me and use it to hobble back to the car. You can't hold a walking stick with a stump.'

Gerald noticed the indefinite article. Stump was no longer the name of a little pet the two of them shared.

Gerald drove. Steve sat in the front passenger seat, Abby at the back. 'I've been thinking,' Abby said, leaning forward into the space between the seats. 'I think you can hold a walking stick in the opposite hand from your bad leg, if you want. So you could have used your good hand after all, Steve. I mean your hand. Then you lean over to the good side and swing yourself along. You sort of whirl your bad leg out as you go. A bit flamenco. I think that's what I did when I sprained my ankle that time. Is that what I did, Gerald?'

'I can't remember you being a bit flamenco, to be honest.'

'Maybe I meant can-can.'

'I just saw you hobbling along with your stick and thought, Oh God, what now?'

'That's not fair. You make it sound as if I get injured all the time.'

'That's *my* privilege,' said Steve. 'I'll just be a torso in a month or two. Maybe just a head.'

'Unless you get decapitated,' Abby said.

'Thank you for that.'

'All I meant was my heart sank,' Gerald told Abby. 'I suspected straightaway that what had happened to you must be my fault.' He couldn't remember if he'd actually suspected that or not, but it seemed best to appropriate the guilt, particularly now Abby had her own share. 'Subconscious intuition.'

'The subconscious has a lot to answer for, if you ask me,' Abby said. She sighed. 'Do you rely on *your* subconscious, Steve?'

'What?'

'Your subconscious?'

'You can't *rely* on your subconscious, Abby,' Gerald said. 'The whole point is that you don't know what it's up to at any given moment.'

'I just meant, to generate your animals,' Abby told Steve. 'They seemed to come streaming out of you. I thought they might be streaming out of your subconscious. And the lovely curves on your vases. His vases have beautiful curves, Gerald – you ought to see them. Classical.'

'My animals come out of a ball of clay. And my vases. End of. For Christ's sake.'

'Like the statue in the marble.'

'No,' Steve said, voice rising with irritation. 'Not like the statue in the marble. Like I said, from a ball of clay.'

'No need to get aerated,' Abby said. To Gerald: 'Artistic temperament.'

Steve lived in an ex-council house in Twerton, the poorest area of Bath. To Gerald's surprise, the tufty littered front garden looked as if it had been neglected for much longer than could be accounted for by his accident. In his early days as an academic, Gerald had had an elderly colleague who was shot in the head in the war and who, as a result, suffered from a strange sort of tunnel vision. He proudly showed him and Abby a Victorian frieze he'd repainted in his sitting room, obviously quite unaware of the blotches and smears he'd left just to each side of it. Perhaps Steve had a similar problem, brought about by the artistic temperament Abby had mentioned, concentrating intensely on the work he was doing, unaware of what lay around it.

By now the pain in his leg seemed to have eased a little. Leaving the field, he had to have an arm round the shoulders of both Abby and Gerald, reaching up to Gerald's, clutching down at Abby's; now he just leaned heavily on Gerald, gasping occasionally.

At Abby's request, Steve got out his key and let them into a garage at the side of the house that had been converted into a studio, complete with kiln. There were shelves round the walls with dusty animals looking down from them: penguins, each with its egg, elephants, tigers, rhinos, crocodiles, assorted fish remote from any sea. Gerald remembered Terence talking about art being portable. Steve's pottery, though, seemed completely static. That egg was never going to hatch. Its parent penguin would never waddle off to dive into the ocean. He felt oppressed by the display, as if he'd died and woken up unmoving, in an unmoving world – his ultimate fear, being dead and knowing it. 'Amazing,' he said. 'Wow.'

'I still believe this garage is a mirror of Steve's subconscious,' Abby said. 'Like you said, Gerald, Steve himself would be the last person to know. In my opinion, some people have a subconscious, and some people don't. I'm pretty sure I don't. My consciousness is all I have to work with, such as it is. You know when you're in the Arctic and the sun never sets? Like Al Pacino in that film where he has to find the murderer and doesn't get any sleep. That's how it is in my head, I sometimes think. I wish I could turn the light out once in a while.'

'Thanks, Abs,' Steve said. 'Nice to know my head is a garage.' He was being sarcastic, but Gerald clocked the Abs.

'What it is,' Gerald said, letting his eyes track the deadness all around, 'is it's life-affirming. Teeming with life.'

'Like Noah's Ark,' Abby said, 'that's what I always think.'

'Was,' said Steve. 'Was teeming. Was like Noah's Ark. My world has been halved, basically.'

Gerald remembered a joke about a pantomime horse and nearly said, which half? 'But you've got Abby. Abs here. She helps out, doesn't she?'

'Abby is my handmaiden. I never thought before that that's

what handmaiden means. Hand maiden. She can use both her hands equally well, so she sort of has a spare one for me. My right hand. Which is what someone being your right hand means as well, at least in my case. My *actual* right hand.' It could have been a light-hearted remark but wasn't. Steve said it in barely suppressed rage. He was shaking a little, though that could have been delayed shock.

'I'm not up to his level, that's the problem,' Abby said.

Steve began, unenthusiastically, to protest, but Abby put up a warning finger, and on that flat note they made their way round the back of the house and in through the kitchen door.

To Gerald's surprise, the back garden was well cared for, and the house seemed neat and tidy. Everything in its place in the kitchen, with no washing-up left to moulder on the draining board. Can you wash up one-handed? Perhaps he had a carer. Perhaps Abby, ambidextrous all over again, a two-handed handmaiden, did it for him. The impertinence of it, appropriating another man's wife. Remember, Gerald reminded himself, a wife is not a servant. She doesn't belong to me, not in that way. But by the same token, she doesn't belong to Steve either. In any case, Abby was hardly house-proud herself. It was Gerald who usually took care of finishing touches.

They sat around the kitchen table on Ikea plastic chairs. Abby fetched over a stool for Steve to rest his injured leg on. 'It means the blood doesn't have to go up and down,' she said. 'Using a lot of energy. It can just slide across from one end of his leg to the other.'

'That helps the healing process, does it?' Gerald asked.

'Bound to.'

'Are you sure you don't want us to run you over to A&E? Just get you checked out,' Gerald asked Steve.

Steve gave a low snarl or growl in response. Gerald couldn't stop himself from sighing with satisfaction. 'I'll make us some tea, shall I?' he suggested.

He was just pouring the kettle into the pot when the kitchen door opened. He looked up and jumped with shock, displacing the kettle and pouring boiling water onto his hand.

Even through his scream he had the need to check that it was what he'd thought it was. It was like trying to make out a figure through sheets of rain or billows of fog, an auditory version of obscurity. A gigantic dark creature was standing in the doorway, its helmet making a huge domed head like that of an insectile alien in a sci-fi film. Each time Gerald was confronted by a policeman out of the blue he saw him with seven-year-old eyes. But nowadays these sudden policemen were always the same policeman, Constable Bennett.

'Fucking hell,' Steve said. 'You wouldn't bloody believe it. We might as well have A&E come to us, it would be more economical.'

'Gerald,' Abby said, 'run it under the cold-water tap straight away.' As Gerald did so, Abby said, 'In my mother's day, bless the silly old so-and-so, everyone thought you ought to put butter on burns, but in fact that's the wrong thing altogether. I think most people were a bit daft in those days, not just mum. You've only got to picture it. It would be like frying bacon in a pan.'

'Thanks for that thought, Abby.'

'Come in, Andrew,' Abby said to the policeman. 'It's your home, when all's said and done. La la, darling, what a welcome. Gerald, do you remember Andy? He came round that time when he had a dead body he wanted you to look at. It was when Judith was staying with us.'

'I remember.'

'He lives with Steve, would you believe? I found out when I started coming round here. He's Steve's *husband*. Small world. Andy, I'm so sorry you couldn't come to dinner with Steve yesterday. We had a horrible time, didn't we Steve? And now he's gone and buggered up his leg.'

'On late shift,' Andy said tersely. 'Are you all right, darling?'

'I fell off a bloody horse.'

'He flew over it, to be honest. Her.'

Bennett took off his helmet, placed it carefully on the kitchen table, and ruffled Steve's hair. Steve patted his hand. 'Are you OK? We don't want you losing more body parts.'

'I'll live,' Steve said.

'There's always trouble when the prof's around, isn't there, Prof? People fall in rivers, or threaten to. Drop dead in pubs. Fall off horses. He's dangerous company, the prof is.'

'I wasn't anywhere near that horse at the time,' Gerald said.

'Her name is Dorothy, remember,' Abby said.

'Near Dorothy. I got warned off *you*, funnily enough,' he told Bennett. 'I went into the police station on Manvers Street not long after that woman died in The Star. I spoke to a sergeant on reception. I thought it was time to get that girl Laura onto a missing persons' database.'

'Oh yes, I saw she was on the database. Fair hair with stumps. I don't think we've had any feedback.'

'The sergeant didn't seem to like you very much. He called you a cunt. I didn't think that was very professional.'

'That sergeant hates me. He's a homophobe.'

Gerald had felt a certain amount of glee in relaying the sergeant's insult. He was tired of Bennett always catching him on the back foot. But now he felt wrong-footed yet again.

'There's not been sight or sound of her, in fact,' Bennett said. 'Are you sure she's missing?'

'If there's not been sight or sound of her, of course she's missing. That's what missing means, isn't it?'

CHAPTER 12

Y ou could have told me that Steve was fixed up with that policeman,' Gerald said as they drove home. Abby was at the wheel. The policeman had bandaged his scalded hand, but the burn stung and puckered beneath the bland white cotton.

Abby was smoking, her privilege as she was in the driving seat, the cigarette drooping from her lips gangster-style. She took a drag, then removed it and held it near the steering-wheel. 'I didn't think about it. What does it matter?'

He could hardly explain that knowing it would have stopped him being jealous of Steve. He thought of Demis, the half-Greek engineer, of the waiter on Crete, of other unindividuated waiters, a shadowy motley crew, people who might or might not have existed, flickering like spindrift. He had assumed the past was fixed now there were no other universes for it to occupy, but perhaps it was more like the future than you might think, indeterminate, undetermined. It melted and reformed. He could try forever to plot Abby's past, even though he'd lived with her for half a century; he could try forever to plot his own, though he had lived with it always.

'It doesn't. Though I never took to him. So officious. But still.' He held up his bandaged hand as if to concede a point. That had been a moment of intimacy, no other word for it.

'You never took to Steve either,' Abby said.

Neither spoke for a moment. Abby raised her cigarette, pulled on it till the tip glowed like a tiny flower.

'Funny the way they neglect the front garden,' Gerald said after a while.

'I think it's a disguise.'

'Oh?'

'There's some rough types live down that street,' Abby said. 'People who never put a shirt on, just wear string vests. I don't even know where you can *buy* string vests, nowadays. Plus they have huge Alsatian dogs with those black muzzles. Like their mouth and nose are just a sort of evil smudge, with teeth behind. And here comes this pair, ping pong, Andy's a copper, Steve's an artist. They're gay. They're not likely to be popular. But letting the front garden go to pot makes them look as rubbish and hopeless as everyone else. That's what I think. If you were hiding in a burrow or a hole, you might put sticks and leaves over the entrance so no one knows you're there. Same same,' she concluded in an echo of the language of long-ago Libya. She sighed with satisfaction at the picture. 'Talking of not liking people, I've never really liked Terence, if you must know.'

'Abby!' His hand began to throb again in shock, and his headache came on as if in sympathy. 'But he's been our friend for years. A good friend. For years and years. Our best friend.'

'*Your* best friend. Do you remember how he took my shoe off after I slid on your dumplings and felt my foot? Gave it little squeezes? I wanted to shriek out loud. Anybody touching my foot makes me want to shriek out loud. Even you. But Terence specially, copping his little feels.'

'I remember you saying he was a treasure. You called him a treasure.' He couldn't tell if this was a trivial matter or the rumblings of an earthquake. Another moment when the verities of the past seemed to give way suddenly under his feet.

'Did I?' Abby said. 'I must have been being sarcastic. I said to Judith, what you ought to buy him, get him some escargots, if they sell them in Wrexham. It'll be nice for Mr. Ooze to have a few friends and relations around.' She wound down her window and threw her butt onto the road.

'For God's sake, Abby. That was really mean. Truly mean.' What was this he was saying? What was his tone? His own tone? You could speak and not be certain how you were pitching it. It was amusement, that's what it was. Disapproving in such a way as to enjoy what he was disapproving of. He had loved Terence for many years, but now he understood how it felt to be in a mob when its sympathies turned.

'Don't worry. I didn't tell Judith that. I just said get escargots, not why.'

'I hope she doesn't give him a hard time, that's all.'

'No no, I think she's smitten. What you've got to remember is that her taste in men is very different from mine. Look at who she married. Having sex with Ken was like going to bed with a gorilla. Except he didn't have any small talk.' She laughed at the absurdity of the idea.

Gerald sat stunned. I need to think about this, he thought. Except that his throbbing head and his throbbing hand were taking up all the space. Must think. He tried to formulate the possibilities between the systole and diastole of the throbs. Did she mean that going to bed with Ken *would have been* like going to bed with a gorilla? Or was it reported speech? *Judith told her that going to bed with him was like going to bed with a gorilla.* Was she just being provocative, trying to wind him up? Or had she actually gone to bed with Ken, to try him out?

'Plus,' Abby continued, 'I've never forgiven him.'

'Who? Ken?'

'No, Terence of course.'

'What have you never forgiven him for? Apart from squeezing your foot.'

'That Laura business; that's what I've never forgiven him for. He was supposed to be a friend of the both of us.'

'But that was *my* Laura business, wasn't it?'

'You know what they say these days. Me Too? To which I would add, him as well.'

'Let's open the window,' Gerald said.

'I'm not sure that's such a good idea.'

'Why not? It's a nice day.'

'I might frighten the neighbours. You never can tell.'

It was strange to hear her being provoking. She looked so demure, so much the bluestocking, sitting on the edge of the bed with her big glasses balanced on her little nose, her neat woollen dress.

He stepped up to the bed. Her dress had big buttons down the front. He raised his hand to undo the top one. She slapped it away.

'First things first,' she said, standing up and taking off her glasses, which she carefully placed on the bedside table. Her eyes looked small and naked, blinking in the light. Freckles swarmed across her cheeks like golden constellations. One, just below her right eye, had little spears like a star, at least like a star in a devotional painting. He lowered his head, kissed it, let his hand drift to her top button again.

Once more she slapped it. 'My privilege,' she said. 'My clothes.' She did a little pirouette. It wasn't an action that suited her, which made it touching. The heavy grey dress hardly flared with the movement. She raised her hands to the back of her head and undid a clip that held her auburn hair in place, letting it drop onto her shoulders. Then she swung her hips, a little stiffly, and began to undo her buttons, looking at him with a stripper's fixed gaze from myopic, hard-reading eyes.

This is what I want, he thought, his heart pounding, this is what I've always wanted, without even realising: knowledge, intellect, made flesh. She understands Jonathan Edwards, and here she is taking her clothes off.

She had a neat little bra, not lacy, just practical, small firm breasts. She dropped the bra on the bedroom floor, still swaying awkwardly as she did so. She was wearing brief white pants with minute blue flowers on them. The whiteness of the cotton was almost translucent, so he could make out through it the brown tuft of pubic hair. She slid a hand in each side of the pants and began to ease them down.

'No, no.' Abby's voice from the doorway. Laura's hands shot from her pants like a child's from a biscuit barrel. 'Oh no. Go and do your homework somewhere else, young lady. This is not the right place for a tutorial. This bedroom is mine. I thought the prat standing here with his eyes out on stalks was mine as well, but that's debatable.'

Laura was bending over, scrabbling for her clothes, the dead white cheeks of her bottom, half exposed, becoming suffused with faint pink patches, as if blushing. 'Shit, shit, shit,' she was saying to herself, almost absent-mindedly. Her flustered clumsy movements made her look about ten years old. She rushed past Abby and out of the room with her clothes in her hand.

'I hope she remembers to put them on before she goes out onto the street,' Abby said.

'Abby I – what can I say? I thought you'd still be at school. Oh God. Poor Laura.'

'Well, that's a good excuse. I would appreciate it, Gerald, if you would confine your shagging activities to your office, like all the other lecturers. I had to go to the dentist this afternoon, if you must know. I told you about it, I'm sure. You were probably thinking about history at the time, or maybe how your student would look when she had no clothes on. Well, now you know. And I know too, not that I was ever curious. I always think that naked men look more fun, but maybe that's just me. E.T. is taking my class this afternoon.'

E.T. was the head teacher, who apparently had a curiously

small cranium. 'It's funny to think we have to call him the head, when he has the littlest one in the whole school,' Abby said once. 'Except for the children, of course.'

'And if you say this is not what I think it is,' she told Gerald now, 'I will surgically remove your bollocks, one after the other one.'

'All I can say, Abby, is it's not – it's quite serious.'

'Well, at least that's original. The standard line, for future reference, is that it *isn't* anything serious.'

'I think I'm in love with her.'

'Gerald,' she said wearily, 'we can all fancy a little extra-mural action now and again. Fair do's. I quite appreciate you showing a bit of initiative in that respect. But don't blow it up into something it isn't. She's half your age. She's a student, when all's said and done.'

'A research student. That's not quite the same thing. Ethically speaking.'

'Since when have you heard me talking about ethics, Gerald? Ever in my whole life? Ethics is not what I do. For goodness sake. Grow up.'

'I think – she's my future. That my future lies with her.'

'Oh dear, it's worse than I thought. I wish now I hadn't interrupted the two of you. If you'd managed to get your rocks off, maybe you'd have returned to normal.'

'You make me sick, Abby. You see everything in such a disgusting way. You know what you are? *Coarse.* Your outlook. Vulgar, that's all I can say.' He stood there, huffing and puffing, aware of his self-righteousness, his ludicrous pomposity. 'Sometimes,' he added, panicked.

'So I'm coarse, am I, Gerald? Thank you very much. Can I remind you it was you who fetched your girlfriend up into our bedroom? Some people might say that *that* was a bit coarse. Some people might even say it was vulgar.'

'What did Terence have to do with it?' Gerald asked.

'He took your side. He egged you on. He was a sort of pander.'

'Are you sure? I don't remember that.'

'You don't remember a lot of things. How convenient. When we got blind drunk and had that awful row and you went round to Mr. Ooze cap in hand, and he wiped your eyes for you and let you sleep in the spare room. And then along toddles Laura, and she ends up in the spare room too. If that isn't being a pander, I don't know what is. I expect he brought the pair of you a cup of tea in the morning.'

'Who told you that?'

'You told me that, Gerald. I couldn't tell at the time whether you were boasting or complaining. I thought to myself, if you have to go off and shag your student, just get on and do it like a man and don't come back to me boasting and complaining about it.'

The rain was pounding down. Gerald bent down to the intercom system for Terence's flat. Through its tinny speaker Terence's voice sounded strained and suspicious. There was something impatient, peremptory, about the way he pressed the buzzer to release the lock. It occurred to Gerald, extrapolating from his own behaviour, that Terence too might be up to something. But when he opened the door of his flat, Terence had that look of having just woken up, a certain beddy unwholesome air. He was tie-less, with his shirttails hanging out, very unlike his normal dapper self. Gerald remembered a dream he had once, where Terence was wearing a pair of shorts and a t-shirt and was seated on the top of a tiny slide. 'Des-hab-ill-é,' Gerald said, remembering the word in fits and starts, hiccups almost.

'*You're* absolutely drenched,' Terence said by way of tit for tat.

'I walked here.'

'But why did you do that? It's tipping it down.'

'I wanted to get good and wet. I wanted to get saturated. I wanted to get a fucking soaking, if you must know.'

Terence got him a towel to dry his hair. 'Whatever's the matter, Gerald?' he asked.

How to say it? Usually it was Terence who had to communicate large, difficult ideas. Gerald felt crushed by all there was to tell him. There was all the past for a start, his relationship with Abby, its limitations and frustrations, but also his respect for her, love even – 'Love, even,' he kept saying. 'Despite everything. Thing is, I'm so unspecified compared to her. Unspecific. Even my head wobbles. From time to time. They used to call me Noddy at school. It's not screwed on tightly enough. That's what Ruth told me, when I said I was worried about it. Shared a cigarette and confided my troubles. She said, not to worry, it'll bed down in due course. But it never did, completely. Maybe it would have if she hadn't died so soon. It might have bedded down then. My head might. *I* might have bedded down then. As a whole. Abby is the least wobbly person I ever met. She's all of a piece. What it is, she grabs at life. She's reckless. I love how she does that. She used to work in a hardware shop, years and years ago. She didn't care. That's how she is. It was so cool, with all the hammers and saws about. Standing behind the counter with a shop coat over her miniskirt.'

Terence had tucked in his shirt, put on his tie, pulled a crew-necked cashmere jumper over his head. He was Terence again, in a smooth carapace like a beetle. He came across with two whiskies. 'Let me tell you something, Gerald,' he said. 'Your head doesn't wobble.' He passed one of the whiskies over. 'Hardly at all.'

Gerald took a swig of whisky. It seemed to burn his gullet like molten lava. 'Jesus,' he said, clutching his throat.

'I know,' Terence said. 'It's good, isn't it? I bought it when I was at a conference in St. Andrews. So smooth.'

Gerald groaned, but luckily it came out wistful, elegiac even. 'I kissed her, Terence. Right on this freckle she's got on her cheek.' He put his whisky down and prodded his own cheek with a forefinger. 'That's a seal of intimacy, wouldn't you say?' She had slapped him immediately after, he remembered.

'Gerald, Abby doesn't *have* any freckles on her cheek. Not that I've noticed, anyway.'

'Not Abby. For goodness sake, haven't you been following anything I've been telling you?'

'To tell you the truth, no, I haven't. I've hardly understood a word of it. Might as well have been gibberish, as far as I'm concerned. In my world a seal is something that eats fish and balances a ball on its nose. I thought being incomprehensible was my. I can say whole paragraphs without people understanding a word. You ought to go to one of my lectures sometime. My prerogative. Students nodding off all over the bally room.'

'I've met the love of my life, Terence. Do you understand *now*?'

'I thought *Abby* was the love of your life. I've always envied you and Abby. So different from each other. Living with difference. That's what you don't get when you're a bachelor. You see your own reflection in everything you do. It becomes very boring. Do you know, people detect each other's pheromones, even without knowing they do? The only person I ever get a sniff of is me. You can get tired of the scent of yourself.'

'What I've been looking for, without knowing I've been looking for it, is someone I can talk to.'

'For heaven's sake, you've got Abby to talk to. Look at me. I spend a large part of my time chuntering. That's onomatopoeic, by the way. It's the sound I actually make when I'm all by myself in this flat, brooding, which is almost all the time. Think yourself—'

'Proper talk, I mean. About life.'

Terence recoiled, ready to object again. Gerald, with a certain drunken alacrity, knew exactly how he would counter. *Abby* could talk about life, Terence would tell him. Life was her special subject, true enough. She was the world expert on it. She was composed entirely of life.

'Of the mind. Life of the mind,' Gerald said. He'd never put a lot of faith in his own mind, as it happened. It was mediocre, when all was said and done, when compared with truly original ones. A plodder's mind, needing stimulation. Not like Terence's. He had the sort of mind that could brood upon silences. And at intervals lay a large egg. But wasn't that the whole point? Gerald needed another mind to elevate his own. To trigger it. Fertilise it, even. 'And now I've found it. Her. But the physical side as well, that's the thing. Mind and body. Both at once.'

'Gerald, you've not fallen for one of your colleagues, have you? I'm trying to recall which one has a mind. Not to mention a body.'

'What? God, no. Terence, she's beautiful. Not beautiful beautiful. But.' He waved his hand ineptly, to suggest the kind of unbeautiful beautiful Laura was.

'I would have said Abby is pretty good-looking, when all is said and done. I've always thought so, anyway.'

'Inside as well. Inner. She's a vegetarian. Her mind also.'

'I'm sorry, Gerald, I'm not following this. If you don't mind my saying, you must have had a few. What are you trying to tell me? She thinks vegetable *thoughts*?'

In some way or another, that *was* what he was trying to tell Terence. That Laura's thoughts were refined, rarefied, not fleshly (except when they were, of course).

'Do you know, Gerald?' Terence continued. 'You can actually get fed up with the mind. And that's me saying that.'

'Abby humiliated her. She made her run for it. It wasn't nice. She has freckles.'

'So you said.'

'Auburn hair.'

'Like me, then.'

'Terence, you're ginger. You always have been ginger. Ginger as in biscuit.' He found himself laughing at the comparison.

Terence gave a long reflective look from his ginger eyes, slightly to one side of Gerald's face. 'She's not a student, is she?' he asked. 'Oh God. What's her name? Did you say Ruth? No, no, that was your sister, I remember. Tell me she's not a student.'

'She's not a student. She's a *research* student. Her name is Laura.'

'She *is* a student. Gerald, this is not a good idea.'

'Laura is not an idea. She's a woman.'

'You're the one who keeps talking about mind.'

'Terence, you must ring her up for me.'

'Me? What on earth's it got to do with me?'

'I'm frightened if I ring she'll just hang up. Abby humiliated her, Terence.'

'So you say. But this Laura person doesn't know me from Adam. Why don't you just go round to where she lives?'

'She shares a house with other girls. Women. With other women. They will all stare at us. We've been stared at enough already. I want her to come here, in the rain. Like *I* did. I've got her glasses to give back. She left them on the bedside table.'

Gerald took Laura's glasses out of his top pocket, unfolded their arms, and held them out towards Terence, hoping somehow that the spectacles would imply the fascination of the face that normally lay behind them, the penetrating eyes that looked through the lenses. Terence glanced at them without particular interest. 'She was in such a rush to collect up her clothes,' Gerald said.

Terence shook his head wearily. Gerald folded the glasses up again and replaced them in his pocket. Rain, he reminded himself, as if it was an item on a to-do list. 'I want you to tell her to come *here*, in the rain.' The rain seemed somehow to be an essential part of her coming, spangling her auburn hair, running down her freckly cheeks like surrogate tears. 'You're neutral territory, as far as she is concerned. You're not here nor there. As far as she is concerned."

'Calling me neutral territory is not the way to get in my good books, Gerald. I spend too much of my life being neither here nor there. I don't need reminding of it.'

Her hair wasn't spangled. It was tied up tight in its clip, at the back of her head. She'd used an umbrella on her walk through the rain.

Gerald passed her spectacles over. She opened them carefully and put them on. Her eyes seemed to nose towards him through the thick lenses. He took a step backwards to diminish the strength of her gaze. She was wearing a maroon anorak and jeans. Terence had tactfully retired from the scene as soon as he'd made the call.

'OK, here I am,' Laura said. Even in those three words the difference was clear. Previously her superior brain had performed for his approval, hoping to please like a precocious child trying to impress its parents. Now it was just a superior brain, free of obligation. 'Perhaps you can explain what the fuck happened back there. Why wasn't your wife at work?'

'I'm so sorry, Laura. She went to the dentist's.'

'For fuck's sake, Gerald, why didn't you tell me she was at the fucking dentist's?' There was a pause. Gerald shrugged disconsolately, impotently. 'Gerald,' Laura went on, 'have you ever heard about the relativity of time?'

'What?' He looked at her in astonishment and relief at this apparent swerve. 'Yes, of course I've heard of it. My friend Terence talks about it practically non-stop. He's the one who owns this flat. He went to bed.'

'You sit for hours, Gerald, in the dentist's chair, being drilled. Then when you get up and leave, you find out only a few minutes have passed. Which is how come she came home fucking early and found me taking my pants off.'

'She didn't *tell* me she was going to the dentist. She told me she told me, but I don't remember it. She can be a bit scatty at times. She doesn't always say what she thinks she's said. I thought she was in school.'

Laura sighed impatiently. 'What a mess,' she said. 'Still, I suppose we might as well get on with it. Does this Terence person have a spare bedroom?'

In the spare bedroom, Laura unzipped her anorak and put it on a chair, then took off each article of clothing in turn as functionally as if she was stripping for a medical examination. Gerald observed she had changed her pants. The fresh ones were large and business-like, in an anonymous off-white colour.

She stood naked. Gerald was amazed at how un-turned-on he felt. There was her body, to all intents and purposes just as it was before, or almost was, but now it seemed . . . he couldn't quite pin down the right word. Secular, was the nearest he could get. Her body seemed to have become secular. Neutral territory.

'Come on, then,' she said.

He took a step towards her and put out his hands, thinking she was asking to be caressed or grasped. She slapped them down, just as she had in the afternoon when he had tried to undo the top button of her dress. 'Gerald,' she said impatiently, 'you can't have a fuck with all your clothes still on. I do not wish to screw a pair of trousers.'

'The dishwasher has broken down,' Abby said. 'Anyway, I like getting my hands in hot water from time to time.' She was standing on a small wooden box – she had always complained that the sink in their kitchen was too high for her – washing up the dishes from the glum, dazed supper they'd silently eaten the previous night, not long after they'd both said, and shouted, and drunk, far too much, and just before he had rushed off whimpering into the rain. 'You wipe.'

Gerald picked up a tea towel, and they stood working side by side. Gerald realised she wasn't going to ask him where he'd been. 'I'll ring a repairman,' he said.

'Gerald, the days of repairmen are over. Plus it's well out of warranty. What you do is go out and buy a new one and get them to take the buggered one away. That's how it's done nowadays.'

'OK. Will do.' He raised the tea towel and touched his forehead with it. 'Yip,' he added feebly.

They were nearing the end of the washing-up. He felt a flutter of panic at what to do next. Silence, left to itself, has a tendency to thicken. He could feel it happening already. It would get denser and denser until neither of them would be able to speak, or move. He pictured them standing side by side staring at the kitchen wall, she on her box, he at the draining board, standing there perhaps forever.

'I went to Terence's flat last night.'

'How nice.'

They both spoke at the wall.

'He rang Laura for me, and she came round.'

'What a little party you must have had. Did she do her striptease again?'

'Terence went to bed before she arrived. Laura and I slept in the spare room.'

There was a pause.

This is what you wanted, Abby, so you said, Gerald told himself. You said you thought I ought to get my rocks off. 'We had sex,' he said.

'What fun.'

'Not really. She was weird. It wasn't what I expected at all. She was wild. It was as if she hated me for some reason.'

'Oh dear. I wonder why that should be.'

There was another long silence.

'It was horrible, Abby. It felt out of control, but not in a good way.'

'Did you talk about history afterwards? You know, in that time when people are supposed to share a cigarette under the covers? Remember the old joke, do you smoke after sex? A bit of history, back and forth, do no harm. Interesting little nuggets. Like what date was it when they chopped off the Queen of Scots' head. I intend to take up smoking myself one of these days. It would be easier than doing *history* after having sex.'

'That isn't history, Abby. Dates are just what they bang on about in school. No, we didn't talk about history. We didn't talk at all. She seemed to be someone completely different. Some*thing*, you could almost say.'

'I suppose that's supposed to make me feel better.'

'I'm just saying she wasn't the person I thought she was. She was like an animal.'

'I thought that was what you professors yearned for. Going to bed with a brainbox who suddenly turns into an animal.'

'I suppose it depends what sort. Laura turned into a gorilla.'

They continued staring at the wall, Abby on her box, Gerald resting his palms flat on the draining board. After a while there was a squeak, the sort that might come from an unoiled bicycle wheel or small animal. Gerald didn't like to move his frame but slid his eyes sideways so far they hurt. Abby was vibrating, like a glass before it shatters. Then she was laughing as if it hurt to laugh, tears streaming from her eyes. Gerald started to laugh too, in a different way, modestly as if he had said or done something clever, proprietorial laughing.

Gerald said, 'I told her this morning it was all over between us.'

'And what did she say to that?'

'She said, "You better bloody believe it."'

SUMMER

CHAPTER 13

It was something Gerald had been putting off for months, ever since that fateful conversation in the pub last winter. He changed the title of his book from *Quantum History* to *The Road Not Taken*. Brian Chandler's baggy face gloated down at him from above, or maybe up from below, like the moon in a puddle. All the romance and daring drained from the subject, leaving it diminished, secular. The multiverse had been reduced to a thought experiment.

In his heart Gerald knew that this was the end of the project. Time to face facts. He would never have the willpower to carry on with the book. Quantum history had been too good to be true. He had never really understood it. His intellect was too mediocre to cope with such strangeness.

Abby was out, potting or riding, so he decided to go for a walk. It was a lovely June day, and soon he found himself on the river walkway where he'd looked out for Laura many months before. Bath as a city had never made much of its river frontage, and this was a dull, functional place, even though the Avon itself was blue with sky, the surface not rippling but sliding in flat planes, as if made of sash windows. He stood watching the river for a while, overcome by an intense nostalgia, though for what he couldn't say.

When he got back to the house, Abby still wasn't there. The afternoon was getting on by now, and he needed to know if she wanted him to book a table for dinner or intended to produce something herself. He dialled her number but heard her phone ringing on the hall table.

I will cook something, he thought. I will make a cottage pie. He'd done no cooking since that disastrous Chinese, months ago.

He took a pack of minced beef from the freezer. It seemed rather large for the two of them. He got out a carving knife and tried to cut the mince in two, but the knife kept slipping. He pressed his finger to the tip of his nose, as if it was a button that would switch something on in his brain, a habit he'd learned from Abby. He would make two pies and freeze one of them.

He cooked the mince in a frying pan with stock, onions, and sliced peppers, then added a few peas. Abby seemed to believe peas were facile or crass, except with lamb. 'Tough,' Gerald told her. He put the cooked mixture to one side and boiled the potatoes. As he mashed them with some milk he recalled the curse of cottage pies, of shepherd's and fish pies too: lumps in the mash, curiously resistant to pulping and difficult to spot. Nail one, and another would appear somewhere else. As the pie browned under the grill, those you missed became visible as translucent blotches, like glare in a photo.

It wasn't worth lighting the grill until Abby returned. He put the spare pie in the freezer and poured himself a beer. It felt good to prepare a meal without anyone getting hurt. Then he set about doing the Guardian crosswords on his iPad.

When he surfaced, it felt quite late. Yes, half past seven, and still no sign of Abby. Because he'd not thought about her for some time, he felt a sudden slight panic, as if a lapse of attention could let disaster in. Remembering that night last September, he looked about for a note and then checked their bedroom to make sure she wasn't asleep. When he had established for certain that he hadn't overlooked her somehow, the emptiness of the house seemed to intensify.

He remembered something Terence once said to him. They had been waiting to cross London Road. 'Have you ever thought how odd it is waiting for a gap to come?' Terence said.

'A gap isn't anything, yet we wait for one in the traffic as if it is *some*thing. What we should say is we're waiting for cars to *not* come.'

'Isn't that the same thing? Just a matter of how you express the negative?'

'That's the whole point. We make the negative a positive. Something *is*n't there. Nothing *is* there. So then we are able to see a gap in the traffic driving up towards us even though there's nothing to see. It's a sort of ghost. We see a ghost.'

'You're a clever so-and-so, Terence.'

'It's not me being clever, it's all of us being clever. Brains wired accordingly. Same as calculating with minus numbers. Facility,' he concluded. 'Facil-i-ty.'

That was how the negative presence of Abby now seemed, as if she was implicit in the very atmosphere. It was what haunting must be: the contours of absence, a silhouette of what is no longer there, like the shape of Desperate Dan after he has broken through a brick wall.

Gerald lit the oven grill and, when it was hot, roughened the surface of the cottage pie with a fork, then put it under to brown. When he took it out again, its surface looked like a neatly ploughed field, not a single scab of unintegrated potato. He must somehow have eliminated every last buggering lump. What a shame Abby wasn't here to see it. Still, she could always eat later.

He scooped out a neat spoonful of pie, poured himself a glass of red wine, shovelled a forkful into his mouth, for some reason chewed it by moving his jaw from left to right like a baby being weaned, forehead frowning, eyes fixed on inwardness, always on the alert to spit if necessary, the baby they had never had.

Ten o'clock came and went. It would be logical to ring Steve, given that he was the explanation for her last absence. Maybe he and Abby were doing their three-handed potting together and had just lost track of time. But he couldn't risk it. The phone would be picked up by Constable Bennett, and Gerald would make a fool of himself yet again. At eleven he went to bed. Where else was there to go?

Of course he lay for hours without sleeping. For weeks he and Abby had gone about their daily lives as if that cascade of revelations hadn't taken place. They had managed to avert their gaze from it. At least he had – perhaps Abby hadn't felt the need to, perhaps she was better able to live with complication and betrayal. But now she was missing again, just as she had been on that night last September, and somehow her absence, a sort of lacuna of the body as a whole, brought it all back, the discoveries he had made about her, assuming they *were* discoveries, the ones he'd made about himself. It was like one of those coy Jane Austen dances you see on TV, shifting and changing as the dancers prance from hand to hand.

Eventually his brain began to throb, tired of dealing with the intricacy of it all. Slowly, as he grew sleepier, the detail melted away, leaving only a deep sense of unease at Abby's absence. Then even Abby slipped out of focus and only his unease remained.

He was in his office in the history department of Manchester University. It was a dour November afternoon. A few large raindrops had run down his window so that it looked as if there were cracks in the glass. He liked to sit at his desk and watch people scurrying across the bleak space between the humanities building, where his office was situated, and the refectory opposite, the two structures cunningly arranged to ensure a chill wind always blew between them, even when the air was perfectly calm everywhere else. But today his stomach was tense with anxiety. He was due to have his monthly meeting with Laura to discuss the progress of her thesis, their first session since that night in Terence's flat.

The way to handle it, he thought, was just to get down to business, academic business. There were times when you were naked, and times when you were clothed. None of the business of the world could be accomplished if those two states were allowed to overlap. When a doctor sat down opposite his wife for dinner, he didn't visualise her liver and kidneys and guts, even though he knew they were there in a heap in front of him. Instead he would keep his eyes fixed on her twinset and pearls, dab his lips with a napkin. Your skin covered one level of nakedness, your clothes another. We are layered like onions. Decorum was a matter of keeping in mind what layer the particular intercourse was taking place on. The trick was not to get the layers muddled up. But of course that was just what he had done, when he switched from being Laura's mentor to being her lover.

For what seemed like a long while, he continued to look out of the window at the spitting rain, the hunched and hurried people, without glancing down at his watch, as if knowing how late Laura was would make her *officially* late in some way, eliminate a margin. But when he finally raised his wrist, just ten minutes had passed. As yet, she was hardly late at all. She was still inside her margin. He had the waiting still to do.

When you wait for something you secretly dread, Gerald thought, you simultaneously want it to come so that you can get it over with and want it not to come so that you don't have to cope with it. The anxiety of expecting a knock on the door is not anxiety about whether the knock will take place but whether you will be relieved or disappointed when it does or doesn't. The issue is not what is happening (the approaching along the corridor, the knuckle rising towards the door panel) or not happening (empty corridor, smells of polish and cigarettes) on the *out*side of the door, but what is taking place on the *in*side, the sitting silently at the desk, the staring at the rain-streaked window. The anxiety is about what you yourself are thinking, not about what may or may not be about to happen.

Understanding that didn't help, as it usually doesn't. Sometimes, Gerald thought, as the rain intensified and began to rattle against the glass, sometimes I get fed up with investigating the psychopathology of every fucking thought I've ever fucking thought.

She didn't come. By the end of an hour he was exhausted. Now what should he do? If he wrote asking her why she hadn't turned up, there was a danger that she might actually tell him, and if he made any official enquiries he would in effect be dobbing on her.

A week went by, two weeks. She didn't send a note. She didn't phone. Every time he worked in his office, his ear, both his ears, were cocked towards the door. He felt like a windblown dog. And every time someone did knock – some random colleague or student – he had to say come in without letting his voice crack or flute in fear.

The following morning he decided to ring Judith. She often knew of Abby's comings and goings, despite being all the way off in Wales.

'Hello.'

'Terence?'

'Hello, Gerald.'

'Good grief, Terence, are you still there? It's been weeks.'

'Not still. Again, is how I'd put it. I come and go. Judith comes and goes too. To my flat. We seem to be shuttling from one to the other. I think it's metaphorical, to tell you the truth. My flat is me, and her house is she, to a certain extent, so we are getting to learn how to inhabit each other, so to speak. Don't tell her I said that, because she always claims Wrexham is a kind of accident. As if the whole town just happened to fall on her head. As I said to her, we live in a universe in which everything is an accident and nothing is an accident. I think she took my point.'

'Well I'm damned. I had no idea things had gone as far as that.'

'She's a wonderful woman, I have to tell you. Nowhere and everywhere at the same time, like a quantum particle. I always feel Abby has that same quality. To saturate space while still being a very small entity.'

Leave my wife out of it, Gerald thought.

'But Judith is Judith,' Terence said, as if reading his mind.

Gerald recalled that moment when he saw Judith in the café on Deansgate, her lipsticked lips, the way she held herself in reserve, like a cat being called to in a garden, something arch about her. 'I suppose she is,' he said. You couldn't describe Abby as a femme fatale in that way, even the first time he set eyes on her at that Cambridge party, long ago. She simply sat on a chair being intensely Abby.

'She is more . . . bubble-like,' Terence said. 'Judith is, than Abby. Like a bubble. No offence, but I need that quality in my life. At this stage. Probably in previous stages for that matter, could have done with. Drifting along. She gave me snails for our first meal, just saw them in a shop. Mind you, getting them down felt like an initiation rite in a New Guinea longhouse. They have teeth on their tongues, snails do. I mentioned it to Judith, but she said she preferred not to know.'

'Talking of Judith, is she there?'

'Somewhere. Give me a minute.'

Terence took the phone with him in his search. It seemed touchingly domestic, him calling for Judith, even more so hearing her distant replies.

'Hello poppet.'

'How are things?'

'Things are grand.' She lowered her voice. 'We got off to such a good start. Do you remember me telling you about those snails? Terence gobbled them up. I think they helped to make him take me seriously. Nobody has ever taken me seriously before.'

'*I* take you seriously.'

'How's Abby?' Judith asked, as if to remind him where his allegiances lay.

Her question answered his unasked question. 'She's fine. Not in at present.' Gerald recoiled from saying he had no idea where she was; it seemed so hapless. 'She asked me to ring. She wants to invite you and Terence down next weekend.'

For God's sake, why did I say that? Gerald asked himself. He must have felt that by pretending he was acting on instructions he was establishing an alibi for Abby's disappearance. But why did he need one? He imagined Abby's reaction when he admitted he had invited Judith and Terence down without consulting her. Of course, she loved her sister and in the past had asked her to stay without discussing the matter with *him* – those were valid points, but no matter, Abby would not be pleased, Abby would be unhappy. For one thing it wasn't a question of Judith coming, but of the two in tandem. And apparently Abby didn't like Terence, had never liked Terence in all these years. But even that wasn't the nub of the matter. She would be upset because he had appropriated an area that didn't belong to him.

It was a tiny act of adultery. Not that Abby would use such a term. She would regard that kind of conceit as pretentious. She would just say: you should have kept your nose out.

Another day went by, and still no word from Abby. He had the sense that he was going about his daily business under false pretences, as if he had buried her in the back garden. Steve rang, asking if he could speak to her. 'She's out at present,' Gerald told him. Judith rang too, to say that she and Terence would be arriving early on the Friday afternoon, if that was OK. Gerald told her it was. She asked to speak to her sister. Gerald said that she was again unlucky, that Abby had just gone out.

'That's funny,' Judith said.

'Why is it funny?'

'Well, as you know, I'm a bit psychic.'

'Are you?'

'Don't pull my leg, Gerald, you know I am.'

'Do I?'

There was a pause. It occurred to Gerald that he might be a bit psychic as well, since he could guess what Judith was referring to, that meeting in the coffee house on Deansgate all those years ago. Was she implying that she had installed herself there on purpose, that in some sort of psychic way she had summoned him from the Manchester University library, that she had been able to exert a kind of magnetic or gravitational pull on him?

There was a certain consolation in that thought, since it suggested that he needn't feel responsible for what happened subsequently.

'Not *exactly* psychic,' Judith said. 'I think there's a lot of mumbo-jumbo talked about being psychic. I don't speak to the dead, for starters. Well, a bit to Ken, of course, but that's only to be expected, we were together for so long. By the way, I don't think he's exactly delighted that Terence has come into my life.'

'Is he not?'

'That's the impression I've got. But of course he's not likely to be happy in any case, is he, being dead?'

'Good point.'

'It must make you feel a bit left out. What I would say I am is intuitive. For example, I can usually detect whether Abby is about or not about. I had the strongest impression that she was about. That was why I phoned now. I thought I'll phone now while she's in. That's what I would say was being intuitive, don't you think?'

'Except she *is*n't in.'

'No. That's caught me on the hop, I must admit.'

It was on the tip of Gerald's tongue to say, Me too. Then he could tell Judith how Abby had gone unexpectedly missing, could bring this charade to an end. Instead he said, 'Oh well, you'll be seeing her on Friday anyhow.'

After a couple more weeks had passed, Gerald found a note from the office for graduate students in his pigeonhole. It stated simply that Laura Cunningham had withdrawn from her PhD programme. No explanation given. The assumption, of course, was that Gerald would have discussed it with her at length, would know the reason why. His role was what the university referred to as the primary point of contact – too much so, as it had turned out. Too primary, too much contact.

He wondered what he ought to do, if anything. He could get in touch with the office and ask if they had any further details. Presumably research students abandoning their studies must have to fill out a form. None of those he was responsible for had ever previously walked out on him. They had never had reason to. Yes, why not stroll over there and casually enquire, as if merely to check what they had in their records. Hopefully some junior administrator would be on duty who wouldn't ask penetrating questions.

As luck would have it, Marcia Greene, the director of graduate studies, was the only person around. An aura always hung around senior university managers, like that curtain concealing the Wizard of Oz. She wore a grey suit with a white blouse, her hair grey and white to match, grey eyes slightly magnified by black-framed specs. Most people are more or less clean, but usually you don't notice it. With her you did.

'Ah, Gerald,' she said when he came in, as if they met routinely instead of once in a blue moon, 'I was hoping you would pop in.'

'Well. Here I am. Popped.' For some reason Gerald grimaced

and opened his own eyes wide, as if to register the absurdity of what he'd just said.

'Yes. *Yes*,' Marcia said. 'You have popped. As you say.' She pressed her lips together by way of putting a stop to this *jeu d'esprit*. After a suitable pause: 'Laura Cunningham.' She tapped each syllable home with a little hammer.

'Indeed.' Gerald sighed. 'Laura Cunningham,' he repeated wistfully. They looked at each other in silence for another moment. 'Gone. Left. Such a shame.'

'So it would appear. Judging by your reports to the graduate committee, she was an extremely promising student.'

'Indeed. Was. Is. I mean, she's not dead, after all. She will continue to be promising, presumably.'

'But not here.'

'No, sadly. Not here.'

'Not my area, of course, the history of American thought.'

'No, I suppose not.' Another pause. Marcia was one of those people who could create a silence so immediately deep and dizzying that it could suck any sort of garbage out of you to fill up the space. 'Insects, wasn't it?' Gerald asked. He was aware of his hands trembling and thrust them into his trouser pockets.

'Insects?' Marcia frowned. 'What insects?'

'Insects, I was under the impression.' People joked about Marcia counting beetles. Oh God, perhaps beetles *weren't* insects? Perhaps they were just beetles? He felt humiliated that he could be a university lecturer without having such information confidently to hand. 'Your area?' he asked.

'Oh, I see. Insects.' She seemed to test the word against her palate. 'I think it would be more accurate to say *area* was my area.'

'Really? Area? I thought it was beetles.'

'Beetles come into it, of course. Come into the area, that is. Beetles come into most areas. My field was micro-ecology.

Take a cube. Say a metre by a metre by a metre. A cubic metre. It wouldn't be exactly that for various technical reasons, but let's call it a cubic metre. Imagine it's a sort of transparent box. Bit of air. Bit of surface. Bit of underneath, as you might describe it. Explore every living thing in it. The grass growing. Flies buzzing. Worms worming. As you say, beetles. Beetling. Right down to the microbial level. How it all interacts. That's what I used to study. How a cube of *world* actually works.' She seemed to bloom for a moment, enthused.

'It sounds important work,' Gerald said. He was aware that he sounded ingratiating even though he was in fact being quite sincere. The notion of a cube of world, constructed of glass perhaps, or some other see-through material, was captivating. He imagined being inside one himself, like being a fish in a tank, or some animal in a vivarium. There you were, stuck in your finite box, your life, while beyond it the world stretched away indefinitely in all directions. Ultimately the box wasn't authentic. That is to say, it wasn't strictly speaking *part* of the world. It was imaginary, or psychosomatic. Perhaps you needed the feeling of security it gave, its very finitude. It was like a prison cell where unbeknownst to you they never locked the door, so you could walk out at any time. As long as you weren't thinking about where, or rather who, you were, the walls dissolved, and you could beetle around in the big wide world without restriction. It was like the way toys came to life in the middle of the night, when nobody was looking. As soon as you became aware of what you were doing, you found your-self back in your box again.

'It was important, and it was unimportant,' Marcia replied modestly, to his surprise. 'Like so many things we do. But any-way, one of life's ironies is that when you start organising research you stop doing it yourself.' She gave a distant look for a moment, as if saying farewell to that cube of world, before snapping back into her own personal cube. 'Which brings me to Ms. Cunningham. We were wondering – can you shed any light on what happened with her?'

Gerald clocked the we, the implication of muscle behind her routine question. 'To be frank,' he said, feeling as unfrank as it was possible to be, 'I was wondering what she had told you. Officially.'

'Officially, hardly anything. Personal reasons, that's all she wrote on her withdrawal form.'

'I thought as much.'

'Did you?'

'There are some personal issues swirling about. She confided in me a little, as her tutor. But I'd better stay mum. Respect her . . . ' He felt his face redden. Respecting her was hardly what he'd done.

'So we are just left with generic personal issues. It's a bit bald.' Marcia gave him a long look through those beetling spectacles of hers. Gerald felt she was saying, And *you're* the person, I bet. 'We must respect confidential information acquired in the course of our duties, it goes without saying. Except.'

'Except?'

'Except when it conflicts with our duty of care. If, for example, there was evidence that the student involved was suffering mental-health problems.'

'Oh no, I don't think she had any of those.' Though *did* she? he wondered, remembering the extraordinary wildness, violence was almost the word, of their sexual encounter in Terence's flat. It was as if she hated him, had reason to hate him.

'Would you say that she was unnaturally *calm*, then? That's the alternative possibility.'

'Calm, yes,' Gerald said. God, he thought, this is agony. It was as if Marcia had access to every thrust and parry, bite and grope, of that endless night, the rain hammering against the windows, the sudden animal lunging under the covers, the necessity of stifling cries so as not to shock Terence in the other bedroom. As if she was coolly aware of every twist and turn of the whole sordid episode, was determined to make him suffer for it. 'But not unnaturally so, I would say.'

'Because it's possible for a student to appear numb and alienated. Almost languid. And then, in a sort of fugue state, to take their own life. I've seen it happen, sadly.'

'No, not languid,' Gerald said. 'I can say for certain she showed no signs of being languid.'

Gerald was sitting in the sitting room reading, or rather half reading, while watching, or half watching, a day-night 20/20 cricket match on Sky. It was mid-evening, mid-summer, and twilight was just beginning to encroach from outside. A blackbird was singing its evening song. I've learnt my ornithology from the Beatles, he realised. Same as I learned my quantum mechanics from chatting in a curry house with Terence. How shallow I am.

He had a single table lamp lit but no other illumination except what came from the big screen of the TV and the little one of his Kindle. Crunch time was approaching. In two days, Judith and Terence would be arriving. No word from Abby. He hadn't mentioned her absence to anyone. He kept telling himself that at least he should ring her sister and warn her, but it would bring the problem too close to the surface. He would feel like a liar, as if he was covering up something he'd done.

As the evening darkened, so did his thoughts. A deep sense of guilt had been gathering for days, ever since the memory of his affair with Laura had come back to him with such terrible clarity. How could he have stood in their kitchen in Manchester and laughed about the disgusting scene that had taken place in Terence's flat, the scene he himself had orchestrated? How could he have compromised Terence for that matter, the most innocent and well-meaning of men, his closest friend? Abby had laughed too, but her perspective was different. Hers was the sardonic laugh of the wronged wife: she was entitled to it. But he wasn't. What could he have been thinking of? He had brought about the humiliation and betrayal of one of his students. There was that phrase, *in loco parentis*. It didn't have much literal meaning any more, not since the age of majority had been lowered to eighteen. In any case, as he'd kept insisting at the time, Laura was older, a research student. But still a student, his responsibility, a responsibility he'd betrayed utterly, a relationship he had perverted. Because she was cleverer than he was, he had forgotten that she depended on his good faith. He cringed at the memory of his devious dishonest performance with Marcia, covering up his tracks, covering up Laura's tracks for that matter, ensuring the university didn't seek her out and hear her side of the story. Because of him, Laura had left her research, left the university, even, for all these years, vanished from his memory. No wonder he had become addicted to alternative history.

And now Abby had disappeared. Perhaps he was responsible for that, too. Perhaps he'd said or done something to her that had driven her away, and then conveniently forgotten all about it. He seemed to have the ability to keep secrets secret even from himself. He remembered Abby talking about a detective story in which it turned out that the investigator was in fact the murderer. Could he, Gerald, be a murderer too, burying his victims not in some grave in the middle of a wood, but deep down in the depths of his psyche, where the bodies wouldn't be stumbled upon for years and years?

When his mother died he found among her things some of his old school papers, including a composition written when he was seven or eight on the subject of holes. As soon as he saw it, he remembered being asked by his teacher to write about his hobby. It was the first time he'd had to say what he did rather than merely be who he was, whoever that might be. The world was out there, and you needed to show you had an impact on it. He sat at his desk in class and wondered what it *was* he did, the first of many times he would face that question. He thought of holes.

He'd dug a den hole on a bit of untended land near the old Anderson shelter at the bottom of their back garden where chickens roamed and put a plank of wood across it to sit on. It was like sitting in a boat on a sea of earth; you almost expected to rock on the swell. The ground here, wired off from the regular green waves of lettuces, beans, and onions, was pitted and rough, stamped on and battered by years of pecking and playing. He pictured worms and moles swimming beneath him like so many eels and fish.

Dug another, a deep narrow hole, just to see where it went, which was nowhere, it turned out. There seemed no end to just dirt. Also some smaller holes, to hide things in. He and his father had buried the family cat when she died. He remembered the formality of that event, a hole made official, some sort of ceremony, maybe just a ceremonial state of mind, standing by the grave, the sky grey, rain raining, damp monochrome cat prone in the dun ground as if her dying had sucked colour from all around her, sharp little teeth showing over black lips because her mouth wouldn't shut tight any more.

Also holes to store things in. He stored a can of tomato soup, like a squirrel burying its nut. Even now could recall his mother searching the kitchen, saying, 'I know I've got some soup somewhere unless I'm going mad, which would not surprise me,' him not daring to explain, digging it up in secret like a big tin egg, then not daring to replace it in the kitchen so burying it again. Maybe it was in that garden still.

Something twanged in his chest, a deep note like a cello's. Could he have buried that bag of farthings too, and not told anyone, *including himself*? Buried it in a hole in his brain as well as in a hole in the garden? That would explain why he was so fearful of the policeman who came to the house and seemed to loom over them all. That was why he had felt such terror of his father going to prison, because it should be *him* going there. A sob rose in his throat from the depths of his childhood. You could be frightened all over again by the memory of fear, weep retrospectively from the guilt and sadness of long ago. Ancient emotions could knock at your door and enter, pristine, irrational, cans of soup and bags of farthings hatching like cicadas do after years and years in the ground.

But his father hadn't *gone* to prison. Of course he hadn't. It was all a dream. Except it wasn't a dream, more a matter of being at cross purposes with reality itself, misunderstanding historical truth, a false memory you could call it, a memory of something that hadn't quite happened, an almost memory, the memory of an event several universes away, or down. Dig a hole deep enough and there they would be, the farthings, the father.

Between Christmas and New Year, a threat of snow, the sort of looming weather Gerald loved. Judith and Abby had gone down to London for the sales, having arranged the trip in lieu of Christmas presents from their respective husbands. Not that Abby was bothered by that aspect. 'I'm not interested in *things*,' she'd said.

'I thought you wanted a horse,' Gerald said. 'You mention it often enough.'

'A horse is not a thing, Gerald. In fact, that's the whole *point* of a horse. Not being a thing.' She sighed, obviously thinking of the horse she'd never had. 'In any case you can't buy one in Oxford Street. I just want to get Judith out of Ken's clutches for the day, that's all. Even if I do have to watch her trying on fluffy jumpers.'

Mid-morning, Gerald drove over to Marple for a walk along the canal towpath. The sky was sagging by now under the weight of all the snow it was carrying. There were patches of ice in the water, a few glum ducks, nobody about, not even a narrowboat venturing beyond the moorings in the little Marple marina, where the vessels seemed to hibernate in a dense huddle like a cluster of beetles.

Gerald walked away from the town, looking across the canal at the humps of the Pennines rising beyond tatty midwinter allotments and fields. The silence was intense. No sound from the water, not a tweet from a bird or any noise of wings. He couldn't hear his own footfalls, which gave him the odd feeling that his legs had been cut off at the knee.

He intended to walk for half an hour then turn around and walk for the half hour back. After which he would call in at the Ring of Bells and have a sandwich and a pint before going home. The thought made him sigh with pleasure. Nothing better than venturing into bad weather and then getting out of it again.

A few flakes began to spiral down. A woman was now approaching along the towpath, tucked into a maroon anorak, its hood fastened round her face. She too was silent and unobtrusive like the rest of the scenery, hardly impinging on his solitude. They didn't even say hello as they passed each other. But after a few more paces, Gerald stopped in his tracks.

It was as if there had been a delay in his vision. His eyes had seen her, but his brain hadn't registered. The hood concealed her auburn hair, but he'd glimpsed the scatter of freckles on her cheeks. It was over a year since he had last set eyes on her, and he'd had no idea she was still in the Manchester area.

He stayed quite still, not daring to move. The snow began to fall more thickly. He didn't breathe.

From behind, a huge splash.

He spun around. A swan was swimming in the canal. It must have just landed. There was no sign of Laura. He stared down the towpath, hoping to make out her form moving silently through the falling snow towards the marina, like a dim shape on a fizzing TV. A flake landed in his eye, and he blinked it away. No, no sign of her.

The towpath ran straight, and he could see along it for hundreds of yards. There was a tall hedge to the right of the path, pretty well impenetrable as far as he could make out. She couldn't possibly have pushed her way through it or climbed over its twiggy top. But where was she?

Oh God, perhaps the splash had been *her*. He couldn't quite bring himself to look directly at the surface of the canal to check, though out of the corner of his eye he could see the swan serenely swimming. Surely if she had fallen in he would have the impression of flailing arms, would hear her cries penetrate the muted atmosphere.

Where could she be?

He might have paused to identify her for longer than he thought. Maybe many minutes had gone past while he registered the shock of that glimpse. How long would it have taken for Laura to walk out of view while he stood looking the other way altogether, staring with blind eyes at the dumb hills while painstakingly reassembling her image in his mind? It was all a matter of perspective. Given the impossibility of leaving the path to right or left, she would have had to keep going till she simply dwindled with distance and finally vanished altogether. Had he stood pondering for as long as that?

Things you never knew you might need to know. How loud is a swan's splash? Can you confuse it with the sound of a woman tumbling into a canal? Is it possible for a person to fall into freezing water without waving her arms about or shouting for help? Even in this muffled weather, the snow silently falling, the senses, hearing, sight, feeling, all withdrawing, sliding shut their hatches, smell and taste becoming vague and metallic, even in these obliterating conditions the shock of the cold and wetness would surely have squeezed a scream from her.

The cricket was long over though the TV still burbled on. A battery-low warning had appeared on his Kindle screen. The dusk had deepened, and the pool of light from his lamp left the edges of the room in darkness. He switched the TV off with the remote then regretted the sudden silence. After a lifetime of marriage he wasn't used to being by himself in the house at this time of night.

The dimness seemed to flicker a little. He could hear his own breathing and just out of time with it a sort of echo, the breathing of someone else. He sat frozen, not even daring to feel fear, though he was aware of it as a separate entity inside himself, like a figure hunched in a cave. As his eyes grew accustomed to the dim conditions, he made out a small dark silhouette in the armchair opposite. His heart pounded so loudly the room as a whole seemed to pulse.

'There you are,' Abby said.

'For God's sake, Abby. You nearly gave me a heart attack.'

'You were miles away. I thought I'd wait here till you came back. I felt frightened myself, if you must know, sitting here in the dark. I felt just as if I'd turned into a ghost. It's quite frightening, frightening people.'

It was Abby who had been miles away. People could slip out of your life, quietly disappear. He thought of that splash in the canal, the loudness in that numb atmosphere, the insistence. He was simply unable to accept the finality of it. People would vanish, but later they might return, reaching towards you out of the darkness, the exits and entrances of your world opening and shutting without a sound, or nearly so.

They were in Wrexham for a barbecue. Ken had all the accessories: a gas-fired grill, rack of tools, an apron, and a tall chef's hat, worn sincerely. He was a smallish, barrel-chested man, but the gear made him look almost architectural. On a trolley beside the barbecue an array of meats: spare ribs, drumsticks, sausages, lamb chops, steaks, each marinading in whatever gloop Ken deemed appropriate.

'He wouldn't be seen dead doing the cooking in ordinary life,' Judith whispered to Gerald and Abby. 'He eats baked beans from the can if I'm not there. It's only when he can dress up.'

'That's the point of a different costume,' Gerald said. 'You can be someone else for a time. That's why they put soldiers into uniform.' He hadn't thought that particular thought before, but as so often spoke as if he'd pondered it deeply.

'If soldiers wore chef's hats they'd never kill anyone, I imagine,' Judith said.

'I don't know about that,' Abby put in. 'There are a lot of dead bodies on Ken's trolley.'

'Oh well, as he's been promoted area manager, animals have to die, obviously.'

'What about not wearing any clothes at *all*?' Abby asked. 'Is nakedness a costume, or is it the real you?'

'Hey up,' Ken said from over by the grill, alert as a bat to the word nakedness, 'the party's hardly started.'

'Real you,' Judith said. 'Or real me, at least.'

'I don't know,' Abby told her. 'You wouldn't want people running about in their birthday suits waving their willies at everybody.'

'Perhaps there's no such thing as a real you,' Gerald said. 'Or a real me.' He avoided looking at Judith as he said this. The conversation seemed to have got close to the bone. She was wearing a summer dress in lemon, above the knee, with green high heels, but he could picture her naked.

A hiss from the barbecue. 'Chicken's on the grill!' Ken announced.

Some motley cheers, people toasting the launch of the drumsticks. Ken waggled his bottle of beer in response and took a swig.

'Dad?' It was Rita, pushing her way through the throng. She was eight or thereabouts, with the absolute skinniness of a certain kind of child, hair in bunches, big teeth waiting for her mouth to catch up. She had the pink ears of a small mammal.

'Don't get too near. It's hot,' Ken said without looking up.

That warning mode, both familiar and distant, had echoed through Gerald's childhood, his father keeping threats at bay. He realised how rarely, in a childless marriage, you needed to say don't.

'Can I go and play with Lily? Dad. *Dad*,' Rita said, glaring at his absorption in the drumsticks.

'Can *I* go and play with Lily, too?' asked Jed, appearing somehow from between the legs of those clustered round the barbecue as if he was being reborn, a smaller, grubbier version of his sister.

'No you can't,' Rita told him, switching from entreaty to imperative. 'Lily's *my* friend. Go and play with your own friends.'

'I haven't got any friends.' Said as a simple fact.

'Dad, Dad,' Rita said, switching back. '*Please*, Dad.'

'Rita, why don't you play with the kids who are here, instead of going somewhere else? Both of you.'

'Because,' said Rita, then stopped, stymied.

'Because,' repeated Jed. There was a pause. Ken vigorously shovelled a spatula under the drumsticks to prevent them sticking. 'Because,' added Jed, suddenly inspired, 'there's no kids here.'

'There aren't any kids here,' Rita said, repeating the point by rote. Then the penny dropped. 'There's *no* kids here,' she announced triumphantly. 'Not any.'

'Not any,' Jed said.

'Don't keep saying what I say,' Rita told him, snatching away his copyright. 'No. Kids. Are. Here,' she repeated.

'Oh come *on*!' Ken said. At last he raised his eyes from the chicken and began to inspect the throng, lips pursed ready to count. Gerald looked around too but saw only adults holding their glasses and beer bottles and talking. How static they were, as if growing up had turned them into vegetable life, just mouths opening and closing like the flowers, or mouths, of carnivorous plants. 'Where've they all got to?' Ken asked, taken aback.

'Everybody must have thought it was a grown-ups-only do,' Judith said. 'Perhaps because we never said kids were welcome. They'll have left them all at home.'

'I didn't know you could leave them at *home*,' Abby said. 'What a bonus.'

'They'll have got babysitters, Abby. You can't just walk off and let them run riot. Look at my pair. Give them half an inch and they'd set themselves on fire.' Gerald looked at the pair to check, or as if to check. They were standing quite still at a safe distance from the heat. They looked like a couple of small robots, blank eyes pointed at their father, ready to resume petitioning when the moment was right. 'Louise says a whole bunch of them are at Lily's house, as a matter of fact. A girl's looking after them, the Atkins girl. She's training to be a nurse.'

'Daddy,' Rita said, 'she's training to be a nurse. Dad, a *nurse.*'

'Sausages next,' Ken said, laying each flaccid cylinder alongside the cooking drumsticks with finicky care, as if he was taking gloves off finger by finger.

'I wouldn't eat that man's sausages if you paid me,' Abby whispered to Gerald.

'We might catch on fire,' Jed pointed out, trying a random shot.

'Daddy, *Daddy!*' cried Rita, as if coping with deafness or distance.

'Oh, for goodness sake.'

'We'll only be a nuisance if we stay here,' Rita warned.

'We'll be a *nui*sance,' Jed echoed.

'Blackmail,' Ken said.

'I better see them across the road,' Judith told him.

Ken nodded. 'Behave yourselves over there, kids,' he said, turning back to the grill.

'We will, Daddy,' Rita assured him.

'We will, Daddy,' Jed repeated.

'The barbie smells lovely,' Rita added gushingly as she skipped off.

'Smells lovely,' Jed agreed, following her.

'The barbie smells love-ly,' Ken said in imitation, making camp little movements of his hands and spatula, clearly half irritated by, half admiring, their panache. Chips off the old block, no doubt.

Hours passed. Gerald talked with various locals, then with a colleague of Ken's who had read a novel and wanted to recommend it. He sold it the way he might a shiny new car. Gerald ate a sausage while he listened, raising it to his mouth like a cigar. The man couldn't remember the author or title but unfortunately recalled the book as a whole, which he recounted. Finally he sloped off in search of a drink. Other people entered Gerald's small orbit. It had long ago got dark, and now he noticed it was getting cold. He peered at his watch and discovered to his amazement it was almost eleven. He had the sensation of having woken, Rip Van Winkle style, from a long sleep. Judith materialised, compounding the effect. She looked like a memory, still wearing her lemon dress. 'Aren't you cold?' he said.

'I've been indoors – don't you fret. Not my idea of fun standing in the garden all night, watching the grass grow. You should have come in. It's all happening in there. Abby's there. Even Ken, now he's cooked all his animals. Practically everyone's indoors, except for the ones who aren't indoors, like you.'

Gerald looked over the dim lawn. Sure enough, only a

handful of people remained, mostly clustered round the dying coals of the barbecue. He had an urgent, childish sense of having been left out, of missing the boat.

'I've just come out to get the children in. Time for bed. To be honest, I forgot all about them. It was time for bed hours ago.'

'They're not here. They must still be over the road with their friends.'

'Oh Jesus. Can you be a darling and go and fetch them? It's the house right opposite. I'm frozen. I need to go back indoors.'

It was one of those cement roads that have no traffic and go nowhere, with a single street lamp at a distance. The house opposite looked dark and hunched. Gerald walked round the side, hoping to find the children playing in the back garden, but there was no sign of life. A light was on in the kitchen, though. He tapped on the back door. After a few moments came a tremulous voice: 'Who's there?'

'I'm from over the road. I've come for the kids.'

There was the sound of the door being unlocked, then a young woman's head poked round it. 'Hi,' she said.

'Hi. Rita and Jed. They came over to play with Lily.'

'Oh, yes. They're not here. Lily's fast asleep. All the other kids went home hours ago.'

'Rita and Jed didn't.'

'Oh goodness. I just assumed. Oh God, I hope they're all right. They all sort of went off while Lily was getting ready for bed.' She looked up at him, big-eyed. She even put a hand over her mouth, then removed it to say, 'I assumed they were going back to their houses.'

'It's all right. It's not your fault,' Gerald said. No, it wasn't. It was more like *his* fault. He was the one who had spent the whole evening hanging around in the garden at Ken and Judith's, while the dew fell. He should at least have noticed that the children hadn't come back.

There was a copse a street away. Ken and a bunch of other men decided to search it, while Gerald and Judith, along with some of the others, went along the road. Abby said she would stay in the house in case the children turned up there of their own accord.

The road had a white low-wattage glow of its own when your eyes grew accustomed to the dimness. The houses each side were mainly unlit. They looked like blocks of solid shadow, dark on dark. The owners were presumably still at Ken and Judith's, or on the search, if they weren't in bed themselves. The people in the search party called 'Rita! Jed!' in uncoordinated voices, like crows cawing from the top of a tree. When a house had a light on, one of them would scuttle to the front door and knock, but no one had seen the children.

The road was a long one, at least a quarter of a mile. When they reached the end, Judith suddenly said, 'The children are all right. Don't worry.' She was wearing one of Ken's jackets draped over her shoulders, as if she was being seized from behind.

'How can you know?' Gerald asked.

'I'm a bit psychic, to tell you the truth. And in any case a mother would know when her children are dead.'

It was extraordinary to hear the word 'dead' uttered out loud. Judith's assurance had exactly the opposite effect on Gerald from the one intended. He had an instant sense of loss. It was as if the word itself had allowed the worst to happen, as if a word, merely by being said, could give permission. Rita, dead. He had known her since she was a baby. She was the child he and Abby had never had. He felt a sort of vicarious ownership, if that wasn't self-contradictory. And Jed, her small shadow. Their disappearance suddenly seemed like the end of possibility itself, as if all that was left was the empty darkness.

They turned and began the walk back, still calling out as they went. Their voices became more raucous, a note of desperation entering them, except in the case of Judith's, where it was a note of confidence, as if she was calling the children in for bedtime, which is what she *was* doing, of course. Gerald found himself lagging a little behind the others as he tried to inspect each garden they passed, just in case, forcing his eyes to penetrate the dark, to make out the glum lawns and the black flowers in their rows.

After a while he became aware of small noises following behind him. He stopped, intending to turn and look, but realised the noises had stopped too. The hairs on his head, on his neck especially, began to rise and prickle, and his chest felt tight. He started walking again, and the sounds resumed. Abruptly he turned, as if to surprise whatever it was before it could become nothing. And there they were, Rita and Jed, stopped in their tracks, their small forms dwarfed by the night. It was as if they were the rearguard of the very party trying to find them. Gerald's heart thumped so loudly he put his hand on his chest to muffle it, to hold it in place even.

He bent down towards them. 'Where've you been?' he asked. He whispered it as if they were his secret. He was aware of the others in the group marching onwards in their search.

'We've been at Tony's,' Rita whispered back.

'Tony's,' Jed said, also in a whisper.

'Where is Tony's?'

'There,' Rita told him, pointing to a house a few houses back.

'There,' said Jed, pointing too.

'We went past there when we went *up* the road,' Gerald whispered, aggrieved. 'And we just went past it coming back again. We were calling you all the time. We were worried about you.'

'We were watching TV with Tony and his grandad. They invited us. We watched *Charlie and the Chocolate Factory*.'

'We heard you calling,' Jed said.

'Why didn't you come out then, if you heard us calling?'

'We didn't think you were calling *us*,' Rita explained.

'For heaven's sake,' Gerald said, still whispering. 'Did you think we were looking for *another* Rita and Jed?'

'We're not the only Rita and Jed in the whole world,' Rita pointed out.

'Not the only ones,' added Jed.

'Ah, there you are, kids,' Judith said, striding up as if nothing untoward had taken place. 'Don't you know how late it is?'

Gerald had the sensation of flirting with rage, as if it was an option you could take or leave. 'Where on earth have you been, Abby?'

'You know full well where I've been.'

'I have no idea where you've been. I've been worried sick.'

'Don't be silly. I've been on a residential pottery course, down in Exeter. I told you all about it.'

'No you did not.'

She switched on the table lamp beside her chair in order to give him a long-suffering look. 'Come on, Gerald, you're not that absent-minded.' She dug into her handbag and produced a pack of cigarettes. 'I'm sorry, you'll have to do a bit of passive smoking. My nerves have gone all jangled.'

'*Your* nerves! What about mine? I've been rattling around the house like a pea in a box wondering what on earth had happened to you. You could have popped your clogs for all I knew. Or run off with somebody else. I had no idea what was going on.'

'You're always so melodramatic, Gerald. I told you I was going on this course. You must have just forgotten. Didn't you notice my rucksack was gone, and half my undies?'

'I don't make a habit of riffling through your undies.'

'That's because you've grown old. And I've grown old. We've both grown old. Undies don't have the same impact. I wanted to go to Exeter to get stuck into some proper potting for a while.'

Gerald wondered whether she had told him, and he hadn't been listening or hadn't taken it in. It was possible, these days especially. Or Abby being Abby, she might have *intended* to tell him and taken the thought for the deed. 'I rang up your sister,' he said, 'to see if she knew where you'd gone.'

'Oh, for heaven's sake! She'll think one of us must have gone bonkers. Or both of us. *Judith* is supposed to be the flaky one in this family.'

'I was discreet about it. I said I was ringing to invite them for the weekend.'

'Gerald!' The tip of her cigarette glowed as she drew on it. She looked across the room with dark fierce eyes. 'How *could* you? Are they coming? Yes, of course they're coming.'

'They're arriving on Friday afternoon.'

'Buggeration.'

'You invited Judith to stay that time and only told me later. What's the problem?'

'Her. *Her* to stay. Not *them*. *That*'s the problem.'

'Now they've become an item, we might as well get used to it. She used to come with Ken, after all. You never liked Judith being with *him*. Now you don't like it because she's with Terence. Perhaps the problem is you.'

'What do you mean by that?'

'Maybe you're possessive.'

Abby swallowed as she took the word in and forced it down. Gerald was aware how alien it was to her. He felt a momentary satisfaction in being unjust. 'What I want is for Judith to be herself,' Abby said. 'That's all. I never liked Ken, but at least she was never going to turn *into* him. He was too much of a toad for anyone to want to do that. But I know exactly what's going to happen with Terence. It's as plain as the nose on your face. She is going to aspire. She is going to try to be something she isn't. I don't want to see it, that's all. I want to avert my gaze, at least for the time being.'

'You can't seriously imagine that Judith is going to turn into Terence. She is hardly likely to become a quantum physicist all of a sudden.'

'Why not? You did. She won't be any good at it, of course.'

'To be honest,' Gerald said, 'I wasn't very good at it either.'

'You could have fooled me.'

'I think I fooled myself.'

Abby surveyed him again, more sympathetically this time, he thought. How perverse that we all want to aspire when you get so much more credit for confessions of failure.

'You were better than she will be, that's for sure,' Abby said. 'At least you could talk the talk. But poor Judith is only good at one thing.'

Gerald could feel his face redden.

'Being Judith,' Abby said.

'It must run in the family,' he said. 'Oh, and by the way, I made you a cottage pie.'

'I'm not that hungry.'

'Cott-age pie-ie.' Gerald stretched the words in hopes the touch of lyricism would bring her round. She might be refusing because she was pissed off with him, a small-scale hunger strike. 'I made two. I ate the other one. I made them with care. I was thinking about you even though I didn't have the faintest idea where on earth you were. It's got no lumps in it, I promise.'

'Yum,' Abby said cursorily. 'But I'm all right, honestly. I had something on the train. I'm not sure what it was, but it was something.'

'Oh well.' Gerald sighed.

'Tell you what,' Abby said in a relenting voice. 'Let's have the cottage pie tomorrow night, before the visitation on Friday. It'll be like the Last Supper. What I fancy for now is just a crumpet with Marmite on.'

He went to the freezer and rummaged for the crumpets. They were stuck together, so he got out a kitchen knife and slid it underneath the top one to lever it off, then did the same for the one below. He put the two of them in the toaster and set it to defrost.

They ate them in the sitting room. Gerald asked how the pottery course had gone. He was conscious of putting the question in a fake sprightly tone: he wanted Abby to know that he was taking an interest even though he wasn't interested, wanted both the interest and the absence of interest to be clear.

'Do you remember when Judith and Ken went to Scotland three years on the trot?' Abby said. 'Then they went somewhere else. Sicily, I think it was. And when they came back we asked them how they liked it and they said, "It was very nice but it wasn't Scotland"?'

'Oh God,' Gerald said, remembering. Ken had winked, as if Scotland had a secret meaning.

'Well, that's a bit like how I felt on this course in Exeter. The teacher was very good, but he wasn't Steve. He couldn't breathe life into the clay, like they say in the Bible, or maybe it's the Book of Common Prayer. Not like Steve could when he still had both his hands. I wanted to get more skilful, so I could give Steve a surprise. I made some nice things, but they were just things. I didn't bother to bring them home. They were too heavy in my rucksack, so I put them in a litter bin.' She sighed at the futility of it all.

Somehow the binning of the pottery swept away the remnants of Gerald's annoyance. He put his plate on the coffee table, stepped over, and kissed the top of her head. 'Hey ho,' Abby said.

Before going up to bed, Gerald took their plates into the kitchen. He picked up the kitchen knife and was about to put it in the sink along with the plates when he noticed its point was missing.

'Abby, come and look at this,' he called in a preoccupied voice, not taking his eyes off the truncated blade.

'Oh for goodness sake,' Abby said. He heard her feet stomping down the stairs and her rasping breath. 'What's the matter now?' She spoke as if they were working through a list. 'I was just about to hop into bed. I've got one of those horrible Scandi noir books to read. It's about people being murdered in Iceland. I started it in the university hall of residence in Exeter, where the pottery people put us. You know what I'm like getting to sleep, especially in a strange place, but it seemed to do the trick. It's really depressing. I love novels that are full of bad weather.'

'Knife,' he said, holding it up above his shoulder, still staring forward over the sink.

'I can see it's knife.' She paused a moment. 'Buggered knife, in fact. What I suggest, put knife in bin.'

He turned to face her. 'Abby, this is the knife I separated the frozen crumpets with. I calculate a quarter of an inch has gone missing from the end.'

'Is that what you calculate, a quarter of an inch? From the crumpet knife? Ooh la la.'

'The question is, where has it gone? The point? The fucking *point*?'

'Over on the work surface by the fridge, I expect.' She stepped over and inspected that part of the work surface. 'Not here. Maybe on the floor.' She knelt down then got on all fours to inspect the floor. She sniffed like a dog, face close to the quarry tiles. 'Not here, either.' She got to her feet again and dusted her hands together. 'Gone,' she concluded.

'But *where*'s it gone?'

She shrugged her shoulders. 'Just gone,' she said. 'Sometimes things just go.'

'Abby, nothing in this world just *goes*. Stuff can't cease to exist. It's against the laws of physics.'

'We're not talking about the laws of physics. All we're talking about is a little bit of a knife.'

'I don't think you get it. If the blade isn't in the kitchen any-where, it must have snapped off in a crumpet. While they were being levered. When the crumpets were hard and frozen. And we ate the crumpets.'

They stared at each other for a few moments. 'It's like a lot-tery,' Abby said. 'One of us has drawn the short straw. Is it you or is it me?' She blinked solemnly. She had blinked in exactly the same way all those years ago, at the party in Cambridge when he was approaching her chair, blinked with eyelids that seemed to become heavy and long-lashed like a doll's, so that you could almost imagine a small delicate noise, the faintest chime, as the upper and lower ones made contact with each other. How strange, the body's memory, that a blink can sur-vive half a century.

'We could be being cut up on the inside. One of us. You or me.'

'Gerald, can you feel your gullet?'

'What kind of a question's that?'

'What I mean is, when you ask yourself if you can feel your body or a part of your body, you can feel it and not feel it both at once. It's like a low hum that most of the time you blot out. Except it's not a hum, it's just your body ticking over.'

'I can't feel a pain in my gullet, if that's what you're asking.'

'What about your stomach?'

'Nor in my stomach.'

'Or your guts?'

'Guts neither.'

'There you are then.'

'What about you?'

'Same same. Just my body ticking over.'

'What should we do about it?'

'Well, since there's nothing actually wrong with us, nothing.'

'But the crumpet might just be muffling it for the moment. The point of the blade.'

'There you are then. Muffled by crumpet. Clogged up with
Marmite. The blade might pop out of us, out of one of us,
whichever one it might be, like an owl pellet popping out of an
owl.'

'What?'

'I saw it on TV. Beaks of eaten birds and bits of claw all
packed safely inside a little parcel.'

'Abby, we're not owls. Otherwise that analogy would be
very comforting.'

'What I think,' Abby said, 'is that the end of the blade
could have snapped off before you used it. Maybe in the dishwasher some time.'

'But I would have noticed when I slid it between the crumpets.'

'That will be the day, when you actually notice something.
The thing about you, Gerald, is you have to make a song and
dance about whatever you do, even if it's just toasting a crumpet. What happened, happened. Or didn't happen. There's no
point in worrying about it. I don't know about you, but I'm
going to bed.'

He watched the local news, but there was no mention of
anyone drowning in the canal. Perhaps she'd got stuck on the
bottom somehow, tangled up with a shopping trolley or old
bike. It might take weeks for the body to bob up, presumably
when the gases had inflated it to a certain level.

Don't be ridiculous, he told himself. People don't do anything as melodramatic as dying in a canal in real life, at least in
my vicinity. Also, swans are big birds. They must make a con-
siderable commotion, splashing down. Mustn't they?

He actually visited the lake at Lyme Park, the stately home
situated to the south of Stockport, in hopes of hearing one do
exactly that, but none cooperated. He felt furtive, standing for
half an hour in the snowy parkland with children tobogganing

down the nearby slopes, aware that no one else would be able to guess why he was here, trying to look like a bird-watcher while conscious of his secret agenda. He slapped his gloved hands together every now and then like a man with nothing to hide, a man without the least interest in, for example, watching children at play, or at least only the interest anyone might have. There were a couple of swans peering out of a patch of reeds with that built-in frown swans seem to have, but they obviously had no intention of flying anywhere.

Why on earth hadn't he checked the canal at the time it happened? He imagined staring down into the depths and seeing nothing down there, the let-off of it. The relief. But canal water was so opaque. You wouldn't even be able to see nothing.

Maybe this uncertainty was a form of self-punishment for his previous unforgivable behaviour. He was tormenting himself with the possibility that he might have driven Laura to suicide, even murdered her. It was a way of establishing the extent of his betrayal. Out of the tiniest ingredients, a glimpse of someone passing by on the towpath, the splash of a swan landing on the water, he had concocted a melodrama, even an allegory. It served him right to have the issue unresolved, to keep the wound open. He found himself holding the possibilities in balance, searching the local rag for any mention of canals, checking up on conference reports and fellowship appointments in his field in case Laura was continuing her research somewhere else. It was as if she inhabited two separate universes, or rather as if she inhabited one and lay dead in the other, steadily inflating with gases.

And then, eventually (to preserve his sanity, he concluded looking back on it), he must have forgotten about her altogether.

Gerald lay awake for much of the night. He had the sense that at any moment he would experience a flash of agony. Meanwhile, Abby had fallen into a deep sleep as soon as she put down her book, comforted by the thought of chilly crime in Iceland just as she predicted she would be. He would draw the short straw, he was sure of that. There was something impervious about Abby, as if her optimism was a cocoon, keeping her safe.

Finally he fell asleep. Hours later, he almost flung himself into wakefulness as you do when you've missed something important, a plane, a job interview, a big lecture. He sat up in bed panting and rubbing his fist over his mouth, until he remembered.

He went through Abby's sequence: gullet, stomach, guts, every one in order. Nothing but the low hum.

He couldn't just leave it like that. He couldn't cope with the sense that an event, or non-event, was biding its time, waiting to suddenly leap out at him like a jack-in-the-box. He decided to go to the drop-in surgery at the health centre as soon as it opened.

A locum was on duty, a young woman with an eager interested face and a habit of repeating what he said to her, barely moving her lips and nodding, not in approval, he soon realised, but as a way of indicating that each unit of meaning had arrived home. She both nodded and shook her head when he had completed his story. 'Dear God,' she said.

'I don't suppose it's anything to worry about,' Gerald said hopefully. He watched as her lips subtly repeated the words.

'When I was on holiday,' she said, 'I drank this glass of wine. I'm not much of a drinker as a rule. And when I got to the bottom I discovered there were glass fragments in it. I went out and bought a pack of cotton wool. Have you ever tried swallowing cotton wool? It's very hard to get down.'

'Is that what we must do? Eat cotton wool?'

Cotton wool, her lips said. 'I don't think cotton wool would be enough for a knife blade.'

'We thought the crumpets themselves might have a muffling effect.'

Muffling effect. 'No. What you'd better do, you'd better fetch your wife and the two of you go straight off to the X-ray department at Bath Hospital. Do you have a car?'

'Yes, we have a car. We even have a horse.' Why did I say that? Gerald immediately wondered. Anything to be amusing, as if that would make the blade go away, or not have existed in the first place.

Horse. 'The car would be best, I think. The last thing you need is being joggled about. Try to keep on an even keel. You can't take chances with something like this. I'll ring them now to tell them you are on your way.'

'For heaven's sake, Gerald,' Abby said. 'What were you thinking of, going up to the health centre? You might have known what they'd say.'

'Abby, it's not the doctor's fault. She just wants to be on the safe side.'

Abby obviously thought that going to the doctor had made what had happened official, so to speak, in other words *real*, so that if he'd stayed at home instead, the problem would simply have gone away. But come to think, he was just as idiotic himself. He'd thought that by *going* to the doctor that same outcome would be achieved. He had expected the doctor just to tell him not to worry, not share her own experiences, not repeat his words, not reveal that doctors could swallow sharp objects too.

The two of them went up to the reception desk in the radiology department. It was still early, only a little after nine, so they were the first patients to arrive. 'Ah!' the middle-aged woman on duty said. 'You must be the crumpet couple. The doctor telephoned me.' She gave them a bright look, eyebrows raised, her big toothy smile giving nothing away.

'That's us,' Gerald said.

Chapter 16

Gerald woke abruptly. There was a face above him, peering down. Two dark, implacable eyes. They were watching him with such intensity the gaze was almost tangible. He could hear himself whimpering in fright. It was like seeing a face before you know what faces are. As an alien might see one, coming from a world without faces. Then slowly it resolved into familiarity. Abby, propped up on one elbow, leaning over him.

'Hello, hello,' she said.

'Hello.' I didn't recognise her, he thought. It was only a second or two of lostness, but. Is that how it will be? Everything, everybody, becoming distant and unfathomable, a world entirely inhabited by strangers. Like being a toddler in a vast department store, separated from its mother.

'Bad dream?'

'Yes.' Gerald's lips felt loose. 'Bad dream.'

He hadn't dreamt at all, or at least had no memory of a dream. That was just an alibi for his fright on waking up and not knowing who or even what Abby was.

'What about?' Abby, plunging in. She wouldn't leave well enough alone. There was something sceptical about the way she asked the question. Gerald felt as if his bluff was being called in an interview or cross-examination.

'It was about my mother,' he said.

'Oh dear.'

'Oh dear,' he agreed. Oh dear indeed. Why had he said

that? What was the matter with him? It was like that time he told Steve he'd gone fishing with the man who'd lost his hand at the rubber-composition factory. Perhaps this lie was because just a moment or two ago he'd thought the word mother. He *never* dreamed about her. His father, yes. He dreamed about his father often. Or at least remembered him in a dream-like way, as if memory had slipped its anchorage in the chronology of his life and hovered or shimmered in his consciousness, a fragment of reality that was as real as a dream.

It was a sunny summer's day, and they were at the seaside. Not Stokes Bay, the local Gosport beach, which was shingle, but further along, where it was sandy – West Wittering, on the Sussex coast. He was thirteen or fourteen, a bit old for family days by the sea, and he was embarrassed at being with his parents. He should have been mooning listlessly at home, like teenagers were supposed to do. Maybe coming here was a consequence of Ruth's death. Maybe he was here because Ruth wasn't, because he had to take on the whole burden of being his parents' child himself.

He went into the sea, wading out, watching the sunlight glitter on the soft swell. Then, gently, hardly disturbing the tempo of the water, he began to swim. The water, the air, his body, all seemed to be the same temperature. It was as if he was nowhere, or everywhere. He felt at peace. He hadn't known that he wasn't at peace before, but now he understood. It was as if, all his life, or at least for years and years, or for what seemed like years and years, he'd had to hold Ruth in the world through sheer power of imagination, like holding a large slippery fish, so that if his concentration faltered for an instant she would flip out of his grasp and be gone forever. And now at last he didn't have to any more. Like Gerald himself, she was everywhere, implicit in the scene.

A cold hand grasped his shoulder. How can it be cold, he

wondered, when everything else is warm – no, not warm exactly, blood heat. It was his father swimming beside him. 'Where do you think you're going?' his father asked.

Gerald had had no idea he was going anywhere. 'Out,' he replied. He looked towards the horizon, nodded awkwardly at it. Though the day was bright and clear, there was a fuzzy ambiguous area where the sea fused with the sky, as if the fictional meeting between those elements had real impact, generating a light fog.

'That's what your sister did. She went out. She went out one evening with her boyfriend and never came back again.'

Or perhaps he didn't exactly say it. Perhaps Gerald just articulated it on his behalf as he peered back at the scene through time. Knew that that was what his father would have said, or if not said, at least have thought. Knew that he hated the very word *out*. There was a sort of telepathy with people of the past, just as there was with people in dreams. You knew what they wanted to say.

They were treading water now, looking at each other. Gerald twisted his head to look back. Yes, the shore was a way away, swarming with tiny brightly coloured people living intricate lives on the beach as if sea matters were no concern of theirs.

Gerald's father's eyes were hard. With love presumably, the hard sort of love. He pointed towards the shore. 'Back,' he said. The way he pushed his face towards him, the grim straight line of his mouth, made Gerald think of a turtle or tortoise poking its head out of its shell. People said bullies were weak, which mostly couldn't be true, because they hurt you, which was what bullying was, after all, hurting you, and if they could hurt you that must mean they were strong, stronger than you were, at least for the time being, until the tide or the tables turned. But not in his father's case. *His* rigour was the hardness of fear, a carapace over the heart. He had to hold Gerald in the world just as Gerald had had to hold Ruth. He was holding him now, a hand under the armpit, as if Gerald couldn't swim.

'For goodness' *sake!*' Gerald said. He kicked backwards, freeing himself from his father's grasp, then swam to shore, back to where his mother was sitting on a towel, buttering bread for their picnic. For some reason she never made sandwiches in advance. Maybe she liked to have something to be getting on with, since she didn't swim, or at least Gerald didn't recall ever seeing her swim, buttering bread instead while the sun turned the butter liquid. His mother didn't do a lot of things, in fact. She would be content to occupy just a corner of his memory, buttering her bread, slicing sweaty cheese, inserting floppy lettuce leaves. Maybe that was her way of reacting to Ruth's death, taking up as little room as possible. If she was hardly in the world, that would mean she was mostly somewhere else, like Ruth was.

He stood by his mother. Perhaps she asked him about his swim. He looked back out to sea, and there his father was, out, out, far out. He hadn't bothered to escort Gerald back. He was a tiny figure, black against the shiny water, his insectile arms circling with each stroke of the crawl. The hypocrisy of it stunned Gerald for a moment. But then, somehow, he understood the imperatives at play. His father didn't care how far out he went himself, now that Ruth was dead. It was only Gerald who had to stay safely *in*.

'What did she do?' Abby asked. 'Your mother? In your dream?'

'Not a lot.'

'It doesn't sound like much of a nightmare to me. Do you remember *Nightmare on Elm Street*? *That* was a nightmare.'

'Maybe my dream was really about *not* dreaming about her.' That was the nearest he could get to admitting he hadn't dreamt at all. 'You can go through life not seeing someone, not taking any notice, then when it's too late, you think, why didn't I look, why didn't I bother to look? Maybe that's what I was dreaming about.'

'Gerald, you know what's the matter with you? You're too clever by half – that's what's the matter with you.'

'I don't think it's possible to be too clever.'

'I didn't say you were too clever. I said you were too clever by half, which is a different thing altogether.'

They lay side by side in their bed. Gerald thought about his mother's quiet grief, the years and years of sadness, unexpressed. There was a sort of humility in her restraint. As if she didn't feel important enough to shout and scream and make a fuss. His father didn't do those things either, of course, but there was a tough explicitness about his sorrow. He had been hardened by loss while his mother had been softened, so much so that she had hardly any shape in his mind at all. He felt a wistful longing to reach out and comfort her. When you caress someone, you describe their form to the world, and that's what his mother had needed. She had needed her form to be described, to be reaffirmed, so that she could remember it herself, so that she could remember herself. Her husband was too sad and too desperate to do it, so Gerald should have done it instead. It would have been like the sculptor who brought his statue to life – not like Steve, who turned living things to clay. But now it was too late, ages, centuries (it seemed like centuries) too late. His poor lost mother was lost all over again, lost to history. She was a woman who had chosen to have no history of her own.

She lived on for years after Dad had gone. That seemed inevitable. She used up so little of life, day to day, it was no wonder hers lasted longer. Gerald had had a friend at Cambridge who always kept a big jar of boiled sweets in his room. When given one, Gerald would crunch it within a minute or two, causing Mark to wince at the sound of the crack. Mark's sweet would go on indefinitely. When they compared notes, it turned out that Gerald had been trained as a child to crunch his promptly, by Dad, of course, to avoid any danger of choking, while Mark had been brought up never to offend others by making a noise while eating. You could crunch, or you could suck.

Gerald and Abby would visit his mother as often as they could, not easy all the way from Manchester, and Gerald always felt taken aback that she had nothing to report about her existence in the intervals.

'What does she *do*?' he asked Abby after one visit.

'Gerald,' she replied, 'she isn't your student, you know. She doesn't have to *produce*. What she does is, she just does her *thing*. The trouble with you is you're like a bluebottle.'

'What? How do you mean?'

'Buzzing at a windowpane. Desperate to get out into the big wide world and do stuff. Do whatever it is bluebottles do.'

'Abby, I'm not talking about me. I'm talking about Mum.'

'Well, that's the point. You want *her* to be a bluebottle too. You want *me* to be a bluebottle, come to think. You want all of us to be bluebottles.'

Abby had an airy tolerance of other people doing their thing, as she would call it. Gerald's fear was that his mother didn't in fact have a 'thing' at all. That was precisely why he worried about her. He would picture her on dim February afternoons, alone in her house, with no 'thing' to be getting on with. Perhaps Abby was so relaxed about it because in her heart of hearts she didn't believe the 'thing' each person allegedly did had any ultimate meaning or even content – maybe that was why she called it a thing. She was able to accept people for what they were because in her equations everyone, or at least everyone's strivings, came to nought. There was a sort of levelling in futility.

In the end, Gerald decided that his mother's thing was in fact to monitor Ruth's non-life, her post-life life. He came to this conclusion because that was what he did himself, though only intermittently (clutching that slippery fish), and less as time went on. Mum must do it twenty-four seven, or at least during waking hours and wakeful nights. She would get up in the mornings, sit in her chair or grub in her garden, all the while visualising Ruth pursuing her career, getting married, having children, being happy, being unhappy even, getting divorced, losing her job, suffering a miscarriage, going shopping, being alive. Monitoring her spectral existence day after day.

It was almost a relief when his mother finally died, all skin and bones, in some sort of dying room to which she had been trundled from her hospital ward. She made a few baffled moans and groans – mute noises, as Gerald thought of them, the sounds you make in a nightmarish dream when you have forgotten how to speak or even scream. The nurse showed Gerald a hypodermic and raised her eyebrows in query. He nodded. Talk about mute noises. After that his mother fell into a sleep and then, at some unidentifiable point, she died. Death seemed nothing more than a matter of degree. She had surrendered her life to her daughter who wasn't even there. Gerald wished he'd explained to her about the multiverse, so that she could have had a heroic vision of her sacrifice, supporting an alternative dispensation, another world, on her bent back and narrow bony shoulders.

A tear trickled from Gerald's eye, ran across his cheek and down the side of his head to the pillow.

After some minutes had passed, Abby asked, 'Do you know what I was up to, Gerald?'

'When?'

'What do you mean, when?'

'When were you up to what you were up to?'

She turned her head towards him. His remained looking up at the ceiling. 'Just *then*, of course. What I was up to just then. What did you think I meant?'

'I sometimes wonder what you *do* mean, nowadays.'

There was silence. Sometimes Abby seemed to digest patches of dialogue almost literally, as if breaking the words down was a physical process. There had been a companionable quality to their conversation, and Gerald wondered if he'd broken their mood, whatever their mood was.

Luckily Abby swallowed his testiness and moved on. 'What I was doing,' she explained, 'when I bent over you while you were still sleeping.'

'No, what *were* you doing?'

'I was trying to transmit sex vibrations.'

'Jesus, Abby.'

'I don't think Jesus had a lot to do with it.' Gerald was glad his weeping eye was on the far side of his nose, where Abby couldn't see it. 'That was my plan,' she said. 'Get you on the way, given we'll have visitors the rest of the weekend. Little did I know you were busy dreaming about your mum. Or not dreaming about your mum, whichever one it was.'

'Ah *ha*,' Gerald said, pitching the phrase carefully to get a certain amount of lasciviousness into it. He directed his attention to his genitalia. It felt like ringing somebody up and being told to leave a message. Think tit, he told himself, tit, bum, cunt, the sex trinity. As if she could overhear, Abby propped herself on her elbow again and leaned towards him. Her nightdress gaped open. There they were, familiar and other, much like the world as a whole.

'I'd better take a pill,' Gerald said.

'Oh for God's sake!' Abby flumped back on her side of the bed, thwarted. There would be a lag. They would go off the boil while waiting for him to *get* to the boil. The injustice of it (going off the boil, *blame* for going off the boil) filled Gerald with despair. Fuck you, he thought, which of course was what he couldn't do for the time being. Fuck you.

There was silence. Abby was nothing more than a sullen

lump under the duvet. Then after a few moments she turned back towards him. 'Crumpet couple,' she said, smiling. She reached across and tweaked his ear (his enlarging ear). 'It'll be OK, love.'

What was she saying? That we will get older and older and *then* it will be OK? How would that work? Would things eventually go into reverse, ears shrinking, prick growing, rage abating, headache fading, memory expanding? She would become a little girl in a minidress again, and he would be whoever he once was. The trouble with being a person was that you had no idea who that person had ever really been, let alone who they would be in the time to come. Crumpet couple: the phrase suggested a state of cosy impotence. The impossibility of Abby's reassurance was like an insult, yet it wasn't intended as one. It rubbed salt into the wound. It was consolation that couldn't console.

CHAPTER 17

J udith and Terence came early Friday afternoon. They arrived in Judith's little car, Terence sitting in the passenger seat in the upright alert pose non-drivers adopt, as if riding shotgun. Judith backed straight into the small space available.

Terence got out. He was wearing a short-sleeved shirt with green and red stripes and lightweight brown trousers. His comb-over was gone – in fact his head was shaved, which had the effect of clustering his features and giving them a sharper focus, almost as if he was scowling.

Judith came round from the other side. While Terence was dressed more casually than before, she'd become more formal, in a demure white blouse and blue pleated skirt. Perhaps she's *aspiring*, thought Gerald. If she was wearing lipstick at all, it must be lip-coloured rather than her usual red.

'And where is my sister?' she asked by way of greeting.

'Not in. She's just gone to—'

'Honestly, has she *ever* be been in? When anyone arrived? In is not what Abby does.'

'Abby,' put in Terence, nodding, as if the other two needed reminding who they were talking about. Gerald wondered for a moment if he'd gone a bit senile. He remembered watching a TV programme about the way salmon swim upriver in order to mate, then grow old and die as soon as they've succeeded. No, Terence had always been slightly bewildered, blinking in the light of day, his personal timeline a millisecond behind everyone else's.

'Talking of which,' Gerald said, 'she wasn't in when I came home the other day. She didn't come back for the best part of a week.' It was funny how you could confess to such a thing when it was over with, by means of that alchemy which transforms anxiety, failure, or disaster into the safety of anecdote. I should know, Gerald thought, that's what history's all about. 'It turned out she was in Exeter. *Exeter.*'

'Oh yes,' Judith said. 'I remember she said about going there sometime in order to pot.'

Well, thanks a bunch, thought Gerald. And so much for your psychic powers. 'Judith, you could have said when we spoke earlier on in the week.'

'Oh boo. All you told me was she was out. Out can mean anything. You didn't say she was AWOL. That would have triggered me, I'm sure. I realise in my old age I need to be triggered. Maybe I've always needed it. That's why Terry has come in so useful. He triggers me all the time.'

Terence looked directly into Gerald's eyes, not something he'd ever done before, Gerald realised, and nodded enthusiastically to take credit for this. He seemed to have switched from senility to youthfulness. 'You know Abby,' Judith continued, 'she's always telling you things. They go in one ear and out the other for the most part.'

'Anyway, this time she shouldn't be that long. She said she'd get some olives for my pizza. I need those salted black ones. Greek ones.'

'Homemade pizza,' said Judith in a fake surprised and admiring voice. Underneath the mockery was genuine admiration. The irony was fake, to allow praise to pass unchallenged. Sometimes Gerald felt you had to strip away layers of meaning as if you were dealing with some kind of complex tonal system, a sort of intrinsic Chineseness in things. Perhaps this was due to getting older, becoming aware of the inner mechanics of the world, seeing the skull beneath the skin everywhere you looked. No wonder Gerald's head throbbed and buzzed, with depths and intricacies apparent everywhere he looked and listened. Turbulence in the neurons, like the first growls of thunder.

'I remember you saying pizza is your thing,' Terence said. 'Apart from Stir Fry of Three Deliciousnesses, of course.'

'I made cottage pie the other day, if you must know.'

Judith pinged open the boot, and Gerald stepped into the road to help her unpack, but Terence got there first and hoisted the cases out with the awkward intensity of a man suddenly finding himself doing family things. All Gerald was left to do was point his arm helpfully towards the front door, as if they were explorers needing directions. Once inside, he transferred his point to the stairs. 'You know where the spare room is,' he said, and moved towards the baggage again.

Again Terence got there first. 'You can't take both at once,' Gerald told him, 'up these narrow stairs.'

'Ha,' Terence agreed. He picked up Judith's pink case, leaving his own black one to be carried up by Gerald, Judith bringing up the rear. Terence trotted up the stairs carrying his load with a self-important stiffness of the buttocks that reminded Gerald of how people look going to church.

Terence went into the bedroom, placed Judith's case on the floor, then turned back to Gerald to receive his own. Judith squeezed past and went in herself, leaving Gerald at the door as if it was their room, not his, which of course it was for the time being. 'Oh well,' he said, 'I'll leave you to it.'

'We won't be a minute,' Judith said.

'There's no hurry. You can have a siesta if you need one.'

'I try not to sleep in the day,' Terence said. 'It takes my edge off. Insofar as I have an edge.'

'It takes his edge off,' whispered Judith, as if keeping this information from Terence. She rolled her eyes.

'Not like your Ken, then,' Gerald said, aware of being slightly malicious.

As he intended, Judith had to explain this to Terence: 'My husband Ken used to call it an assisted siesta.'

'An assisted siesta? Oh! Good heavens.' Terence showed just the disinterested interest he might have felt at a scientific or historical fact, not a hint of jealousy in sight. You can be jealous of somebody's lack of jealousy, Gerald realised. For Terence, sex was just anthropology when other people did it. Maybe when *he* did it, too.

'Do you fancy a G and T when you come down?' Gerald asked. 'Or a beer?'

'Oh, no thanks,' Terence replied hastily. 'Not just at the moment.'

'It takes his edge off,' Judith said.

'What about you?'

'I don't think so. Just a nice cup of tea.'

Yes, aspiring, Gerald thought glumly.

Downstairs again, still no Abby. He put the kettle on. He debated whether to pour himself a beer, just to remind Judith of the world she had lost, the sunny uplands of lunchtime booze, but thought better of it. No need to be crass.

They might not be having a siesta, but they seemed to take an inordinate time to come down the stairs. 'Here you are,' Gerald said when they finally appeared.

'Here we are,' Judith said. 'Did we say hello? I don't think we ever said hello. Come here, diddums. Big kiss.'

She gave him a big kiss on the mouth. Presumably it was safe to do so, now she was installed with Terence. And no lipstick to preserve.

'Hello, darling,' she said when she had removed her lips. Behind her, Terence gave a little wave, as if spotting him from a distance. Yes, they were different now. A kiss could be safely delivered across that divide.

'I'll pour the tea,' Gerald said.

'Honestly, *Abby*,' Judith said, when they were sitting round the kitchen table drinking it.

'You know Abby.'

'She's always been like this,' Judith told Terence.

'Ah,' Terence said. He thought for a moment. 'Quantum entanglement.' He nodded at the relevance of the phrase.

'He says things like that,' Judith explained, as if Gerald wasn't already acquainted with Terence.

'When two particles are inextricably connected but not necessarily in the same place. On opposite sides of the universe, even. But still in sync.'

'Isn't he a love?' Judith asked. She gave Terence a proud, proprietorial look. 'It's just like Vera Lynn said, "We'll meet again".'

'I hope that's true. She was only supposed to be buying olives. Abby, I mean, not Vera Lynn.'

'Maybe she was distracted. She gets distracted quite a lot. She always did. Her first boyfriend was always complaining about it. He said he never knew what she was up to, one day to the next.'

'I thought *you* were her first boyfriend,' Terence said. 'Childhood sweethearts.'

'Not far off,' Judith explained. 'Gerald here was number two, weren't you, Gerald? Apart from the odd bods who came and went. I don't think they count.'

'I was number two,' Gerald said brightly. 'Not far off, indeed. Apart from odd bods. Demis.'

'Demis?' Terence asked.

'Demis. His name. He was called Demis.'

'So he was,' Judith said. 'It had slipped my mind. He made her a record player. But he did blow his top quite a lot. She was too scatty for him, I think. That business of always being somewhere else.' There was silence for a moment. 'He was a pal of yours, wasn't he?'

'Who? Demis? No, no way.'

'You were both students at the university, as I remember.'

'So were a lot of people. Men, at least.'

'Cambridge University was very short of girls in those days,' Judith said to Terence. 'That's why Abby and I were able to have such a good time. I suppose women weren't as clever as they are now. *We* weren't, that's for sure. We did know one very brainy girl, though. She was called Dorothy. Abby named her horse after her. She could speak Chinese. Not the horse, the friend. But she went to Oxford in the end. I think a lot of Chinese was spoken there. The point is, Abby had no shortage of invitations. So did I, in due course.'

'I don't doubt it,' Terence said admiringly.

'She used to *accept* most of them, that was the trouble. She would go to parties and dances without telling Demis and put his nose out of joint.' She turned to Gerald. 'He came round to our house the evening before that party where you and Abby got together, as I remember. He said that if she didn't come with *him* the next day, they were finished. Or words to that effect. I think he liked to throw his weight around. I remember thinking, that's a funny way to invite someone to a party. He was a big fellow. He played rugby, or rowed. Maybe both. Do you know what Abby did, being Abby?'

'What did she do, being Abby?'

'She sang a little song under her breath the whole time he was blowing his top. I thought he would biff her one, any moment. I seem to remember what she was singing was "Can't Buy Me Love". But she went to the party with him all the same. Lucky for you she did.'

'I saw her sitting on a chair. I had no idea she'd come there with anyone. She was just sitting on a chair.'

'There you go, then.' Judith sighed with pleasure at the thought. 'Or there you went. You took your chance.'

'Good for you,' Terence said. 'I don't think I ever took my

chance. I'm not sure I ever *had* any chances, come to think. Not until I set foot in Wrexham, at least.'

Judith stretched her hand across the table and patted Terence's. 'Bless,' she said.

'I've got a bit of a headache, to tell you the truth,' Gerald said.

'Why don't *you* have a siesta?' Terence asked.

'That's a good idea,' Judith said. She looked encouragingly at him. Bright-eyed and bushy tailed, Gerald thought, suddenly repelled. How could I have romanticised her all this time, seen her as a gateway into another life, another universe even? All she has is enthusiasm, on tap. Ingratiating, when all was said and done, no challenge in it. He pictured being in bed like some enormous infant taking his nap, while Judith and Terence pottered about downstairs, the grown-ups.

'I'm fine,' he said.

'She *was* all right, was she?' Judith asked, looking concerned.

'You're the one who said she was never in, remember.'

'I know I did. Yes, I did. I just wondered. She did come back from Exeter? It *was* Exeter, wasn't it?'

'What?'

'I just wanted to make sure.'

'Of course she did. She went to Exeter. Like she told *you* she was going to, even though she didn't bother to let *me* know. She went, and then she came back again. You've just been telling me how her first boyfriend got fed up with her always being somewhere else.'

'That's true.'

'Well then.'

'It's just I had a thought.'

'She never stops having them,' Terence said. 'It's like living with a. Now I think back it seems to me I spent years bumbling around my flat without a thought in my head. Except quantum physics, I suppose, which hardly counts. What I mean is, I never thought about the prime minister, or football. Like living with someone who never *stops* thinking. I find it quite. Anyway, it gees me up no end.' He gave Judith a fond, admiring look. Jesus, thought Gerald, it's bad enough seeing adolescents pawing at each other. This pair were pawing at each other's *morale*.

Judith reluctantly took her eyes from Terence and directed them back at Gerald. 'My thought was, she wasn't with you when you phoned me earlier in the week.'

'No, she was not. As we agreed.'

'So she didn't invite us to come. I mean, *you* invited us to come.'

No wonder I never went in for a life of crime, Gerald thought. I'm the kind of person who gets a ticket every time he parks on a double yellow. He'd had an affair, which he thought he'd kept secret from Abby, two affairs in all. But she found out about them both, which proved the point. And he kept watch by the river for altruistic reasons and promptly got his collar felt by a constable. He sighed.

'So maybe she's gone off in a huff.'

'Oh come on,' Gerald said. 'You know how fond she is of you.' He was conscious of a certain half-heartedness in his tone.

'Being fond of someone doesn't stop you not wanting them to come when you've not invited them to come. Believe you me.'

'Judith, Abby doesn't *do* huffs, you know that.'

'What are you talking about, Gerald? Good heavens. Abby is on a hair trigger, always was. Just like her first boyfriend, in that respect. I suppose from that point of view they were a good match. My Ken used to say Abby was the only person in the whole world who could frighten the living daylights out of him. And Ken wasn't a man easily intimidated,' Judith said, turning towards Terence.

'I'm sure he wasn't,' Terence said. He shuddered slightly, as if in fear of a rival, though dead.

'You ought to have been her little sister,' Judith told Gerald. 'Good grief. Demis built her a record player once upon a time, as I said. Quite a crude thing. It was made out of marine ply-wood. I always remember Abby telling me that. I wondered whether it would float, if you put it in water. She got the wood for him from the shop where she used to work in those days. He must have made a box out of it, then bought the parts and stuck them together somehow. I think he was studying that kind of thing.

'One day I was off school, and I borrowed it from her bed-room. Nobody but me in the house. I was dancing to some records. I suppose *they* were hers, too. Then she came back early from the shop for some reason and blew her top.

'There I was, jiving away in my own little world, all of a sud-den, hell to pay. "Demis made me that – it's mine, it's mine!" You'd have thought I'd stolen her whole boyfriend off of her, not just his record player. "It's mine!" she kept on shouting. She was crying with rage, as if it was the most precious thing in the whole world.'

'A talisman,' Terence said.

'That,' Judith agreed. 'I suppose we neither of us owned much in those days. People didn't, did they? Not that she's ever been a materialistic person, as such. Don't tell me you've not had moments like that with her, over the years.' Without giving Gerald time to reply, she said, 'Do you remember the head teacher Abby used to have? The one with the tiny head? E.T., she always called him.'

'I remember,' Gerald said, though in fact he could only remember Abby mentioning him in passing. It struck him that he'd never broached her world as a primary-school teacher. Talk of alternative universes, she had lived her whole working life completely separated off from him. What had appealed when they first met was her working in a hardware store, a place he wouldn't normally go into. He had always admired her self-sufficiency, the way she had her own centre of gravity. Maybe that had been carelessness on his part, a lack of curiosity, self-concern.

'To tell the truth,' Terence said, 'I think I owned quite a lot in the old days, by the standards of the time. My parents were well off. We lived in Surrey, in a house full of ticking clocks.'

Judith patted his hand. 'Good for you,' she said. 'I hope it made you very happy. Anyway, when E.T. assaulted her that time—'

Gerald froze. Judith gave him a piercing look, rather as Abby herself did from time to time, a look like a hook to jerk his secrets out of his head, in this case the fact that he had no idea what she was talking about. Luckily Terence spoke up in the nick of time: 'Abby was assaulted?' he asked in horror.

'She rang me up about it. I have never known a person so mad. He'd done her a favour some time previously, taken her classes when she had to go off somewhere. The dentist, I think it was. So next time there's nobody else about and all the kiddies have gone home to roost, he tries it on. Payback time, he must have thought. Mauled her about, didn't he, Gerald?'

'I don't like to talk about it,' Gerald said.

'She rang me up. She said she had to tell someone. I expect you hadn't come home from work. She was raging; that's the only way I can describe it. He manhandled her and tore her top. It got completely out of hand. She said he got his – well, I might as well call a spade a spade.' She took a quick glance at Terence, as if for approval. 'He got his willy out.'

'That's not a spade,' Terence said. '*Penis* is a spade.'

'The point was, it was very small, she said. Even when it was' – she lowered her voice, and looked quickly from Terence to Gerald, as if to get the nod from each – 'standing to attention. You know Abby, she can always see the funny side. She said she realised small head, small you-know-what. It was like a toy soldier, she said. Being Abby, she was laughing in amongst the rage. It frightened me out of my wits, listening to her over the phone. I've never heard anything like it. Roaring like an animal in pain and then laughs squeezed in between. Goodness knows how you coped when you got home, Gerald. She must have been in an awful state.'

'Hysteria, I would guess,' Terence said.

At that moment there was a knock on the door. For a moment Gerald thought it was his own heart pounding. Why hadn't Abby told him? Why hadn't he noticed? Why hadn't he *bothered* to notice?

'That sounds like Abby now,' Judith said.

'Isn't it a bit loud for her?' Terence said.

'How would *you* know?' Judith asked. 'No offence, but knocking is a very personal thing. You have to learn people's knocks. You can't just assume. I know Abby's knock of old.'

'It's loud in the sense that she would have used her key instead. Surely,' Terence said.

'If I know my sister, she's quite likely to have left it behind. Or can't be bothered to get it out of her bag. She knows we're here, after all. She'll have recognised the car. She said, when I first drove it here, she could tell it was mine by its aura. Do you remember her saying that, Gerald? I thought, pooh, Abby wouldn't sense an aura if it came up and bit her. It's me who can sense an aura, if anyone.'

The knocking came again, even louder.

'The knell of doom,' Terence said, raising his eyebrows. 'I still dread someone coming and accusing me of doing something I haven't done. I suppose it's because I feel guilty myself. If I'd played my cards differently in the pub that time. Knell of doom,' he repeated in a mutter.

'For goodness sake, Terry,' Judith said. 'People die, my boy. You can't go round saving everybody.'

'To be frank, I've never saved a single person in the whole of my life. Watched them come and watched them go.'

Gerald thought of those *he* hadn't saved, those he'd watched go – Ruth sneaking off with Pete, Laura on that snowy towpath, the second Laura, maybe. He'd never saved a single person in *his* entire life either, far from it. Now the pounding was in his head. Knell of doom.

'Cancer mainly,' Terence said. 'Nothing I could do about it. Just wasting away. Apart from that time in The Star, which was heart. I often wonder about that one. The irony is, while I was first-aid officer, only cuts and bruises ever came within my orbit. One of my colleagues felt faint on one occasion, I remember. That was about it.'

'Why don't you go and answer the door, to make up for being so silly. Professors, I ask you.'

Professors. It was funny how the word was used to mean something other than a job title. Being a professor is what I am, Gerald thought, part of my personality as a whole. Personality itself was a sort of disguise, the front garden of the self, hiding darkness and chaos inside.

'Yes, darling.' Terence rose to his feet.

Gerald wondered if Terence had ever called anyone darling before. The word sounded new-minted in his mouth. Even his compliance had a look of novelty about it. 'No. *I'll* go,' Gerald said.

'You've got a headache,' Judith said.

'It doesn't affect my legs.' But as he stood up he seemed to stumble before actually moving off. 'I can still fucking walk,' he insisted under his breath, making his way awkwardly towards the door.

When he opened it he got a shock. 'It's you,' he said.

'Me,' Constable Bennett agreed.

They stood looking at each other for a moment. Bennett's sharp eyes, under the rim of his helmet, seemed to coalesce into a single point of focus. 'I thought nobody was home,' he finally explained. 'I was just about to go.'

'Ah. Well.'

The silence resumed. 'I was in this part of the town. A domestic down in Chilton Road. I thought I'd knock on your door while I was around, to check if your missus was here. Steve was a bit worried about her.'

'Steve was, was he?'

'He said she hadn't been in touch for a while. Look, can I come in a minute?'

He wants to check up on me, Gerald thought. He wants to make sure Abby is in. *And she isn't in.* 'Well, to tell you the truth, we've got visitors—'

Bennett had already stepped forward, forcing Gerald to step back as if they were coordinating dance moves. 'How you doing?' Bennett asked Judith and Terence when he entered the kitchen.

'Oh no,' Terence said.

'I think you met my—' Gerald pointed at Judith as if he couldn't remember her name, though of course he could; he just didn't want to say it. He needed to keep Bennett at a distance. 'And my—' He pointed at Terence.

'Oh yes,' Bennett said, 'we met in the pub that time, didn't we, Professor?'

Terence paled and opened his mouth as if to reply, but said nothing.

'My sergeant said you gave that wino on the chapel steps a right old pasting,' continued Bennett.

'I'm not usually a violent man,' Terence muttered. Then, in that way he had, warmed to his theme: 'The way you could describe it, it was as if the two of us were fighting in our imaginations. Sort of dream fighting.'

'Terence,' Judith said, 'I didn't know you had it in you. Fighting.'

'*Dream* fighting. When we actually made physical contact it felt like an accident.'

'You're more like my Ken than I thought. Not that he ever fought with anyone, so far as I know. But you always had the idea he could if he wanted. Make physical contact, like you said. I sometimes wondered whether that was the reason he sold so many cars. People were worried he might hit them at any moment. I do like a bit of danger in a man.'

Once again a look of alarm crossed Terence's face. 'I'm not as dangerous as all that.'

'I'm sure you're not, Professor,' Bennett said. 'Just dangerous enough, eh?'

'That's all I ask,' Judith said. 'Dangerous enough.'

'That's settled, then. I've popped in to have a word with the professor here,' Bennett went on, taking off his helmet and pointing its little pinnacle at Terence. 'Not *you*, Professor.'

'Oh. Right. Good-oh,' Terence said. 'Not me.'

Bennett pointed his helmet at Gerald. 'Other professor.'

'This is like a plague of locusts, only with professors instead,' Judith said. 'Tell you what, *my* professor and I are off for a short lie-down. We've driven down here all the way from Wrexham and need a nap. At our age. Don't we, Terence? We'll leave you two gents to it.'

'Oh yes,' Terence said, slow on the cue like a poorly improvising amateur actor, 'certainly we do. Do we?' he whispered loudly as they left the room.

Bennett sat himself down in Terence's place at the kitchen table. Gerald resumed his own chair. Bennett raised his eyebrows at the stairs up which Judith and Terence had just disappeared. 'Maybe he's more dangerous than he looks,' he said.

There was a pause, an engineered one it felt like to Gerald, Bennett waiting till a chill had taken hold. 'So, still not back then? Abby.'

'Oh yes, she's *back*. Couple of days ago.' Gerald couldn't

stop himself from being over-emphatic. 'Been on a pottery course in Exeter.'

'A pottery course? I thought Steve was teaching her pottery. What did she need to go to Exeter for? There's not a lot about pottery Steve doesn't know, as far as I can make out.'

'She wanted to get up to speed. Now that she has to give him a hand.'

'He was measured for his *new* hand yesterday. He wants to tell Abby all about it.'

'Great news. Give him our . . . By the way, thank you for bandaging *my* hand, that time.' There was an awkward pause. Bennet gave a little shrug of his shoulders. 'Anyway,' Gerald continued, 'she said it wasn't much good. What she potted down in Exeter. Compared with working with Steve. She made a . . . ' What *did* she make? He couldn't remember whether she'd told him. It seemed important to have a corroborating detail. 'She made a full English. You know, egg, bacon, sausage, mushrooms.' He faltered for a moment. 'Tomatoes.'

'It sounds more like a cookery course.'

'She wasn't very pleased with it. She ended up dumping it in a litter bin.'

'So she came back empty-handed.'

'Empty-handed.'

'But she *did* come back?'

'Oh yes, she came back all right.' He thought of how she had taken shape in the dimness of the room when he surfaced from his doze. Could he have been imagining it? Had she simply arrived in his head, like a ghost?

'And then went off again?'

'Well no, not really *off* as such. She's just gone out.'

'I'm surprised she hasn't been in touch with Steve. I don't think he knew she was planning to go off to Exeter.'

'Maybe she thought it best not to say.'

'So she didn't end up in the river, like that Laura girl?'

'What?'

'Joke.'

'She's just gone down the road to buy some olives,' Gerald said with strained patience. 'Greek ones. The ones that are wrinkled and salty. You have to get them from Waitrose.'

There was a sudden high-pitched cry from up above somewhere. Maybe just the call of a bird. Bennett jerked his head at the sound. 'I best be off,' he said, turning back to Gerald. 'Tell her to give Steve a call if she shows up.'

'When she shows up.'

'When she shows up.'

Gerald sat in silence at the kitchen table after Bennett had left, nursing his headache. After a time that phrase came back into his head, crumpet couple. Of *course* Abby had come home. They had been sent to the hospital as the crumpet couple. The receptionist in the radiology department would have recorded their appointment. Gerald could have told Bennett there was proof he was in the clear.

That didn't explain where she was now, however. He couldn't just sit here at the kitchen table with that happy pair being happy in the bedroom two storeys above. He wrote a note on a piece of paper – *Gone to find her* – and went to find her.

CHAPTER 18

Waitrose on a sunny Friday afternoon. Gerald collected a basket from a pile by the door even though he wasn't going to buy anything. He went along various shelves looking interested in things he wasn't interested in.

Finally he found himself approaching the aisle where the salad dressings, sun-dried tomatoes, cornichons, tapenade, and olives were on display. He took a deep breath before peering round at it. It was stupid to hope that she'd be there, choosing her olives after all this time as though caught on slow-motion nature film, like some plant unfurling its tendril towards a trellis. Of course she wouldn't be there. There'd be nobody milling about in the aisle except people, just people.

He took a step forward, then froze. A picture came into his mind of Laura, the original Laura, the *real* Laura as he thought of her, just around the corner, standing in the aisle holding a jar of olives, offering them to him.

He and Abby were holding a party for his graduate students. Six of them, an unprecedented number, had signed up for his MA on colonial American history, and he had three PhD students as well.

Abby was not pleased. 'I don't see the point,' she said. 'You don't catch me bringing my little nippers home for jelly and cakes.'

'It's hardly the same thing, Abby. At this level there's a . . . '
He wasn't quite sure what it was there was. 'A sort of equality.'

'A sort of equality,' Abby mouthed. She held her hands out,
palms upward as if offering the phrase for inspection. 'You do
talk complete bollocks sometimes, Gerald. What's equal about
it, for heaven's sake? They're the students, you're the tutor.
Get used to it, what I say.'

'*Graduate* students. With graduate students you have to
have a . . . ' He cleared his throat, hardly daring to continue.
'Meeting of minds,' he finally said in a small voice. This time
Abby didn't deign to answer but just gave him a long look.

As the students trickled in, he saw her point. The MAs all
clustered together on the settee, three seated on the seats, one
each on the arms, and the last to arrive cross-legged on the rug
in front. They looked like some sort of social insect with a collective identity. The two male doctoral students meanwhile
talked warily in a corner, clearly torn between wanting to share
their knowledge and to safeguard any original takes they might
have on it. Gerald remembered the problem – how you
inevitably lost the ability to distinguish between the pedestrian
and the unique because what ended up in your mind seemed
to become yours in any case. He had long ago decided most of
his thoughts were pedestrian. Pre-loved, they called it nowadays.

Everyone, he realised, was embarrassed to find themselves
in this sitting room – except for Laura, who introduced herself
to Abby and asked if she could help. She was wearing a bright
summer frock, quite short, with splodgy red and yellow flowers on it, and seemed like an ornate bird as she leaned her
auburn head over drab Abby, in shirt and jeans.

'I was going to get crisps,' Abby said, 'then I thought,
they're *graduate* students. They must eat olives.'

'We have to eat olives,' Laura said, nodding solemnly. 'At
this point in our careers.'

'Tell you what, I have a jar in the kitchen. Let's put them in a bowl.'

'A bowl would be good.'

'A bowl of olives,' Abby said, as if the bowl was Laura's idea and she was just agreeing with her.

A few moments later Laura was offering the bowl around, while Gerald followed her with wine. When she had done her rounds, she stopped abruptly and turned so that she and Gerald were face to face. She was holding the bowl in both hands and raised it towards him, something ritualistic, Eucharistic, about the gesture. He felt as if the two of them were in a painting. Slowly, so as not to dispel the magic, he raised his hand, took one and placed it in his mouth. She took one in turn and placed it in hers, neither breaking eye-contact.

'You OK, sir?' There was a hand on his arm. Gerald realised to his horror he had sobbed out loud.

'Yes,' he said, 'I'm fine.' He turned. It was the Waitrose floor-walker, a gawky boy in a uniform too large for him. There was something touching about the way his cap sat on his head so that the visor was over his eyes. Gerald remembered having to wear a uniform himself, years ago, when he was working as an usher in the local cinema. 'Bit of hay fever.'

'Medicines are in aisle twelve.'

'Thank you. I think I'll be OK.'

The boy gave him a searching look, or at least his visor did. Perhaps he has had an eye on me, it occurred to Gerald. Perhaps he thought I was loitering with intent. 'I'm OK, honestly.'

The boy nodded doubtfully, stepped backwards, and sidled off.

How stupid, Gerald thought, to think Laura would be there, just round the corner, waiting for me in the olive aisle. It would be the other Laura, if anyone. Except you don't eat olives if you live on the street. Even if you're a vegetarian. Or maybe you don't end up on the street if you do eat olives. It just. It just. It just doesn't add up.

At last he stepped round into the aisle, and gasped with shock.

There was Constable Bennett, tall and dark like the shadow of himself, peering at jars of olives. It was as if he was looking for some tell-tale sign, some fingerprint or bloodstain, to mark Abby's passage. Before Gerald could retreat, the constable turned in his direction in that instinctive way one does.

'Can I ask what you're doing here?' Gerald asked.

'I remembered, when you said about Abby, Mrs. Walker, Steve asked me to get some olives. Olives, he said. He's doing beef stew. Beef and olive stew. He's quite nifty cooking one-handed these days. I'm just going off duty.'

'I can recommend the black wrinkly ones. Greek.'

'Black wrinkly ones.' Bennett turned back to the display. 'Black, wrinkly,' he repeated under his breath. 'Greek.'

'What *I'm* doing,' Gerald said, 'I'm trying to track down my wife.'

'She isn't here.'

'No. I can see that. She must be somewhere else.'

'Yes, she must.' It was loaded, the way Bennett said those words. Gerald wondered whether to mention his alibi, the crumpet-couple business, but it would make him seem more idiotic than ever.

'When I was a boy there weren't any olives,' he said instead. 'In this country, I mean. In the shops. Or very few. But then they started coming in. My dad bought a jar one day. He worked in Southsea and got it on the way home, must have carried it over on the Gosport ferry. He used to go to and from work by boat.' Gerald pictured him as he so often did, windswept on the deck, clutching his trophy.

'Ri-ight,' said Bennett. Andy, Gerald remembered, that was his name. Andy was trying to work it all out as if it was a puzzle. Just doing his job. Policemen had to work out puzzles, same as historians. Same as everyone. And Steve had been asking after Abby – why shouldn't he? He was attached to her. Abby and Steve, hand in stump. There must be an infinite web of criss-crossing entanglements even when they weren't visible. The same for him. Ruth, lost so long ago, Laura, absence of, Laura, disappearance of, Alice, death of, Abby, tendency to be somewhere else. Terence said particles could stay attached to each other even when they were at different ends of the universe. Maybe even when they were in different universes, for all Gerald knew.

'Everybody said at the time that olives were an acquired taste. That that was why they seemed so horrible. You had to serve an apprenticeship. My dad and the bloke next door sat in our garage and drank beer and ate their way through the whole jar. I don't know why they ate them in the garage. Dad kept a couple of old armchairs in there. We didn't have a car at that time. He had sold the family car. My dad would take an olive, then the bloke next door would take one. I went in the garage for a while to watch them. Each in turn would pull a face, almost gag, then have a swig of beer. Laughing their socks off.'

Dad laughing. The memory caught him by surprise. Gerald never normally thought of Dad laughing, except for that evening when he died, and he'd always imagined that particular bout of laughter was a sort of death rictus. But Abby had said there was no reason why a person can't laugh and die at the same time. He wondered if he'd edited his father's laughter out of his memories just as he seemed to have edited out so many other parts of his life. Perhaps in some way it had suited him to endow his unwitting Dad with a sort of reptilian severity as part of the punishment for Ruth's death, his own punishment, his dad's punishment, even, in a tenuous way, Ruth's punishment too.

And on the other hand, maybe merriment was intrinsically forgettable, being sudden and transient like blossom or snow, just a quick flash of teeth.

'It's OK if you're born into it. Them,' Gerald continued. 'Olives, I mean. I remember seeing my niece, Rita, no more than two years old at the time, gobbling olives from a jar happy as Larry. Next generation. Next generation but one, come to think.'

There was an awkward silence after he stopped talking. 'Greek ones,' Andy said finally.

'That's the fellas.' Gerald picked a jar off the shelf and passed it over.

'Ah. Greek ones. Thank you.'

'Give my regards to Steve, when you get back home.'

'Will do, yes.'

'Tell him I'm sure Abby will be in touch shortly.'

Gerald felt cheerful as he left the store, but then he stood outside the doors, nonplussed. He had gone in hoping to find Abby, but she hadn't been there. She had disappeared. It was all very well making his peace with Andy, but the man was right to be suspicious. He, Gerald, was suspicious himself. Was suspicious *of* himself. How did he know she would be in touch shortly? What exactly had happened after the fiasco of this morning? She had said crumpet couple, but what then? Had he deleted yet more from his mind, accusations, recriminations, bitterness? He seemed to spend his time nowadays both forgetting and remembering. Episodes from his past would disappear, then return. When your experience flickered and fluctuated in this fashion, it was next to impossible to account for what you had done, who you had been. Maybe the drip drip of resentment and jealousy, of bad faith, on his part at least, had overflowed at last and washed their marriage away? So that Abby had run off who knew where, communing with her horse in its field perhaps, oblivious of Judith and Terence's arrival, or just not caring about it.

Gerald felt dizzy, as if he might fall over. He hadn't had any lunch. Had he offered Judith and Terence any lunch? He couldn't remember.

He stood on the pavement wondering whether to go back inside the store and buy something. It would be awkward bumping into Andy again, if he was still there, now they had parted on good terms at last. It was funny how social niceties remained relevant even in a crisis, if this *was* a crisis. How peculiar, not to know whether it was one or not. And then there was that floor-walker in his big cap hovering about, waiting for an excuse to pounce. But he needed to eat something. The pavement was wavering up towards him, then down again. His headache intensified.

He remembered that sausage vendor on Milsom Street. That was the answer. A hot dog was exactly what he was looking for. He almost whimpered at the thought of it.

There was a queue at the stall – not students this time of day but tourists, mostly Japanese, as far as he could make out. Those who had been served seemed to be nodding in polite puzzlement at their half-eaten buns. A year ago he'd felt too awkward to buy a hot dog for himself, fearing to look a fool. But he was the tallest person in the queue. He had nothing to worry about.

'Hot dog?' asked the boy at the counter when he arrived there.

'Hot dog,' Gerald said. The boy pressed a sausage into a roll and smothered it with onions, then passed it over and nodded towards the sauce and mustard dispensers. Gerald squirted mustard along the length of his sausage, closed the bun tighter, stepped away from the stall. He raised it towards his mouth. *Finally*, he thought.

Just as he was about to take a bite, he caught a glimpse of redness flittering beyond a Japanese couple standing nearby. Surely not?

He stepped hurriedly round them and there she was, wearing a large maroon anorak.

'Hello,' he said.

'I was just going to go into Waterstone's.'

'I bought you a hot dog.'

'Oh, that's nice.' She put it in her mouth and took a bite, then passed it back so he could have a bite too.

'Abby, where have you been all this time?'

'Oh, here and there. I've been looking at the charity shops. I bought myself this anorak.'

'It seems a bit hot to be wearing it today.'

'I was trying it out. You have to run clothes in, even anoraks. I thought it would be good for wearing on Dorothy. You know how windy it gets up there. I'm going to buy myself a detective novel so I'll have something to read while the love birds are with us.'

'They're here already.'

'What? I thought you said they were coming this afternoon.'

'It *is* this afternoon.'

'I assumed you meant they would be driving *down* this afternoon. I expected them to arrive in time for pre-dinner drinks. I bought you a jar of olives for your pizza. Look.' She drew a jar of Greek olives out of her shopping bag and wagged it at him then put it back, took the hot dog, and had another bite. 'Where *are* they then?'

'They're back at the house. Having a lie-down. An assisted siesta, Judith called it.'

'Oh no.'

'They were crying out like seagulls.'

'God, it's even worse than I thought.'

They stared at each other across their shared hot dog, then laughed.

ACKNOWLEDGMENTS

Certain ideas about the many worlds theory in quantum mechanics were derived from the physicist Sean Carroll, speaking in a podcast entitled 'In Search of Reality', no. 124 in the series *Making Sense with Sam Harris*, recorded on 21 April 2018. Needless to say, all errors in relation to this mind-boggling area are down to me. Steve's pottery was provided by my friend Bernard Zberro, whose craftsmanship I love and admire (unlike my character Gerald, who has his own reasons for disapproving of it).

Thanks to Lucy Atkins, to Richard Kerridge, to Kat Aitken of United Agents, and to my children William and Helen, all of whom read drafts of this book, offered encouragement, and made valuable suggestions. As always, I owe so much to Caroline Dawnay, my friend and agent. I am delighted to have Christopher Potter as my editor once more. He worked on the text with his inimitable combination of scrupulousness, commitment, and energy. Sarah Ream, my copy-editor, removed many errors and solecisms. And my wife, Jo, was involved throughout, as always.

ABOUT THE AUTHOR

Richard Francis is a novelist, biographer and historian. He lives in Bath with his wife, Jo. Visit his blog at http://richardfrancis.wordpress.com